THE CURSE OF SKULL CANYON

A LONNIE GENTRY WESTERN

The Curse of
Skull Canyon

Peter Brandvold

FIVE STAR

A part of Gale, Cengage Learning

GALE
CENGAGE Learning·

Farmington Hills, Mich • San Francisco • New York • Waterville, Maine
Meriden, Conn • Mason, Ohio • Chicago

GALE
CENGAGE Learning®

LIBRARY OF CONGRESS CATALOGING-IN-PUBLICATION DATA

Names: Brandvold, Peter, author.
Title: The curse of Skull Canyon : a Lonnie Gentry western / by Peter Brandvold.
Description: First edition. | Waterville, Maine : Five Star, a part of Gale Cengage Learning, [2016]
Identifiers: LCCN 2016003811 (print) | LCCN 2016009180 (ebook) | ISBN 9781432831820 (hardcover) | ISBN 1432831828 (hardcover) | ISBN 9781432831844 (ebook) | ISBN 1432831844 (ebook) ISBN 9781432833671 (ebook) | ISBN 1432833677 (ebook)
Subjects: | GSAFD: Western stories.
Classification: LCC PS3552.R3236 C87 2016 (print) | LCC PS3552.R3236 (ebook) | DDC 813/.54—dc23
LC record available at http://lccn.loc.gov/2016003811

First Edition. First Printing: August 2016
Find us on Facebook– https://www.facebook.com/FiveStarCengage
Visit our website– http://www.gale.cengage.com/fivestar/
Contact Five Star™ Publishing at FiveStar@cengage.com

Printed in the United States of America
1 2 3 4 5 6 7 20 19 18 17 16

For Bill and Amy Schmidt
longtime friends from the old home country.
For their daughter Olivia,
who I hope enjoys this one, too.

CHAPTER 1

Fourteen-year-old Lonnie Gentry didn't care if he never heard another gunshot again in his life.

In fact, after his many recent near-death experiences at the hands of the outlaw, Shannon Dupree, who'd hunted him and Casey Stoveville like game through the Never Summer Mountains a year ago, he hoped he'd *never* hear the blast of another rifle.

But now as he stopped his buckskin stallion, General Sherman, on a high-mountain trail not far from timberline, and cocked an ear, he was sure that the raking, echoing cough he'd just heard was gunfire indeed.

What else could it be? Surely not thunder, for there wasn't a cloud in sight against the high, dry arch of cerulean blue.

Lonnie looked at his horse. General Sherman had turned his head to stare toward a granite-capped outcropping jutting several yards upslope and behind a ways. The General's eyes were wide, and those dark copper orbs were twitching. The black nostrils worked as the stallion sniffed the breeze.

"Ah, heck," Lonnie said, his gut tightening with anxiety. "Let's head on down the mountain, General. I think we've done found all the bogged cows we're gonna find today."

With that, Lonnie clucked and touched spurs to the General's flanks. The sleek buckskin seemed to want to hightail it as much as Lonnie did. The General gave an agreeable snort and broke into a trot, following the game trail they'd been on for the past several hours, on down the steep slope and into the cool shade of firs, pines, tamaracks, and a salting of white-stemmed, verdant-smelling aspens.

This day and the day before, Lonnie and the General had been scouring this neck of their mountain range for any cows or calves that had gotten left behind last week, when Lonnie had moved his and his mother's herd to another range in the southern reaches of the Never Summers. Now, he'd head on back to the line shack and call it a day, maybe return here for one more look early tomorrow.

He had work to do on the corral flanking the shack, anyway, and, besides, he didn't want to be anywhere around where there was shooting.

Even if it was just someone shooting at elk or deer.

No, he'd had enough of shooting, thank you very much.

Lonnie gave the General his head, and they made good time descending the slope. They reached the bottom of a ravine through which a creek ran. As they were about to turn onto an intersecting game trail that would take them even lower, toward where the line shack sat at the base of Eagle Ridge, an eerie buzzing sounded just off Lonnie's right ear.

Then there was a loud *thud!* as what could only have been a bullet smashed into a fir bole just ahead and to Lonnie's right.

The rifle's blasting, echoing report followed a half a second later.

"Jesus!" Lonnie shouted, ducking instinctively and then glancing back over his left shoulder.

A cold stone dropped in his belly.

Four horseback riders were galloping toward him, spread out side by side and weaving amongst the columnar pines. One was just now aiming the carbine in his hands, pumping a fresh cartridge into the rifle's breech. The carbine's dark maw blossomed smoke and fire.

The bullet screeched toward Lonnie before searing a hot path of torn cloth over his right shoulder. His right arm went instantly numb. The bullet continued on past Lonnie and over the General's head to bark loudly into a granite boulder.

As the rifle's report reached Lonnie's ears, the General whinnied shrilly and pitched sharply up off his front hooves. Lonnie had grabbed at his right shoulder, dropping the rein he'd been holding in that hand, and hadn't been prepared for the horse's sudden, violent buck.

"Ah, *hell*!" Lonnie cried as, kicking free of his stirrups, he felt himself being hurled back over the General's left hip.

The sloping ground came up to slap him hard about the head and shoulders. Lonnie heard his breath slammed out of him in a loud *"Ghahhh!"* of expelled breath. As the General galloped on down the mountain, stepping on his trailing bridle reins, Lonnie rolled, losing his hat and cursing.

Unfortunately, he'd been through his before. So, when he'd stopped rolling and found himself still alive and able to use his limbs, he heaved himself to his feet. With one quick look behind him to see the four galloping riders closing on him fast—one shouting, "Get him!"—Lonnie took off running as fast and as hard as he could, trying to ignore the aching burn in his right arm.

He'd been through this before, all right, but he didn't have time to reflect on the bad turn of his luck. He could now feel the reverberations of the galloping horses through his boots as he sprinted for an outcropping of black granite rising ahead of him.

He hadn't planned to head for the rock. But, then again, he hadn't planned on getting bushwhacked again in these mountains, either—nearly exactly a year since the first time!

As Lonnie ran, he could hear the horses growing near—hear the squawk of tack and bridle chains, the raking of the air in and out of the horses' straining lungs. Guns popped. The bullets tore into trees around Lonnie and chewed up the turf around his hammering boots.

Lonnie glanced back once more. The riders were fifty yards away now and closing fast.

Another bullet burned across the nub of Lonnie's right cheek.

The boy sucked a sharp, pained breath and turned his head forward. He gained the escarpment and fairly hurled himself up into the first nook he saw—leaping and throwing his hands up to grab for hidden holds. He found the holds he was looking for, and hoisted himself up into a natural flue in the side of the outcropping. Breathing hard, in a frozen-blooded panic, the boy continued climbing—scrambling, really—following the natural route that opened before him.

"There he is!" one of the men now below him shouted.

Two more rifles blasted. The bullets slammed into the rock around Lonnie, peppering him with stone shards. Another rifle belched. The slug slammed into the heel of Lonnie's boot as the boy pulled himself over the top of the outcropping and hurled himself across the rock and out of sight from below.

Lonnie lifted his right foot to look at his boot heel. The bullet was poking its evil head out of it. Lonnie swiped at it, trying to dislodge the malicious thing, but it was in there solid. He didn't have time to worry about bullets that weren't in his hide, anyway. He fell back against the escarpment, catching his breath.

Air sawed in and out of him loudly. His heart thudded in his ears.

He was shaking.

He could have lay there a long time, the sky swirling over him, but a horse whinnied below the scarp. A man said, his voice pinched with fury, "Get after him, Jeb!"

"Why me?" Jeb asked.

"I got twenty years on you, you son of a buck! Get after him and kill him!"

A man cussed. Boots scraped against rock. Someone was climbing up the scarp.

Lonnie heaved himself to his feet, and looked around. The scarp was nearly solid rock with only a few tufts of grass and wiry brush cropping up occasionally A few irregular stone formations jutted from its surface, speckled white and gray with what Lonnie figured were bones of some kind. Ancient bones of animals or maybe men. He'd seen them before throughout the Never Summers.

But the only bones he was concerned about now, however, were his own.

He ran across the uneven surface of the escarpment. It shelved downward after several yards, and several stone corridors opened around him. Lonnie considered taking cover in one of these, but if the man after him found him, he'd be trapped.

He glanced over his right shoulder.

The man was behind him, all right. He was behind him and just now aiming a rifle at Lonnie, cheek snugged up to the rifle's rear stock.

Lonnie lurched forward. The rifle thundered. Lonnie tripped over a thump of stone rising from the escarpment floor, and stumbled wildly forward before falling and rolling.

Lonnie gained his feet in mid roll and continued running. Behind him, the rifle thundered again. The slug spanged shrilly off a rock to Lonnie's left.

He ran hard. The escarpment floor dropped more and more. He ran down a steep decline through a narrow corridor.

When he came out on the other side, he saw a narrow gap in a rise of black stone to his left. Instinctively, knowing he didn't have much time, he threw himself into the gap, vaguely hoping it was more than a nook or a cranny without another exit but had a back door to somewhere . . .

To anywhere but where he was now, with a man out to kill him hot on his heels.

Lonnie had hoped in vain.

The gap, only about three feet wide, was only about five feet deep.

Lonnie found himself staring at a cold stone wall of solid rock streaked with bird droppings.

Boots thudded behind Lonnie. The boy winced as the raking breaths of his approaching pursuer grew louder and louder.

CHAPTER 2

Lonnie whipped around to face the mouth of the gap.

The boot thuds grew louder. Spurs trilled softly.

Lonnie slid slowly down the rear wall of the gap until he was sitting on his butt, making himself as small as possible. He brushed his fist across the bullet burn on his cheek, wrapped his arms around his knees, and sat staring out of the gap.

His heart tattooed a desperate rhythm against his breastbone.

His stalker moved slowly into view from Lonnie's right. Lonnie tightened his jaws. He hugged his knees tighter, vaguely wishing the stone floor would open and swallow him.

The man was tall and lean and unshaven. He wore a long, black duster and a low-crowned hat with a thong dangling beneath his chin which was sharply spade-shaped and carpeted in lusterless brown whiskers. That angry chin gave a mean, belligerent cast to his face—at least to his profile, which was all that Lonnie could see from his angle.

He held a Winchester carbine up high across his chest as he continued moving from Lonnie's right to his left. As he did, he limped on one foot, as though he'd injured himself on his run across the irregular floor of the escarpment.

He turned his head as he looked around the stone knob. All he had to do at this moment, now that he was directly out in front of Lonnie, was turn his head a little more to the left. Then he'd see Lonnie cowering in the shadowy gap.

The man lurched to a standstill.

Here it comes, Lonnie thought. Now he'll see me and after two or three quick blasts of his carbine, that will be the end. Ma will never know what happened to me, because once this fella drills me, he'll leave me here in this gap and I won't be found till someone finds a reason to scout around up here, which, given the remoteness and ruggedness of the place, will likely be never.

I'll molder here alone . . .

Ma will die wondering what happened to her fourteen-year-old son, Lonnie Gentry. She'll likely leave the ranch and move to town because if there was one true thing about Ma it was that she hated being alone. She'll likely find a man in town and . . .

Lonnie let the fast train of his half-conscious thoughts trail off. The man before him wheeled away from Lonnie and went limping back the way he'd come, cursing and lowering his rifle to his side.

Lonnie blinked in shock. He couldn't believe the man was giving up on him. All he'd needed to do was turn a little more to the left, and *bam-bam!*

Lonnie listened to the man's spur-trilling footsteps fade to silence.

Lonnie couldn't believe his luck. Was it too good to be true? The man might be setting a trap for him. Did he want Lonnie to believe he'd given up and gone back to his kill-crazy partners? Then, when Lonnie showed himself, the lead would fly.

Lonnie sat there a long time. It was as though he had turned to stone. His heart slowed, the hammering in his ears grew less and less violent. An hour must have passed, for the shadows in the gap grew thicker and thicker and Lonnie detected a cooling in the air that sharpened the smell of forest duff and pine resin.

From somewhere that Lonnie couldn't see, a hawk gave its ratcheting cry. The ratcheting came and faded several times as the bird glided across the skies, hunting the forest floor for mice or squirrels.

Lonnie heaved himself to his feet. His boots feeling like lead, he stepped up to the mouth of the gap and slid a cautious gaze around the wall on his right. He stared in the direction his pursuer had gone, half believing that the man would be squatting there only a few yards away, carbine ready.

Nothing.

The only sounds were the hawk's cry and the breeze playing in the forest canopy surrounding the escarpment.

Lonnie moved out of the gap and looked around. Should he go back the way he'd come? No. The three shooters might be waiting for him at the base of the scarp. Of course, they might have fanned out and were waiting for him at various points around the scarp, but returning the way he'd come seemed the least desirable of his options.

His instincts told him to try to find another way off the knob.

Crouching, keeping his head low so that he wouldn't be seen from the forest floor, he moved off along the scarp, following what was now a gradual drop toward the ground. The scarp continued to drop until Lonnie found himself at the edge of it, crouching, sweeping his gaze across the forest floor only ten or so feet beneath him now. The pines were spread six or seven feet apart, affording little cover for anyone waiting for Lonnie to show himself.

Deciding—or at least hoping—that his pursuers had given up on him—Lonnie dropped to his butt, turned to face the scarp, and crabbed his way down the wall, using small cracks and fissures for hand- and footholds. When he reached the ground, he dropped to his butt once more and pressed his back to the wall he'd just descended and held very still as he again surveyed the forest around him.

After a couple of minutes of seeing no more movement

beyond that of squirrels, chickadees, and nuthatches flicking amongst the branches, Lonnie rose and began moving down the slope toward the east. He had no intention of moving back directly toward where he hoped to find General Sherman, because his pursuers might be looking for him there, possibly even using the buckskin stallion as bait.

Instead, he decided to move in a roundabout way in that general direction, watching, listening, and sniffing the breeze. Lonnie had a good sniffer on him, and he could smell horse or man sweat from fifty yards away. He wasn't sure how his senses had become so keen. Probably because his youth made him vulnerable, and he spent a lot of time alone in these rugged, remote mountains, moving cows around and hunting calf-killing coyotes and wolves—and even the occasional grizzly—while his mother tended the ranch headquarters and her newborn baby, little Jeremiah, several miles away and at least a thousand feet below.

Lonnie Gentry had developed an unusual sharpness to his senses out of necessity.

Without it, he might very well be dead by now.

He made his way around the base of a stone ridge, the wall towering a couple of hundred feet above. Eventually, the wall opened on his left, forming a forty- or fifty-foot gateway into a canyon. As Lonnie stepped into this gateway, which was the mouth of the canyon, he heard something that ran a chill up his spine and caused chicken flesh to rise between his shoulder blades.

"Help me," a man was calling, half moaning. "Help me . . . please. Someone . . . please . . . help me!"

CHAPTER 3

Lonnie stared into the canyon, his lower jaw hanging.

The man's moaning pleas had died, so all he heard now was the eerie soughing of the breeze and the occasional, soft thud of a pinecone tumbling from a tree.

Another moaning sound rose from deep inside the canyon. A louder sound than the soughing sound of the breeze or the previous moaning of the injured man. This sound was made by occasional gusts of late-day wind blowing through a high, porous, distant ridge at the west end of the canyon and then funneling down the canyon's sloping floor toward where Lonnie stood now.

The wind carried with it that eerie, hollow, ratcheting lament that sounded like the agonized moaning of a dying man.

Another chill slid deep into Lonnie's bones despite his knowing that the moaning was not that of a dying man but merely the wind as it sluiced through a rock formation. That formation, standing tall atop the far ridge that Lonnie couldn't see from this vantage, bizarrely resembled a giant human skull.

Thus the canyon's name.

Skull Canyon.

Lonnie had always tried to avoid the canyon when possible, though occasionally he'd had to ride into it looking for lost cows and calves he hadn't been able to find elsewhere. Over the years, he'd found three or four cows inside the canyon, and never dallied but had hazed the befuddled beasts back out of

17

the canyon and down the mountain.

Few people around here dared enter Skull Canyon, for it was said—and had been said for generations of non-Indian settlers throughout this neck of the Never Summers—that Skull Canyon had been cursed long ago by a young Indian brave who'd sought refuge inside the canyon and had perished there after he'd been run down and tortured for several long days and nights by the mountain-man husband of the Indian's white lover.

The white lover had been a young Norwegian girl named Ingrid, a pretty blonde with cornflower-blue eyes. Thus the name of the creek curling down out of Skull Canyon to form a falls farther on down the mountain—Ingrid Creek. The dying brave had summoned a dark Indian spirit who had conjured the curse that was said to cause any man who saw the sun go down in the canyon to suffer shortly thereafter a violent death.

Of course, most folks didn't give the legend much credence. Such stories abounded throughout not only the Rockies but across the entire frontier. The story had probably been made up by some old-timer who'd discovered gold in the canyon and had merely wanted to frighten others away from his mine.

He'd probably been inspired by the skull formation at the canyon's far end, and the eerie sound the wind made as it passed through and around the giant skull.

Lonnie hadn't taken the legend overly seriously, either, though his young imagination was vivid enough to make him want to stay as far away from the canyon as possible whenever he could. He'd noted, however, that the cows he'd found lost inside the canyon had seemed unusually nervous and afraid and had seemed relieved when they'd been hazed on out of it.

But that might have been Lonnie's overactive imagination, too. Most beasts—whether they be with four feet or two—did not enjoy being lost.

Just as the cries he'd heard only a few minutes ago had likely been a trick of his imagination, fired to a frenzy by his recent, harrowing escape from the four men who had been determined to kill him. They'd most likely been rustlers worried he'd spied them at work with their running irons—branding irons long-loopers used to doctor the brands of the cattle they stole. Rustling was a hanging offense. Lonnie's hunters had likely felt the desperate need—even if that need meant shooting an innocent young cowboy—to keep the law from playing cat's cradle with their heads.

That was all he'd heard, Lonnie decided. Merely the wind playing its usual tricks in Skull Canyon.

Relieved, Lonnie swung around and started back down the mountain, deciding to follow the narrow, bubbling creek to the falls, where he'd fill his canteens and water the General, and then continue riding down into the lower reaches.

"Help!" a man yelled behind him.

Lonnie swung back around to stare once more up into the canyon, his heart thudding with exasperation.

"No," he told himself, shaking his head. "It's . . . it's the wind, galldangit."

"Help me!" the man cried, louder.

Then Lonnie saw him. The man was maybe a hundred yards away, stumbling through the knee-high grass along the creek, tracing the bend the creek made as he continued stumbling toward Lonnie.

"Help me!" the man yelled, his voice strangely clear now in the cool, dry, high-country air, aided by the canyon's good acoustics. "I've been injured. I need a hand!"

His arms were crossed on his lower belly.

He took three or four more steps and then he dropped to his knees and pitched forward. He was hidden now in the tall grass behind a thicket of chokecherry shrubs sheathed in brightly flowered wild peas and columbine.

Lonnie hesitated only for a second and then strode forward, into the canyon. He was wary of this place and all the more so because of what he'd just been through. Still, a man was injured. He needed help. It didn't occur to Lonnie that the men who'd been out to kill him might be laying a trap for him until he was within ten feet of the man lying before him.

The possibility hit Lonnie like a slap across his bullet-burned cheek.

He stopped and looked around, half expecting to see the smoke and flames of guns opening up on him.

But there was nothing anywhere around him. Only this man lying on his back, breathing hard, his hands pressed to his belly rising and falling sharply.

"Help," the man cried, squeezing his eyes closed and lifting his head and hardening his jaws as he looked down at his bloody hands and his bloody belly. "Help me. You gotta . . . help me!"

It was as though he were speaking only to himself believing that no one else were here.

Lonnie moved forward. He stepped around the chokecherry thicket, the creek murmuring to his left, and stood over the man who'd laid his head down again now, squeezing his eyes closed. Sweat glistened on his forehead and cheeks, which were very smooth and from which very thin strands of beard stubble sprouted like down.

He was young. Maybe only a few years older than Lonnie. He was dressed, like Lonnie, in the trail-worn gear of the working cowboy—checked shirt, suspenders, faded denims, and brush-scarred chaps.

Lonnie cleared his throat, which felt like sandpaper from all the running he'd done. "I'm . . . here . . . mister."

At first, the young man did not open his eyes. It was as though it took some time for Lonnie's words to make their way into his consciousness. Then, when they did, the eyes opened, slitted against the sun quartering westward over Lonnie edging toward the ridge jutting on the far side of the creek.

"I'm hurt," the man said, wincing with the anguish of his wound. "My stomach . . . hurts real bad."

"What happened?"

"Gut shot."

"I see that. By who?"

"Some jaspers . . . who didn't want me lurkin' around here . . . I reckon. Didn't see 'em."

"Were there four?"

"I didn't see 'em close enough to count. They shot me an' rode away, took off after my partner, Dwight Halsey. I thought maybe you was him, when I first seen you. Dwight . . . he's prob'ly dead now."

Lonnie looked around, a nearly palpable sense of danger closing around him once more. The men who'd ambushed him must have thought he'd been Halsey. He doubted it would matter now if they found out he wasn't Halsey. They'd kill him to keep him quiet about shooting this man, whom they'd likely finish off, to boot, though it didn't seem necessary.

The man was bleeding bad. He'd already lost a lot of blood, judging by the crimson weeds charting his path down the canyon. He was due to lose a lot more unless that wound was closed.

"What's your name?" the man asked, squinting against the sun again.

Lonnie glanced around once more then dropped to one knee beside the man. "Lonnie Gentry."

"Cade McLory."

"Pleased to make your acquaintance. Wish it were under more favorable circumstances. You got a horse around here, McLory?"

The wounded man lifted his head to glance around. "Well, I

did. But I ain't seen hide nor hair of him since they shot me out my saddle."

"Why'd they do that? Why'd they shoot you out of your saddle, McLory?"

McLory tensed as pain rippled through him. Then he licked his dry, chapped lips. "I reckon that's a long story. Don't reckon I got time to tell it . . . less'n we can figure out some way to stop the bleedin'."

"Are they rustlers?"

McLory merely shook his head and shrugged.

Berating himself for not having done so sooner, Lonnie untied the man's billowy green bandanna from around McLory's neck, took it over to the creek, soaked it, and returned. He pressed the bandanna down hard against the wound.

McLory lifted his head, cursing. "Ah, Jesus that hurts!"

"You're gonna have to press down on that until we can figure another way to get the blood stopped."

"Mister Lonnie," McLory said, "do you think you'd do me the favor of helping me over to the creek so I can get a drink of water? I'm powerful thirsty."

"I don't know. If you move around too much . . ."

"I'd very much appreciate it. I'm so galldarned thirsty that gettin' that drink is about the only thing I can think about right now." McLory gave a bleak, choking laugh. "Reckon I can't say's I even care if it kills me!"

Lonnie looked around. He couldn't see anyone else out here.

There was only that moaning wind as it sawed down from the giant skull. It seemed to be giving voice to Cade McLory's own agony. But then it always seemed to be giving voice to *someone's* agony.

Maybe it was giving voice to Lonnie's own agony, now, too— the agonizing fear of what would happen if the four riders returned, which they might very well do before he could get the wounded man to cover.

CHAPTER 4

"Can you stand?" Lonnie asked McLory.

McLory rolled onto his belly and then climbed to one knee. "Let's give it a shot."

Lonnie wrapped the man's left arm around his shoulders and helped him to his feet. "There," McLory said. "That wasn't so hard—now, was it?"

Lonnie helped McLory walk through the high grass. McLory put a good bit of weight on Lonnie, who grunted with the effort of holding the bigger man up. McClory was about four inches taller than Lonnie, and he probably outweighted Lonnie by at least thirty pounds.

When they'd reached the creek, McLory dropped to his knees and groaned miserably, clutching his hands to his belly again. He leaned forward. For a moment, Lonnie thought he'd pass out. But then McLory lifted his head, crawled a foot or so nearer the creek, and lowered his head to the water, cupping the cool, running liquid to his lips.

When he had his fill, he lifted his head, smiled with satisfaction, and then, his eyelids growing heavy, swayed from side to side. Lonnie crouched beside him and wrapped an arm around him to keep him from falling forward into the water.

"Look, McLory," Lonnie said, glancing back toward the mouth of the canyon. "We'd best get you somewhere safe. We're too exposed out here. If them shooters come back . . ."

"Yeah, I know," McLory said. "We'd be sittin' ducks."

Lonnie looked around. His gaze gravitated toward the western ridge wall, which was strewn with gravel, boulders, pines, and cedars. Above and behind a nest of boulders, there appeared a black, oval-shaped gap in the ridge wall. Possibly a cave.

Lonnie's eyes swept the creek. When he saw a shallow place atop a natural shelf over which the water dropped, Lonnie said, "Let's get you up into them rocks yonder. I see a place where we can ford the creek without gettin' too wet. Think you can make it?"

McLory nodded dully. He appeared to be only about half conscious. He was no longer pressing the bandanna to the belly wound. Fresh blood glistened in the waning sunlight, the stain over the young man's belly growing larger and darker.

Lonnie helped McLory to his feet once more. He led the young man upstream a ways, and then they crossed, the cool water just covering their boots and inching up toward their ankles. Once across the creek, Lonnie led the cowboy up the gradual slope rising to the base of the ridge.

From there, the walk got harder, for they had to negotiate the steep slope up through and around behind the sandstone-colored boulders. Loose scree caused them both to slip and slide, both going down once on their knees.

When they'd finished negotiating the hazardous trail, Lonnie was glad to see that the trip had been worth the effort. There was indeed a cave behind the boulder, which shielded the cave from the canyon floor.

The cave was about five feet high and maybe twice that long. The scat and tracks inside told Lonnie that rabbits and a bobcat or two had called the place home within the last few weeks. There didn't appear to be any fresh sign, which meant the place wasn't currently occupied. The last thing Lonnie wanted this hectic day was to be fending off a bobcat or, worse, a mountain lion.

He had no gun, as he'd left his Winchester in the boot strapped to his saddle. He'd already taken note that McLory's holster, which sat high on his right hip, was empty. He'd probably lost the pistol when he'd been shot off his own mount.

Lonnie helped McLory sit down inside the cave. Then he removed his own, navy-blue bandanna, and gave it to the wounded man. "Take this. Press it hard against your belly or you'll bleed out. I'm gonna see if I can't fetch my horse. I have a few medical supplies in my saddlebags, and a small bottle of whiskey. We need to get that wound tended."

McLory leaned his head back against the cave wall, and grinned through his misery. "Whiskey, huh? I didn't take you for an imbiber, Master Gentry."

"It's medicine," Lonnie said, though he knew the man was only pulling his leg. "Best thing for cleaning cuts and wounds and bad rope burns, and I get plenty of all that out here."

"You got a nice cut across your cheek."

"I got another across my shoulder. Compliments the same rustlers that shot you, most like."

McLory studied him. "Young cowboy, are ya?"

"That's right."

"Live around here, then?"

"My ma and I own the Circle G down in the valley."

McLory shook his head. "Don't know it."

"You're not from around here, then."

Again, McLory shook his head. "Not by a long shot. Texas, born and raised."

"What're you doin' here? What're you doin' in the canyon? I thought maybe you rode for one of the other outfits."

Before McLory could open his mouth to respond, Lonnie said, "Never mind. Save your strength. I'd best get off after my horse before it gets too dark to see him."

McLory looked at Lonnie. His face was slick with sweat and the color of parchment paper. The walk up here had taken it out of him. "You really have to go?"

Lonnie looked at him, vaguely puzzled.

McLory licked his lips. "It's just that . . . I don't . . . I don't wanna die alone. I'm really afraid of . . . dyin' alone, for some reason. Never knew it till I thought I was all alone out here. I reckon that's why I was makin' such a fuss. Lost my head." He swallowed, sucked a sharp breath, wincing against the pain it caused him. "Don't wanna die alone, that's all."

"You ain't gonna die." Lonnie wanted to believe that was true, but he wasn't sure. "Not if I fetch my horse and bring some cloth back for bandages. That whiskey'll clean out the wound till we can get you to the sawbones in Arapaho Creek."

Lonnie placed a hand on McLory's shoulder, trying to comfort the young man. "I won't be long."

McLory nodded, though Lonnie could see the darkness of fear mixing with the pain in his eyes. "All right. You go ahead. I'm sorry for the trouble, Master Gentry."

"I'll get a fire goin' as soon as I get back. I'll boil some coffee."

"Good on ya, good on ya."

Lonnie stepped back out of the cave, and straightened. He looked once more at McLory, who rested his blond head back against the cave wall.

He was breathing hard and sweating though he appeared to be losing more and more color from his face. For a moment, Lonnie hesitated, wondering if he'd made the right decision to go after the General.

What if McLory died while he was gone?

That would be an awful thing, his having left him while knowing how fearful he was of dying alone.

But then Lonnie told himself that while the Texan looked bad, he didn't look like he was about to die. Not within the next hour, anyway. And Lonnie would give himself only an hour to look for the General. If he hadn't found the buckskin in that time, he'd head on back to the cave though he sure didn't like the idea of spending the night in Skull Canyon.

CHAPTER 5

Lonnie found the General grazing near the pool beneath the falls that Ingrid Creek made as it dropped over a granite cliff.

At first, the horse ran, still skittish from the shooting. He couldn't hear Lonnie's voice above the falls' loud pattering. When Lonnie worked his way upwind of the stallion, the General recognized the scent of his rider and came running, dragging his reins, one of which the horse had stepped on and broke.

Lonnie was relieved that he hadn't run into the four trigger-happy riders. But his caution had caused his excursion out from Skull Canyon to take longer than an hour. By the time he rode the General back through the gap into the canyon, he judged by the low angle of the sun that he'd been gone a good ninety minutes.

He remembered the curse.

He remembered McLory's fear of dying alone.

Anxiety rippled through him as he galloped the General across the creek and around behind the boulders a ways up the steeply slanting ridge base. He leaped down from the stallion's back before he was fully stopped, dropped the reins, and ran up the gravelly shelf and into the cave.

His spine turned to ice when he saw McLory lying on his side at the base of the cave wall, where Lonnie had left him. The young man's eyes were closed. His chest was not rising and falling. His face looked waxen.

Trembling, horrified that McLory might have drifted off while he'd been alone here, with no one to comfort him, Lonnie dropped to a knee. He placed a trembling hand on the young Texan's shoulder. McLory did not respond. Lonnie thought his flesh felt cold beneath the flannel cloth of his shirtsleeve.

Lonnie nudged the young Texan. "McLory?"

He was about to say the young man's name once more when McLory turned his head toward Lonnie. He opened his eyes and looked up at the young cowboy. For a moment, it was as though McLory were trying to place him.

Then he glanced around and pushed up off his shoulder with a rattling sigh. "Reckon I done drifted off."

Relief washed through Lonnie though he didn't like the amount of blood that McLory had left on the cave floor, where he'd been lying. "How you feelin'?"

McLory smiled, his gray-blue eyes slanting devilishly. "Never better. Where's the girls? Ain't it Saturday night? Me—I'm ready to dance, Master Gentry!"

"I don't think you'll be doin' any dancin' anytime soon, McLory," Lonnie said, straightening but keeping his head bowed so the low ceiling wouldn't scrape his hat off his head. "But I found my horse, so I'll fetch my possibles."

"Don't forget the whiskey!" McLory raked out as Lonnie ran down the steep gravelly slope to where the General waited for him. "Uh . . . for medicinal purposes only, ya understand."

Lonnie retrieved his saddlebags and canvas war bag and hustled back up into the cave. He dug around in the saddlebags, found his flat bottle wrapped in burlap, and handed it to McLory, who took it and, struggling a little with the cork, tipped it back.

McLory took two hard swallows and then pulled the bottle down, blinking and turning even whiter than before. "Oh, jeepers," McLory said. "Oh, boy . . . maybe that wasn't such a good idea."

"Burns?"

"Yeah."

"Better go easy on it."

McLory scrunched his face up and stiffened and then gradually relaxed and rested his head back against the cave wall. "I'm . . . better now. Once the liquor gets into my blood . . . it eases the pain."

"But when it hits your belly, it probably kicks like a mule."

"There you have it." McLory held the bottle up to Lonnie. "Snort?"

Lonnie shook his head as he rummaged around in his bags for his flannel wrappings and the small, buckskin pouch of ointments his mother had prepared for him when, here and there throughout the year, he'd begun spending several nights by himself in the line shack, when he was working their herd.

"You don't drink?" McLory asked him.

"Nope."

"Good for you." McLory took another, small sip from the bottle and winced as the fiery liquid seared its way into his belly. "Many a desperate man has turned to drink for comfort . . . only to find it's about as much comfort as a woman. No comfort at all when the chips are down."

"Speak from experience, do you?" Lonnie asked him.

"Sure do."

"You've had bad experiences with both, then, I take it."

Lonnie was unbuttoning McLory's shirt. McLory put a hand on Lonnie's, stopping him and narrowing one eye. He already seemed drunk. "Kid, when you're as old as I am, you'll get savvy to the ways of men and women . . . and firewater. And you'll learn the two don't go together."

"How so?" Lonnie was genuinely curious despite his urgency

31

at wanting to get the young Texan's belly bandaged, the blood stopped.

McLory merely shook his head. Releasing Lonnie's hand, he took another drink from the bottle.

"Best save some of that for the wound," Lonnie said. "I'm gonna need some for the cleanin'."

"Don't bother."

"What's that?"

"I'm a goner, kid."

Lonnie looked at McLory. McLory was staring hard at Lonnie. He was trying to be tough just as he'd been trying to talk tough and sound worldly. But a fear blazed through that hard stare, giving the lie to the young man's braggadocio. He was young and sick to death with the fear of dying, with the fear of leaving this world before he'd really had the chance to experience it.

Lonnie knew that fear himself. He'd experienced it last year with Shannon Dupree, and he'd experienced it just a couple of hours ago, when he'd nearly been blown out of his saddle.

"It's gonna be okay, McLory," Lonnie said. "I'm gonna patch you up. Then I'll take you down to our cabin and send for the sawbones in Arapaho Creek."

McLory looked at him, and now his gaze was even more fearful than before.

Finally, McLory rested his head back against the cave wall and let his gaze slide past Lonnie and into space as his fears set to work on him with even more intensity, chewing away at him the way the whiskey probably was.

CHAPTER 6

Lonnie cleaned and bandaged McLory's wound, but it continued to bleed. Lonnie could see the blood staining the flannel pad he'd placed over the wound and held in place with a long, slender strip of flannel he'd wrapped around the young Texan's lower torso.

If McLory noticed the blood, he didn't let on.

He sat back against the cave wall, dozing as Lonnie fed and watered the General then gathered wood and built a fire in the middle of the cave, far back enough that the flames wouldn't be seen from the canyon floor. Lonnie emptied his war bag and brewed a pot of coffee.

While the coffee cooked, he tended his own wounds, cleaning them with a flannel swatch dipped in whiskey. Neither was bad enough to require a bandage.

When the coffee was bubbling over, the smell awakened McLory.

Lonnie filled him a cup and gave him a bacon-and-biscuit sandwich that Lonnie had made earlier that day, before he'd left the line shack. It was his favorite food to nibble on throughout the day, until he could head back to the shack and cook a pot of pinto beans with a rabbit from one of his snares. Though only fourteen, Lonnie Gentry was an impeccable if rudimentary cook.

Night descended on the canyon. A metallic chill stitched the air. Mornings up this high, there was usually frost on the ground. Lonnie had given McLory his bedroll, and the Texan curled up in the sewn-together blankets, his head resting back against the wool underside of Lonnie's saddle.

Lonnie kept the fire built up, knowing the night would grow colder and that McLory needed to stay warm. Even now, he could see the Texan shivering beneath the blankets. McLory's coffee steamed up from where the cup sat beside him on the cave floor. He hadn't drunk much of it. He'd taken only a couple of small bites from the biscuit Lonnie had given him.

"You want some jerky?" Lonnie offered when he'd returned with another load of firewood. "I got some in the saddlebags there. Help yourself."

McLory shook his head.

"How come you're not drinkin' your coffee?" Lonnie asked him, biting into his second biscuit, and chewing. "You don't like the way I make it?"

McLory didn't respond to the question. He seemed to be staring right through Lonnie from where he lay back against Lonnie's saddle. Lonnie studied him, feeling a little queasy with worry for the young Texan whom he'd found himself taking a liking to.

McLory seemed a lot like Lonnie. In McLory, Lonnie thought he could see something of his later self. Besides, being young, he had a raw fear of death that could probably be attributed to his lack of understanding of death, despite having witnessed it when he'd killed Shannon Dupree and Dupree's two rotten, thieving partners and even having lost his own father to a heart stroke several years ago.

All he really knew about death was that it was a horrible thing, and he wanted nothing to do with it. But now, as he stared back at the dull eyes of Cade McLory, he had the chilling feeling down deep in his bones, that he was staring into the face of death itself. It might have just been his imagination, but he thought that McLory's eyes were sinking deeper into their sockets and that the waxy skin was drawing back tight against his cheekbones. It was as though the young Texan was becoming a skeleton before Lonnie's very eyes.

McLory smiled, then, as though to put the younger man's mind at ease. "You got you a girl, do you, Master Gentry?"

Lonnie felt heat rise into his ears. The topic of the fairer sex always seemed to embarrass him for some reason, though it once did more than it did now. Now he felt a thrill of pride to say, "I reckon you could say that."

"I had a feelin'—a good-lookin' kid like yourself. A neighboring ranch girl, is she?"

"No. A town girl." Lonnie refilled his coffee cup, using a thick leather swatch he'd fashioned for the maneuver, to keep from burning his hand. "Her name's Casey. Casey Stoveville. She works at Hendrickson's Mercantile in Arapaho Creek." With a touch of pride, he added, "She's sixteen."

"How old are you?"

"Fourteen." Lonnie felt his upper lip curl a grin.

McLory whistled. "An older woman—imagine that!" He looked at Lonnie askance, and Lonnie knew he was being teased now. "She don't . . . she don't work the cribs on the side, now, does she, Master Gentry?"

"Hell, Casey ain't no parlor girl!" Lonnie felt a sudden burn of anger. He and Casey had been through a lot together, when they'd been trying to take Dupree's stolen money over Storm Peak Pass to the deputy US marshal in Camp Collins, and they'd gotten close. As close as a sister and brother, at first. But then Casey had professed to Lonnie her love for him.

The boy's heart had swollen to the size of a mature pumpkin. It had fairly sprouted wings and flown.

While he hadn't had the chance to visit the girl in a while, her living in town and him living thirty miles up in the mountains, Lonnie held her close in his heart, and he was quick to run to her defense. But then he realized that McLory's mockery was all in fun. The young Texan was merely trying to distract himself from his misery and, most likely, his fear of death.

"Must be nice," McLory said, his gaze growing distant again, pensive. "Havin' a girl all your own. I had me one, once. A couple years back. I was gonna marry up with her, back in Texas, but then her pa, a rich rancher—one of the few rich men in west Texas—steered her in the direction of a man who had a better chance of providing for her—you know, *long term*."

"She let her pa convince her of that?" Lonnie was incredulous.

"She sure did. The night before we was to be married, she came out to the little shotgun ranch my brother and I were runnin' at the time. She even brought me a bouquet of wildflowers, as if those would soften the blow of what she had to tell me."

Tears glistened in McLory's eyes. Thoughts of the girl still haunted him, obviously. Lonnie could imagine how he felt. He'd likely feel that way if anything like that happened between him and Casey, though he doubted it ever would. They were too close and too much alike.

They'd be married, eventually, when they were both a few years older. Lonnie had it all planned out in his head—how Casey would move out to the ranch with him, and he'd build a cabin just for her and him, separate from his mother and his little brother, who was Shannon Dupree's child.

They'd raise a family out there—Lonnie and Casey.

"Summer."

"What's that?" Lonnie asked McLory.

"Summer was her name. Summer Nulf. It was like her folks gave her such a purty first name to make up for the humble last name. It fit her, too—Summer did. She was purty as a Texas hill country summer—all jasmine eyes and hair like honey. I can still smell her. She smelled like wild cherry blossoms growin' on the banks of the Rio Grande."

McLory paused. He was staring at the ceiling against which the firelight and shadows were playing tag. "I'd like to see her again. Never thought I would. But, now, I'd really, really, really like to see my Summer again."

Tears dribbled down the young Texan's cheeks.

Embarrassed, Lonnie turned away. He was surprised to find his throat swollen with emotion. He cleared it and then said, "You'll find someone else. Sounds like she didn't really deserve you, her listening to her pa and thinkin' only about money an' such. That ain't how life should be. It's too short. I know that from seein' folks die."

Lonnie stared off for a time. Then he sipped his coffee. Noting that McLory had fallen silent, he turned back to where the young Texan lay back against his saddle, staring dully up at the ceiling. McLory did not blink his eyes. He merely lay there, still, staring at the ceiling.

"McLory?" Lonnie said.

CHAPTER 7

Lonnie set his coffee down on the ground. He rose slowly from where he sat against the cave wall, on the opposite side of the fire from McLory. His heart was beating hard and fast.

Again, his boots felt like lead.

"McLory?" he repeated.

He walked over and knelt down beside the young Texan. McLory's eyes stared nearly straight up at the play of light and shadows on the cave ceiling. He did not blink. Lonnie slowly waved a hand in front of McLory's face.

Still, the Texan didn't blink.

Lonnie set his hand down flat against McLory's chest. He didn't detect even the faintest flutter of McLory's heart. He pulled his hand away quickly, instinctively repelled. He sat back hard on his heels and stared in shock at the Texan, who was now merely the husk of whom he'd been only a minute before.

A minute ago, he'd been a living and breathing man.

Now, suddenly, he was a corpse lying here before Lonnie. There didn't seem anything more hideous to Lonnie than a corpse. His impulse was to hightail it. To leave the cave and set up camp elsewhere.

But then, swallowing, Lonnie made a conscious effort to control himself. McLory was still McLory even if he was dead. Even in death, the Texan needed Lonnie's help.

Lonnie lifted his right hand. It quivered as he slid it out toward McLory's head. Lightly, he ran the tips of his fingers down over the dead man's eyelids, wincing and shuddering at the papery feel of the dead man's skin and the fine prick of his eyelashes. Lonnie gently raked the eyes closed.

Instantly, he felt better. Now McLory looked as though he were merely sleeping, though of course he was just as dead as he'd been before. But those open eyes had been deeply disturbing.

Lonnie stared down at the dead Texan for a long time. Many thoughts ran through him. As his revulsion for the nearness of death faded, they were replaced by sad thoughts of what McLory had lost, dying so young.

McLory's last thoughts had been of the girl who'd spurned him. Now, he'd never be able to see her again or to find another girl and build a life with her. He'd never raise a family. He'd never ride a horse or eat a meal or swim in a creek or know the joy of holding a girl's hand.

Now, he would know only darkness. Or, if the preachers had it right, he'd know Heaven. In that case, he might make out even better than Lonnie, who was still alive and, if all went well, he'd live through this night and eat another meal and ride his horse down out of these mountains. If the preachers had it right, Heaven would be even better than a good life right here on earth.

Heaven seemed like a tall order, but what did Lonnie know about such things? The preachers were older than he was, which meant they were wiser, too, didn't it? Lonnie supposed he was skeptical because he always needed sound reasons for his beliefs, and he couldn't say any grown-ups, preachers included, had ever given him any clear evidence about Heaven.

Enough thinking about all that. What did Lonnie Gentry know about it? He was a cowboy who'd been born in these mountains. He'd likely die in them, too. Just like McLory.

Only, later. He hoped.

Lonnie would see his girl, Casey Stoveville, again soon. That was as close to Heaven as he cared to get for now. In fact, he wanted right now to head down out of these mountains and visit Casey. It seemed the most important thing he could do.

But he could not. He'd see her again soon. First, he had to figure out what to do with McLory.

Lonnie drew McLory's blankets up over the dead man's face. Then Lonnie rose, walked over to the other side of the fire, and sat back against the cave wall, staring toward McLory. The young Texan faded gradually from Lonnie's view as the fire died. It was an eerie sight, seeing him over there, still and silent in death beneath the blankets, his head still tipped back against Lonnie's saddle.

When the fire died down to only three or four small, dancing flames, Lonnie built it back up again. The night was cold. And Lonnie didn't want to be alone in the darkness with McLory's body.

And not with that old Indian's curse on this canyon. He knew he should leave, but it was too dark. He couldn't risk injuring the General on his way out of here. And he couldn't leave McLory.

He had to take his chances that the curse was nothing more than some old prospector's tall tale.

When Lonnie had the fire going again, he sat back against the cave wall, crossed his arms on his chest, and shivered despite the fire's heat. He should take McLory's blankets, but there seemed something rude and crass about doing so, though he needed them more than McLory did now.

Still, he couldn't do it. He'd keep the fire going all night.

But then he opened his eyes and realized that he'd slept there against the cave wall though he hadn't thought he'd be able to. The fire was merely a mounded pile of faintly smoking ashes. False dawn filtered a milky light into the canyon. Birds were chirping and squirrels were chattering.

McLory lay where Lonnie had left him, on the far side of the cave—a dark mound beneath the blankets.

Lonnie shivered. He'd probably been shivering in his sleep all night. But now he shivered at the passing of a young man he'd grown close to in their short time together as well as at his refreshed knowledge of the nearness of death and of having to deal with it somehow.

Lonnie got to his feet. The cold made him feel like an old man. When he'd worked the creaks out of his young bones, he ate a couple of pieces of jerky and washed them down with water from his canteen.

He didn't bother with a fire. He wanted to get out of the canyon as fast as possible. He felt a cold, hard knot of sadness about McLory, but, frankly, the young Texan's body tied Lonnie's nerves in knots.

He decided that he probably couldn't get McLory onto his horse. McLory was too heavy for him. He probably could have found a way to get the dead man onto his horse if he'd been less repelled by him. But he chose to tell himself that it would be best for them both if Lonnie left McLory here, discreetly covered by Lonnie's blankets, while Lonnie fetched the sheriff out from Arapaho Creek.

He owed it to McLory to tell the sheriff about what had happened here, so that the sheriff could find those four rustlers who'd killed him not to mention who'd tried to kill Lonnie. The sheriff would see to it that McLory was taken to town and given a proper burial.

Gently, Lonnie eased his saddle out from beneath McLory's head. He noticed that McLory already appeared to be stiffening. Moving quietly, as though it were possible to wake the dead, Lonnie hauled his gear outside and onto his horse.

The sun had still not risen when Lonnie rode the General

41

out of the canyon, leaving the dead man alone in the cave behind him. He reflected with dread that he had now spent a full night in the canyon.

Did that mean he would join McLory soon?

CHAPTER 8

Lonnie was glad when he reached Arapaho Creek around noon that day. During the ride, he'd been wary of being run down again by the same men who'd run him down the day before.

Now as he rode into the bustling mining camp and ranch supply hamlet lying in a shallow valley in the southernmost reaches of the Never Summer range, he continued to look around cautiously. There was a good chance the men who'd ambushed him—likely, the same men who'd killed McLory— had come to town.

Lonnie felt safer here than he had in the mountains, but he was not yet out of the woods.

He headed directly for the sheriff's office. As he trotted the General along the street, Arapaho Street, which occasionally snugged itself up against the creek running through the heart of town, he weaved through the steady traffic of pedestrians and ranch and mining supply wagons and around the occasional bearded prospector and his pick-and-shovel-laden donkey or mule.

The mercantile was coming up on the right side of the street. That was where Lonnie's girl, Casey Stoveville, worked.

As Lonnie always did when he came to town, he scouted the place, hoping for a glimpse of Casey. He didn't have to look hard today. She was sitting out on the front steps running up to the mercantile's broad front porch and loading dock. Casey wasn't alone. She was sitting next to a man in a store-bought three-piece suit and bowler hat.

The gent had a handsome face though his nose was a little short. Dark-brown hair curled onto his celluloid shirt collar. He sported a neatly trimmed goatee and watch chain. Likely a drummer of one sort or another. Salesmen often swarmed the mercantile, imploring the proprietor, Mr. Hendrickson, to stock his shelves with their company's goods.

Mr. Hendrickson was probably out to lunch at the moment. That was likely why the drummer was talking with Casey, who often ran the place for Hendrickson and who knew how to do nearly everything that Hendrickson himself did. But, then, as Lonnie started moving on past the mercantile, raising his hand to wave if Casey caught his gaze, Lonnie frowned uncertainly.

There was something about the man sitting with Casey that made Lonnie doubt that he was a drummer, after all. One, he didn't appear to have a sample kit with him. Two, his suit appeared of a better cut than your usual salesman. And it appeared fairly new. Drummers didn't usually earn enough for a new suit of fine quality.

Also, this gent—who appeared to be in maybe his mid twenties—didn't look hungry or desperate enough to be a drummer. In Lonnie's limited experience, salesmen were usually the slick, syrupy-eyed, wolfish sort.

But that wasn't all that Lonnie noted about him. This fellow was sitting so close to Casey on the step that their legs were nearly touching, and he was giving Casey his full attention as he talked, smiling in a groveling way. He seemed to be keeping his voice low, so that no one else could hear. It was an intimate conversation.

Casey sat leaning forward, elbows on her knees, her head turned toward the man beside her, one finger twisting up a long lock of her dark-blonde hair as she sat listening to him, rapt.

Lonnie's gut twisted a little behind his belt buckle. Was this fancy Dan sparking Casey?

The General pulled up sharply and gave an indignant whinny.

"Hey, watch where you're goin', young fella!"

Lonnie whipped his head forward to see a freckle-faced, potbellied man in a soiled bar apron glaring at him. Standing ahead and to one side, the man was holding an armload of firewood.

"This time o' day the street's too damn busy to be ridin' through town with your head in the clouds, boyo!" The barman spoke with a thick Irish accent.

A man coming up on Lonnie in a buckboard ranch wagon, chuckled and shook his head in mockery. The barman, whom Lonnie recognized as Paddy O'Ryan, who ran a shack out of which he sold tin buckets of beer and ran a couple of whores' cribs out back, gave Lonnie one more venomous glare, and said, "You damn near ran me down!"

Then he swung around and, shaking his head, stomped through the open door of his low-slung shop.

Holding the General's reins taut in his gloved hands, Lonnie glanced at Casey and the suited gentleman, who were behind him now, as he'd ridden on past the mercantile. Casey and the fancy Dan were still talking back and forth, smiling and occasionally laughing, so involved in their conversation that neither one seemed to have noticed Lonnie despite Paddy O'Ryan's loud harangue.

Lonnie had never really known jealousy before. But he knew it now. It was an ache down deep inside him. It was like an injury though no bones or muscles were involved.

He rode on. He had more important business to take care of at the moment, though his aching gut felt otherwise. He glanced back over his shoulder once more. The fancy Dan and Casey were still chinning as though they'd known each other for years.

Maybe they had. Maybe they were just friends.

Something told Lonnie that wasn't true. Something told him the fancy Dan wanted to be more than friends with Casey. Lonnie had sort of half consciously been worried about that sort of thing. Casey had filled out nicely in the last year, and she'd acquired a certain mature, self-confident sparkle in her eye that meant she was growing up and getting even prettier than she had been before.

She was becoming a young woman, which somehow didn't seem fair to Lonnie, who was still two years younger. At fourteen, he was still a kid. In the worst way, he wanted to catch up to her, to be her equal.

Lonnie managed to sweep the confounding problem aside for the moment, but not before reflecting briefly on the story that McLory had told him the night before, about McLory's girl spurning him in favor of a gent who'd made more money than he had.

That girl, that heartbreak, had been the last thought, the last image in the young Texan's mind before he'd died.

Lonnie drew up to the sheriff's office, a log cabin supported on low stone pylons near the county courthouse on a side street behind it. Smoke issued from the tin chimney pipe to sweep down low over the porch, rife with the sweet tang of pine.

Two men wearing deputy sheriff badges were lounging on the front porch. Lonnie recognized them, for he recognized most folks in the town as well as around the county, having grown up here and also being curious and observant in the way that boys often are, learning the ways of things.

Lonnie dropped down out of the saddle and tied the General's reins to the hitch rack. As he mounted the front stoop, one of the sheriff's two deputies, Chick Bohannon, said, "Well, look what we have here. Mister Big Britches his own self!"

The other deputy, Randall "Walleye" Miller, laughed as he sat back in his timber-framed, hide-bottom chair, sipping a cup of coffee likely laced with whiskey. It was said that Miller, who'd been fired from several mines in the area, had a problem with who-hit-John. Miller was a big man with a thick, curly beard and one wandering, red-rimmed eye. He had a sawed-off, double-barreled shotgun resting across his fat thighs clad in greasy, torn denim trousers.

"You find any more money out in them mountains, Mister Big Britches?" Bohannon asked, referring to the money that Lonnie and Casey had taken over the mountains and delivered to the deputy US marshal in Camp Collins.

The tall, slender man's tone was fairly dripping with sarcasm. Bohannon's lilac eyes were flat and malicious, and he had long, coarse, yellow hair streaked with mud brown.

Lonnie knew from the way he'd been glared at and spoken to in town over the past year that some folks around here still thought, as had originally been suspected, that he'd been part of Shannon Dupree's holdup gang. He wasn't sure how they coupled that notion to the fact that he and Casey had returned the stolen bank money to the rightful authorities.

Lonnie had inadvertently shot one of the sheriff's deputies who'd ambushed him in the mountains. That deputy had been a well-liked man in this area. Lonnie suspected that that was a big reason why it had been hard to change some folks' minds on the subject of Lonnie's part in the initial robbery.

That and the fact that Dupree had been making time with Lonnie's mother, earning not only May Gentry a bad reputation hereabouts, but earning her innocent son a bad reputation, as well.

"Nope, no money today," Lonnie said, trying to keep his tone jovial. "Sheriff Halliday in?"

"What you want him for?" asked Deputy Miller with a suspicious, self-important air, narrowing that odd, wandering eye of his. "The sheriff's too busy to be bothered by the offspring of mountain scrubs."

Lonnie drew a sharp breath, trying to calm himself but finding himself balling his fists at his sides. "My family ain't scrubs, Deputy Miller."

Walleye, who'd been tilted back in his chair, set the chair down with a dull thud, and flared his nostrils at Lonnie.

"Oh, yeah? Well, I say you are. What're you gonna do about it?"

CHAPTER 9

Deputy Miller slowly gained his feet, his dung-brown eyes riveted on Lonnie though the wandering one rolled slightly to the outside of its socket. The man's swollen nostrils and thick neck gave him the aspect of an angry Brahma bull. Long, grizzled dark hair liberally woven with strands of gray hung down from his slouch hat.

Walleye moved toward Lonnie and stopped. "I asked you a question, Gentry."

Lonnie couldn't believe this. He'd done nothing to provoke this man. He tried not to let his exasperation show as he said, "I'm just lookin' for Sheriff Halliday. That's all. I ain't lookin' for no trouble."

"You Gentrys is always lookin' for trouble. Your pa was a troublemaker, too. An uppity troublemakin' Yankee."

"I doubt that."

Lonnie's dim memories of his father were of a gentle, good-natured man. The problem was that for some reason or another, Southerners, some of them ex-Rebels from the Old South, outnumbered Yankees in and around the Never Summer Range.

The lingering differences between the two sides often boiled over in hop houses and whiskey saloons—usually after sundown. Lonnie had heard that his father, a well-liked man with many friends and also a decorated war veteran, had occasionally visited the saloons here in Arapaho Creek, and he'd no doubt been involved in a skirmish or two over the lingering disagreements. From what Lonnie had heard about his father, Calvin Gentry had been a man who'd stood up for his principles.

Apparently, Walleye had been involved in one or two of these likely busthead-induced dustups, as well.

Walleye shoved his shotgun out toward Deputy Bohannon, who took it with a laugh and leaned back against the office's front wall. "You callin' me a liar, Gentry?" Walleye asked.

"Whoa, now," Lonnie said, holding up his hands, palms out. "No one called no one a liar. I don't want no trouble, Deputy Miller. I'm just here to . . ."

"How's your momma doin'?"

Walleye's question surprised Lonnie. He stared up at the big man towering over him. Walleye stood on the porch while Lonnie stood on the middle step leading up to it, a hand on each rail. He didn't like the dark, glowering cast to the big man's eyes coupled, as it had been, with the mention of Lonnie's mother.

"What's that?"

"I asked you how your momma's doin. A purty gal like that, livin' out there all alone with a scrappy shaver to look after, and with her outlaw boyfriend dead . . . she must get lonely."

Again, Bohannon laughed. Louder this time. He said, "I heard she gave birth to Dupree's child, to boot!"

Walleye said, "You tell your momma, boy Gentry, that if she gets *too* lonely, I'm right here. She can come knockin' on my door—"

"Shut up!" The words were out of Lonnie's mouth before he knew it. His ears were burning with sudden fury.

Walleye lurched forward, jaws hard. "What'd you say to me, boy?"

"I told you to shut up, you fat son of a bitch!"

Lonnie was suddenly so riled that his innate common sense

slithered out his ears. He was ready to fight this big, gutter-brained peckerwood, never mind that the man outweighed him by close to two hundred pounds and was nearly twice as tall as Lonnie. As Walleye started down the steps, Lonnie tried to hold his ground, but Walleye lunged like a cat, snatching him up in his arms, and, fight as he might, there was little that Lonnie could do.

Within seconds, Lonnie found himself upside down. His hat went tumbling off his head. Walleye was holding Lonnie by his ankles and jerking him up and down, so that the ground came up so close to Lonnie's face that Lonnie could see every rock, pebble, strand of hay, and fleck of horse manure.

Walleye jerked Lonnie down sharply.

The ground came up to slam the top of Lonnie's head, stunning the boy. His arms fell slack, hands in the dirt. Then Walleye carried Lonnie over to the stock trough behind the hitch rack. He raised Lonnie up and over the hay-flecked trough and then lowered him. Before Lonnie could suck a complete breath, his head was plunged into the trough, cold water engulfing his head and seeping into his ears.

Lonnie's heart was a drum beating away in his ears as the water rushed in to make the drumming even louder.

Lonnie sucked water into his lungs. He convulsed, blowing bubbles around his head as he thrashed his arms and kicked his legs, trying to free himself of the burly Walleye. Just when Lonnie thought his head would explode, Walleye lifted him out of the trough but dangled him in the air above it, his head about three inches above the water.

The General was whinnying and stomping his front hooves, threatening Walleye from the other side of the hitch rack. Walleye was hugging Lonnie's knees hard against his chest.

Walleye glared at the General, and yelled, "Shut up, you mangy cayuse, or I'll put a bullet in you!" He looked down at

Lonnie, who continued to thrash while coughing water up out of his battered lungs. "You ready to say you're sorry, boy?" Lonnie's nose and eyes were on fire.

He looked up at the big man towering over him, and clenched his fists. "You go to hell, you big son of a—!"

Before Lonnie could finish his sentence, Walleye plunged Lonnie's head into the trough once more. Again, Lonnie inhaled water. He strangled, thrashing, his head swelling, his heart hammering like an Apache war drum in his ears. When he didn't think he could go another half second without a breath, his head growing so light he thought he was about to pass out, Walleye lifted him clear of the trough once more.

Above the General's enraged whinnying and hoof stomping, Walleye said, "How 'bout now, boy? If not, you're gonna—"

"Turn him loose, Miller."

Lonnie had only vaguely heard the voice above the General's caterwauling and his own strangling sounds. Then he saw Frank Halliday step out onto the porch and move up to stand beside Chick Bohannon, fingers in the pockets of his brown wool vest, which he wore beneath a black, claw hammer frock coat. His shiny, five-pointed sheriff's star was pinned to the lapel of his coat—up high where everybody could see it.

Pursing his lips, looking like a schoolmaster only mildly annoyed with the current bout of playground roughhousing, Halliday said, "Put him down."

"Whatever you say, Sheriff."

Grinning, Walleye released Lonnie's legs. Lonnie dropped straight down and head first into the trough. His head struck the bottom of the trough, and then his legs splashed into the water, as well.

He grabbed the trough's wooden sides and heaved himself up and out of the water, strangling as he tried to rid his lungs of water while also trying to draw a breath, to keep from passing out. As the sunlit street grew dim around him, Lonnie crawled over the side of the trough, and dropped into the street. He rolled onto his belly and then rose onto his hands and knees, convulsing violently as he fought away the cold, wet hands of what felt like certain death.

As he did, he could feel the General's hot breath against the back of his neck and the occasional, concerned touch of the buckskin's prickly, rubbery snout.

"What's this all about?" Frank Halliday wanted to know.

"The kid comes waltzin' up here, bein' a smart Mcgee, Sheriff," said Chick Bohannon. "You know the Gentrys. Him an' his ma think they're really somethin', when all May Gentry is is a Jane-about-the-mountains."

"Prob'ly shackin' up with another outlaw," said Walleye.

Rage and exasperation continued to boil through Lonnie, but he had no energy with which to vent it, even if he was inclined to bring more trouble onto himself. Walleye likely would have drowned him in the stock trough if Halliday hadn't stepped out of his office.

"Boy," Halliday said, raising his voice so Lonnie could hear above his choking, "what brings you to town?"

CHAPTER 10

When Lonnie thought he'd finally coughed most of the water out of his lungs, and could draw at least half a lungful of air, he rolled onto his back. The General lowered his head, sniffing him again with concern.

Lonnie looked up past the horse to where Halliday was standing on the stoop with Chick Bohannon, who just now tossed the shotgun back to Walleye. Walleye caught it one-handed and turned to glower down at Lonnie.

"I found a man wounded in Skull Canyon."

"A wounded man this time," said Chick Bohannon, mockingly. "No stolen bank loot?"

"Maybe you wounded him," grunted Walleye. "Just like you killed Willie Drake. Willie—he was my cousin." Walleye poked his sausage-sized, grime-encrusted thumb against his lumpy chest. "I take it personal that you shot him!"

Lonnie said, "Yeah, well, I take it personal that he was shootin' at me before he got his facts straight."

Walleye bunched his lips and lurched toward Lonnie once more.

"That's enough, Walleye," Halliday said. "Pull your horns in." Halliday produced a long, black cigar from inside his vest, nipped off the end, and stuck the cheroot between his large, pale yellow teeth. "Tell me about this wounded man you found in Skull Canyon."

"A little . . . a little older'n me. Name was McLory. Cade McLory."

"What do mean 'was'?"

"He died last night. I tried doctorin' him, but he didn't make it."

"You shoot him?" Walleye asked, accusingly. "By *mistake*— same way you shot my cousin?"

Bohannon laughed.

Lonnie sat up and tried to brush water off his cheek. All he did was smear mud on his face. He was sitting in what had now become a bog around the horse trough. "Hell, no!"

"Don't bring your foul language to town, boy," the sheriff ordered. "You leave it back on your ranch. Your mother may let you get by with talkin' that way, but I won't. Not in my town."

"I'm sorry, Sheriff, but I'm tired of him hound doggin' me!"

"I'll hound dog you, all right!"

"Stand down, Walleye. Get the hump out of your neck." To Lonnie, Halliday said, "Where is this dead man you're talkin' about? You leave him out there?"

"He was too heavy. I didn't think I could get him on my horse. I left him in a cave near the entrance to the canyon. Just inside about a hundred yards, west ridge wall. Behind some boulders." Lonnie rose, his wet clothes heavy on him, his sodden boots squeaking. "Four men tried to run me down before I found McLory. Rustlers, most like. They must've shot McLory and thought I was McLory's partner."

Lonnie didn't like the way Halliday was staring at him. It was a vaguely suspicious look. Mostly, it was menacing. Why it was so, Lonnie had no idea.

He picked up his hat, stuffed it on his head, and looked up at Sheriff Halliday, who was a tall man of middle age, with a neatly trimmed, gray-streaked brown goatee to match his thinning hair. He was an elegant man who spent most of his time in the gambling parlors and hurdy-gurdy houses. Dwight Stoveville, Casey's father, had been the sheriff here until Shannon Dupree had shot him when Stoveville had tried to cut off Dupree's escape from the bank holdup in Golden last year.

Halliday, a wealthy dude from Oklahoma who owned a saloon and a freighting business, knew important men in the area. Those men had gotten him an appointment as sheriff. There would be an official election in September though no one was running against him. It was said that no one dared. It was also said that Halliday had gotten rich by sinister means and that he intended to use his position as sheriff to continue cashing in on his sinister ways.

Suddenly, Lonnie wished he hadn't involved Halliday and his no-account deputies. He thought he'd been doing the right thing for both himself and Cade McLory, but now he was starting to feel incriminated in McLory's death, for all three lawmen were regarding him skeptically.

Halliday took a long drag off his black cheroot, blew the smoke out into the wind, and then, keeping his gray-eyed gaze on Lonnie, said, "Walleye, Bohannon—saddle up and check it out. Bring the body back to town. I want a look at it."

Walleye frowned at Halliday. "Skull Canyon's supposed to be cursed, boss."

Bohannon laughed as he dropped lightly down the porch steps, spurs jingling. Halliday looked at Walleye as though he'd just broken wind. Walleye flushed and then, setting his shotgun on his shoulder, followed Bohannon off in the direction of the Federated Livery Stable.

Halliday returned his hard, gray eyes to Lonnie. He didn't say anything for a time. It was as though he were probing the boy's deepest thoughts and motivations with his gaze.

Then he stuck the cheroot back between his teeth, took another long drag off it, and blew the smoke out as he said, "I know about you, boy. I know about the trouble you and your mother got yourselves into last year. I know all about you and her throwin' in with Shannon Dupree and those two tough nuts he rode with—Childress and Fuego."

"We didn't throw in with 'em, Sheriff. That's just a malicious rumor goin' around. Heck, me an' Casey Stoveville, the sheriff's daughter—"

"I know, I know—I heard that story, too. About how you two took the money to the deputy US marshal over in Camp Collins. But I don't think that's the whole story, is it? I think you did that after you killed that deputy and you saw the writing on the wall—that you were going to hang if you didn't do somethin' fast with the money. Somehow you got the drop on Dupree, Childress, and Fuego, and shot them all just to keep them quiet about your part in the robbery."

Exasperated all over again, Lonnie wagged his head.

"Just hold your tongue, boy," Halliday cut him off before he could speak. "I won't take no sass from a no-account mountain boy. I don't know what you and your mother got goin' up there in them mountains, but you best understand I'm gonna keep my eye on both of you. The word goin' around is that your place is a hideout for cattle rustlers."

"*What?*"

"I told you to hold your tongue, boy!"

"But I'm tellin' you that's a damn lie, Sheriff!"

Halliday pulled his cheroot out of his mouth, lurched down the porch steps, and smashed the back of his hand holding the cigar across Lonnie's right cheek. Cigar ash burned Lonnie's eye as the blow hurled him back to the muddy ground.

The General gave a menacing whicker and shook his head, not at all happy with all the abuse being visited upon his rider.

Halliday poked his cigar threateningly at Lonnie, and gritted his teeth. "I done told you I won't allow young folks to talk like drunken Irish miners. Not in my town! Now, you get the hell away from me. When I've investigated the killin' out in Skull Canyon, I'll know where to find you for further questions. If I hear one more word of insolence from you, I'll take the strap to you and throw you in jail for a night!"

Halliday wheeled, marched back up onto the porch, and disappeared into his office.

Lonnie sat up, rubbing his cheek. He glanced around. Several townsfolk—women as well as men—were staring at him. They were regarding him accusingly, muttering among themselves and shaking their heads.

Lonnie cursed under his breath.

He spat mud from between his lips, slogged over to the hitch rail, and untied the General's reins.

He shouldn't have come to town.

He should have kept quiet about Cade McLory. He should have kept quiet about the rustlers who'd tried to kill him. He probably hadn't helped McLory one bit, and he'd only made more trouble for himself.

From now, Lonnie Gentry would make a trip to town once every six weeks for supplies, and that was it. Other than that, he'd stay in the mountains. That was the best place for him.

He heaved his weary self into his saddle. He rode on down the street, back in the direction from which he'd come. He was intending on riding on out of town. He was too beaten up and humiliated to visit Casey.

But then, as he passed the mercantile, he saw her standing on the loading dock waving good-bye to the young fancy Dan she'd been talking to before. The fancy Dan turned abruptly away from Casey, lifting his hat to the girl, and nearly ran smack into the General.

The fancy Dan stopped abruptly, gave Lonnie the hairy eyeball, and said, "For Heaven's sake, boy—watch where you're going, will you?"

Then he waved at Casey once more and strode off down the street.

Casey looked at Lonnie, her eyes raking his soaked, muddy, and generally bedraggled countenance up and down.

The pretty, hazel-eyed blonde planted a fist on her hip, and said, "Lonnie Gentry, what kind of trouble have you gotten yourself into *now?*"

CHAPTER 11

"The usual," Lonnie said, feeling too downtrodden to defend himself. "The usual trouble, Casey."

He turned the General away from the mercantile and continued down the main street. He no longer cared about seeing Casey. He just wanted to get back up into the mountains and be alone. He was feeling sorry for himself. He wanted to hole up and lick his wounds.

"Lonnie—hold on!"

He couldn't ignore the girl, however. He drew back on the General's reins and turned to see Casey moving on down the porch steps, holding the hem of her checked gingham housedress above her ankles, her long, wavy, gold-blonde hair bouncing on her shoulders.

She moved out into the street and stopped near Lonnie's left stirrup, looking up at him, brows furled with concern. "You look like you were caught in a cyclone. What happened?"

Lonnie spat more mud from his lips and glanced in the direction in which the fancy Dan had gone. "Who was that?"

Casey hiked a shoulder, saying, "A friend. You're soaked. What have you been doing? You're all mud. And that eye . . . You're gonna have a nice shiner, there, Lonnie. Did you get into a fight?"

Lonnie could only give a caustic laugh at the question.

"Ride on over to my place. I'm gonna clean you up before you catch your death of cold in those wet clothes."

"Never mind, Casey."

"Lonnie!" She gave him one of those admonishing scowls of hers, both cheeks dimpling, her hazel eyes slitting. He didn't think she was any more beautiful than when she was scowling at him, though he had to admit her warm smiles could turn his heart to putty.

"Casey, you're workin'."

"I was about to close up for lunch. Mister Hendrickson is home sick, though I think it's the bottle flu. I heard he was up all night gambling in the Purple Palace. Lonnie, you ride on over to my house. I'll meet you there in a minute. Don't argue with me, Lonnie Gentry!"

Lonnie had to admit if only to himself that the girl's obvious concern for him made him feel a little better about his lot in life. He didn't let on, however. He sighed as though at another bitter defeat and gigged the General on around the corner of the mercantile and down the side street to the south.

He crossed a tributary of Arapaho Creek, picked up another side street, passed several old cabins—the original cabins of Arapaho Creek, from a time when the town had not been named yet and was only a small, seedy mining camp. The cabins slouched beneath their shake roofs pocked with moss. An ancient, bearded old man in pinstriped overalls sat out front of one, blindly staring toward the far peaks, a shaggy dog asleep in the shade beside him. A stick he'd been whittling lay across his lap.

Lonnie passed a giant cottonwood rattling its leaves in the warm, dry breeze and rode into the yard of the neat, white clapboard house in which Casey Stoveville now lived alone. There was a small stable and corral behind the house, as well as a buggy shed. Lonnie rode around back and after releasing the General's belly strap and slipping his bit, Lonnie led him into the corral and closed the gate.

By the time Lonnie walked back around to the front of the house, Casey was walking into the yard, having followed a shortcut over the creek from the mercantile. She wore a long, faded denim jacket over the dress, and a gray felt Stetson, the chin thong dangling down her chest.

She stopped in front of Lonnie, and reached up to touch two fingers to the swelling area around his eye. "That hurt?"

"Startin' to fuss a little."

"Compliments of whom?"

"Walleye Miller."

Casey grimaced as she turned away and started up the steps of the small, white porch fronting the house that was in need of a fresh coat of paint. The mountain winters were hard on clapboard houses. A floorboard was missing from the porch, as well, and there was a small crack in a front windowpane.

"How on earth did you get mixed up with Walleye Miller?" Casey asked. "You know he's a tough nut who couldn't keep a ranch job because of all the fights he got into."

"Kind of hard to see the sheriff without seein' Walleye first," Lonnie said, following Casey into the house. "You know how all he and Bohannon do is sit out on the sheriff's front stoop, sharpening matchsticks and drinkin' coffee spiced with bust-head. It sure is a different office without your pa runnin' it."

Immediately, Lonnie wished he hadn't mentioned Casey's father. His murder was still an open wound.

Lonnie saw Casey's cheek blanch slightly and her shoulders tighten as she went to the kitchen sink and pumped water into a tin coffee can. She shook her hair out of her eyes, and glanced at Lonnie. "Have a seat, killer. I'll try to get you cleaned up."

Lonnie stood on the rope mat just inside the door. He was trying to pull a boot off.

"Don't worry about your boots," Casey told him, pumping water. "I sort of miss having a man to clean up after around here . . . on occasion."

She gave Lonnie a faint, wan smile then turned away, letting her hair drop down to cover her face.

"Sorry," Lonnie said. "I shouldn't have said that . . . about your old man."

"My father is dead," Casey said, setting the filled can on the table and then turning to open a cupboard door. "I miss him, but I'm used to it."

She came back over to the table and sat down beside Lonnie, turning her chair to face him. She dipped one of the flannel cloths into the can and wrung it out. "It's just that . . . times are tough."

"How do you mean?"

Casey reached forward and began lightly wiping mud from around Lonnie's eye. "I might lose the house."

Lonnie grabbed her hand, frowning. "Why?"

"Taxes. And I'm havin' trouble keepin' up with the payments. Pa was a good provider, but he didn't save much. I was able to get through the first eight months all right, but now I'm starting to backslide. I don't make enough at the mercantile. That's not Mister Hendrickson's fault. He pays me all he can." Casey shook her head as she dabbed at Lonnie's lip. "Still, it's not enough."

As she continued cleaning Lonnie's face, taking special care with the area around his eye and the bullet burn across his cheek, she said, "The house needs a new roof and fresh paint."

"I can shingle the roof for you. And I can paint for you, too. For free."

Again, Casey gave a halfhearted smile. "Thanks, Lonnie, but you got your hands full out at the Circle G."

Lonnie grabbed Casey's wrist again and gave it a gentle, re-assuring squeeze. "Don't worry, Casey—everything will be all right."

"Listen to me go on," Casey said, wringing out the cloth in the can again. "Good Lord—you're the one all soaked and muddy and beaten up. And you haven't even told me why you needed to see the sheriff in the first place."

Lonnie looked at her. At first, all he could see was Cade McLory lying dead in the cave, staring blankly at the ceiling. Another chill swept through Lonnie. He swallowed back his emotion, trying to be strong. But he heard a tremor in his voice as he said, "I saw a man die last night."

CHAPTER 12

Casey just stared at him for a long moment.

"Good Lord, Lonnie. Where? How?"

"In Skull Canyon."

Casey looked surprised now as well as shocked. "What were you doing in Skull Canyon? You know the place is cursed."

Lonnie had never known Casey to be the suspicious sort. But, then, he hadn't known her all that long. Just since last year. She'd always seemed levelheaded, so for her to believe the old legend about the canyon being cursed made Lonnie all the more unnerved about having spent a whole night in the spooky place.

Half of that night with a dead man . . .

"I was chased by four men on horseback. They tried to kill me. They popped off enough lead to cast a cannon."

"Oh, Lonnie, what in the world have you—?"

Lonnie squeezed her wrist a little harder, to forestall the question. "I got no idea who they were. Rustlers, most likely. I seen one of 'em up close, and didn't recognize 'im. I don't think they're from around here. They're probably from Wyoming or New Mexico. I've seen every range rider from these parts at least once, and I got a mule's memory."

"What about the dead man?"

"When I got away from them four shooters, I was workin' my way back down the mountain to look for the General. I heard a wounded man moanin' and carryin' on. He was in the canyon—

Skull Canyon. I didn't see another way, so I went in. He was gut shot. He couldn't walk very far, so I got him into a cave near the canyon entrance. I built a fire and tended him as best I could."

Lonnie swallowed and gave a shudder, remembering last night and wishing some of the vividness had been honed away by time.

"His name was Cade McLory. A nice fella, seemed like. Only a few years older'n me. He was from Texas."

"What was he doin' in Skull Canyon, this Cade McLory?"

"I don't know."

"You didn't ask?"

Lonnie tried to remember. Little but McLory himself and the way he'd died, the way he'd *looked after he'd died,* had stayed clear to Lonnie. The peripheral stuff, what they'd talked about, had turned blurry.

"I don't know. I reckon I did. But . . . if I did, he didn't tell me. At least, I don't remember what he said, if he said anything. He was there with another fella."

"Lonnie, why were those other men chasing you?"

"I got no idea, Casey. I know what you're thinkin'. You an' Walleye an' Bohannon and Sheriff Halliday."

"Don't throw me in the stable with those worthless—"

"All I know is I was up brush poppin' lost cows an' haulin' 'em out of the mud when those four curly wolves rode at me like the devil's hounds loosed from hell. Then I found McLory. I came to town to report it all to the sheriff, but now I'm wishin' I'd stayed in the mountains. I should know better than to ever leave the mountains. Dang near got drowned in a horse trough, was treated like a killer, slapped by a man three times my size— and all that was only *after* I rode by the mercantile and saw my girl lookin' all starry-eyed at . . .'"

Lonnie let his voice trail off when a knock sounded on the door.

The door opened. Fancy Dan himself poked his head into the kitchen, grinning. The grin faded, however, when his large, copper-brown eyes found Lonnie sitting at Casey's kitchen table, still wet and muddy, with Casey sitting within three feet of him, the two of them holding hands.

"Miss Casey," fancy Dan said, looking bewildered as he slid his gaze from Lonnie to Casey and back again, "I just wanted to stop by and tell you . . . when the next dance was . . . out at Vott's Barn, but . . ."

"Oh, Niles!" Casey lurched to her feet so quickly that she nearly knocked her chair over backwards. She hurried over to the door. Fancy Dan retreated out onto the porch, and Casey followed him out, drawing the door closed behind her.

The door wasn't much of a buffer, however. Lonnie could hear the fancy Dan also known as Niles say, "Casey, who is that boy? He and his horse nearly ran me over in town, and . . ."

Casey spoke in a soft, low voice, but Lonnie could still hear the girl say, "Oh . . . he's . . . he's just a boy from the mountains, Niles. I see him from time to time. He gets into trouble on occasion and . . ."

Then they must have moved off down the steps because Casey's voice grew gradually quieter until Lonnie could no longer hear what she was saying.

That was all right.

Lonnie had heard enough.

His bruises no longer ached. At least, they were nothing compared to the driving, burning agony that the invisible fist of Casey Stoveville's hushed words had hammered into his gut.

Lonnie rose unsteadily from his chair.

The kitchen pitched and swayed around him. He felt the way he had when he'd "gentled" half-wild horses to add to his own remuda, riding the green out of them. Those owl-eyed broom-tails would use the lean-to shed off the barn to rake Lonnie off their backs and then pummel him down hard in the dust with their hooves.

He felt the same way now. He felt as though he'd had the stuffing kicked out of both ends.

Dragging his heavy feet, Lonnie made his way out of the kitchen, through a curtained doorway, and down a short hall to the house's rear door. He pushed through the door and outside, leaving the door wide behind him. Regaining his balance, he almost ran to the corral, threw the gate open, and ran at the General so fast that the horse whickered and sidestepped from him, neck arched and tail raised.

"Easy, boy—easy, easy," Lonnie said, moving up on the horse more slowly but with no less urgency.

When he'd slid the bit back into the General's mouth and tightened the latigo strap, Lonnie mounted up and rode out of the corral. He galloped off to the southwest, toward the trail that would take him deep, deep into the mountains where no one else in the world would ever see or hear from him again.

Chapter 13

Crouched behind a boulder sitting like a hat on top of a haystack-shaped bluff, Lonnie slowly pumped a cartridge into his Winchester's chamber and caressed the cocked hammer with his gloved right thumb.

He doffed his hat and edged a look around the boulder.

The trail he'd been following from town snaked around the base of the bluff to climb steeply into pines. A few minutes ago, while Lonnie had been riding deeper and deeper into the mountains, the General had given a warning whicker. Thirty seconds later, Lonnie had heard what the General had heard—the distance muffled hoof thuds of a rider approaching along Lonnie's back trail.

Lonnie had quickly dismounted, led the General off the trail, and climbed the bluff to hide behind the boulder. If he was being followed, he wanted to know by whom and why.

The hoof thuds told him only one man was approaching, but there might be more behind him. Like *three* more. Which would make a total of four—the same number who'd bushwhacked him yesterday afternoon around the same time of day, when his life had exploded like a powder keg.

Now a shadow moved among the pines. Lonnie jerked his head back behind the boulder with a start. Then he slowly slid another peek around the boulder. He drew a short breath and held it.

The rider was moving down out of the trees. He was a lanky

man in a tall gray Stetson and long, spruce-green duster. His pinstriped trouser legs were stuffed down into stovepipe, cavalry-style boots. Lonnie couldn't see his face from this angle, for the man was riding down the slope, and he had his chin down, as well, as though he were scrutinizing the tracks in the trail ahead of him.

Lonnie's tracks.

The man rode a speckle-gray horse that lifted its head abruptly and gave a warning whinny. The horse had winded Lonnie. Behind Lonnie, at the base of the bluff, the General answered in kind.

"Dangit, you old hay burner!" Lonnie snarled at the stallion.

The rider jerked his head up, pulling back on his reins, and reaching for the big pistol holstered for the cross draw high on his left hip. Lonnie licked his lips, drew another, calming breath, and stepped out from behind the boulder, aiming his rifle at the big man on the speckle-gray.

Trying to keep his voice calm, Lonnie said, "Leave the hog leg in its holster or I'll blow you clear back to sunup."

The man froze and slid his head slightly to the side, his eyes finding Lonnie beneath the broad brim of his tall, gray hat. His long, lean face was sunbaked; his hawk nose was brick red. Long, gray hair curled over his collar. He wore a mustache, goatee, and muttonchop whiskers of the same color. Lonnie thought his eyes beneath his hat brim were frosty blue. They resided in deep sockets around which a meshwork of deep crow's-feet spoked and beneath which heavy, dark bags sagged.

Lonnie said, "Who are you and why're you followin' me?"

The man narrowed his eyes as he took the measure of the rifle-wielding kid before him. "Careful, boy. You don't want that thing to go off."

"Neither do you," Lonnie said, consciously keeping steel in his voice. Just because he was young didn't mean he was gonna take any grief from a grown-up. He'd had enough grief from grown-ups.

The man raised his gloved hands slowly, holding his reins in the right one. "I was only wantin' to ask you a few questions, that's all. I don't know who you are or where you're from, but I figure you're from around here. I'm not."

He raked a thumb across the edge of his duster, peeling the canvas lapel back to reveal a copper moon and star badge. "Name's John Appleyard. *Deputy US Marshal* John Appleyard. Out of Denver. I'm lookin' for an hombre who goes by the name of Crawford Kinch. Thought maybe you knew him or seen him hereabouts."

Lonnie kept his rifle aimed at the tall man before him though he eased the tension in his trigger finger. He'd shot one lawman last year. He didn't want to go for another lawman this year. Unless he had to, that was. He knew from experience that not all lawman were lawful. They could kill you just as dead as the worst variety of outlaw.

"I don't know no one named Crawford Kinch," Lonnie said.

"He might be goin' by another name. He's a tall man. About my size, a few years older. Has a gray beard, one blue and one brown eye, and wears a tattoo on his neck. The tattoo is, uh . . ." The lawman glanced away, vaguely sheepish, before turning back to Lonnie. "The tattoo is a naked lady. Big enough so's you couldn't miss it."

Lonnie flushed a little at the image of the naked lady floating around inside his head. "Never seen him."

"Could you lower that gun, son? You're makin' me nervous. And I *am* a lawman. I don't just wear the badge because it looks nice and shiny on my shirt."

"Just cause a dog has a tail," Lonnie said, "don't mean he wags it."

The man smiled briefly at that, and looked away again. "Fair enough." He looked up at Lonnie, narrowing one eye. "You from around here?"

"Yep."

"What's your name?"

Lonnie considered whether he wanted to give the man his name. He supposed it couldn't hurt. He could ask around and find out easily enough. Lonnie told him.

"Would you do me a favor, Lonnie Gentry?" the deputy marshal asked. "If you do happen to see this man, Crawford Kinch, around here somewhere, would you please get word to me in Arapaho Creek? I'm staying at the boardinghouse on Third Avenue."

Lonnie lowered the gun to his side but kept his finger curled through the trigger guard, in case he needed it quickly. "What do you want with this Crawford Kinch fella?"

"Never mind about that. Whatever it is, you'll want to steer clear of it. And you'll want to steer clear of Crawford Kinch, too. But if you do happen to be unfortunate enough to run into him, and live to tell about it, tell me, will you?" Appleyard gave an ironic grin.

Lonnie studied the man, nodded slowly. "All right. I'll get word to you if I see this Crawford Kinch . . . and live to tell about it."

Lonnie wondered if he should tell the marshal about the four men who'd run him down yesterday, and about Cade McLory. He decided against it. He'd been reminded in town only a couple of hours ago that the less he said to the law, the better. Besides, he hadn't gotten a very good look at three of the four riders yesterday, but he was sure he'd have noted a tattoo on one of them.

Especially one in the shape of a naked lady.

He'd already told Halliday about Cade McLory. He'd done his duty, and he'd suffered the consequences for it, and McLory wasn't going to benefit one way or the other if the men who'd shot him were brought to justice.

Appleyard dipped his chin and pinched his hat brim to Lonnie. "Much obliged, boy. Even from here, your lips look blue. You'd best get yourself warm before you catch your death of cold."

Lonnie didn't say anything. He watched the lawman turn his horse around on the trail and then ride up into the pines, heading back in the direction of town.

Lonnie stared at Appleyard's back growing smaller and smaller until the tree shadows swallowed horse and rider. Lonnie scraped a thumbnail along his smooth jawline and mused softly, "Crawford Kinch, huh? A naked-lady tattoo. Imagine that."

CHAPTER 14

Lonnie shivered as he rode higher into the mountains. His clothes were no longer soaked, but they were damp. The dampness had leeched into his bones, muscles, and tendons.

He didn't intend on riding all the way back to the ranch just yet. He didn't feel like seeing his mother and his half brother, whom May Gentry had named Jeremiah. Jeremiah was the offspring of Shannon Dupree, but Lonnie didn't hold it against the baby, only a few months old.

Still, the kid was loud, and Lonnie needed peace and quiet. He felt like being alone for a while, to lick his wounds both physical and otherwise. He headed for the line shack at the base of Eagle Ridge. His mother wouldn't start to worry about him for another day or so. When coyotes or wolves were around, or when he'd spotted the tracks of a mountain lion on his range, Lonnie often stayed with the herd in the mountains for several days and nights at a time, to try and keep his losses to a minimum.

He was used to being alone. In fact, he was starting to prefer being alone. People were too much trouble.

The trail meandered ever higher into the Never Summers. Finally, when Lonnie was a good hour and a half out of Arapaho Creek, he turned off the main trail and followed an old horse trail through a ravine thick with aspens. Eagle Creek flowed down the middle of the ravine, rippling over beaver dams. The air was spiced with the wine fragrance of the creek and green leaves and wild raspberries.

The line shack sat at the head of this ravine and at the base of the towering granite crag known as Eagle Ridge. The cabin was a low-slung, mossy-roofed log structure that his father had built when he and May Gentry had first settled in these mountains. Mostly, his father had stayed overnight in the cabin only during spring and summer roundups or when predators were on the prowl. He'd limited his time here. He'd loved his family, so he'd stayed close to home.

Lonnie tended and stabled the General out back of the line shack. Then he hauled his gear into the cabin. He climbed up onto the roof and removed the coffee tin which he always placed over the chimney pipe, to keep birds and squirrels out, and then went back inside the cabin and built a fire in the sheet-iron monkey stove.

As the fire got going, Lonnie walked over to where the creek ran over its rocky bed through the aspens. He paused at the edge of the stream, near a cool, dark hole of waist-deep water, doffed his hat, kicked out of his boots, and steeled himself.

He took a deep breath and then plunged feet-first into the pool.

The water, fed by a spring deep beneath Eagle Ridge, was as cold as snowmelt. It was so cold that Lonnie thought his teeth would crack. Still, it was the best way to get himself and his clothes clean.

He thrashed around for a while in the water, shivering and yelling, unable to control the outburst. Oddly the cold felt good. It almost pushed Casey and fancy Dan out of his mind.

Almost, but not quite . . .

When he thought his heart could no longer take the bitter-sweet torture, Lonnie crawled up onto shore, and gained his feet. Water sluiced off of him. He shivered and cursed like a sailor, feeling the luxurious freedom of being able to do so in so remote a place, where the hawks, chickadees, squirrels, owls, and occasionally a skunk or two were his only neighbors.

Once, he'd befriended an orphaned fox cub out here, and named it Red. Red had grown up and gone off on his own, but occasionally Lonnie saw a red fox hunting mice in a near meadow, and he believed—at least, he hoped—the fox was his old pal Red.

As he walked back to the cabin, Lonnie peeled off his wet clothes, leaving a soggy trail of blue denims, socks, longhandles, checked shirt and navy-blue neckerchief in a long, wet, twisted line behind him. Gray smoke billowed from the cabin's stovepipe. It was like the fire was beckoning to the shivering youngster.

By the time Lonnie reached the front door, he was naked—dark brown where the sun reached him and as white as flour where it did not, which was almost everywhere except his face, neck, and hands. He went in, closed the door, wrapped a blanket around his shoulders, shoved more pine sticks into the stove, and hunkered close to the open stove door.

The heat pushed against him, hot as a dragon's breath. The fire *whushed* and the stove ticked as the iron grew hot.

Gradually, the chill began to ease its grip on Lonnie though he continued to shiver violently, crouched beneath the blanket. After a time, he rose from the cot, went over to where he'd hastily piled his gear, and rummaged around in a saddlebag pouch. He pulled out the pint bottle of whiskey, and held it up to the window.

Still half full.

Lonnie had never had a desire for liquor before. He'd seen what it had done to the likes of Shannon Dupree. It had turned him into an ugly, wild, violent animal. But Lonnie's mother had given it to Lonnie, mixed with hot water and honey, when he'd suffered from colds and sore throats. The busthead had soothed not only the pain of the illness, but it had drawn the chill from his bones, as well.

Lonnie sat back down on the edge of the cot, close to the crackling, popping fire, and pried the cork from the bottle. He took a sip and made a face as the liquor dribbled down his throat, burning harshly all the way down into his belly. A moment later, however, the burn eased. A comforting flush spread out from his belly, rising from his chest and neck and into his cheeks and ears.

Soothing . . .

He took another sip. That one was too big. It nearly came back up.

Somehow, he managed to keep it down though he thought it would strangle him. He coughed and choked for a brief time, as though someone like Walleye Miller had his hand around his neck. But then the hand eased its grip, and the soothing flush rose once again.

Lonnie looked around. The harsh angles of the cabin softened, and the mountain light slanting through the windows grew less harsh, pleasantly fuzzy.

The chirping of the birds outside in the branches grew keener.

Best of all, the warmth of the fire was finally seeping into his fingers and toes, thawing him out. Still, his heart felt swollen and tender. He doubted any amount of whiskey would heal it.

Casey . . .

Lonnie corked the bottle and set it on the floor beneath the cot. He chunked another split pine log onto the fire and sat back down on the cot, holding the blanket tight about his shoulders. He was no longer shivering. He just sat there now. Beneath the ache in his chest, he enjoyed being mildly drunk and the feeling of being dry and warm at last.

Outside, the General whinnied.

Lonnie snapped his head up.

Now, what?

Outside, another horse whinnied from the direction of the trail. Hooves thudded softly as the horse approached. Someone was coming.

Lonnie held the blanket loosely around his shoulders as he scrambled over to his gear and picked up his rifle. He opened the cabin door, cocked the rifle, and held it in one hand straight out from his waist.

No more, he thought. He would be trifled with no more . . .

Now he could catch glimpses of the sun- and shade-dappled horse and rider moving through the aspens toward the cabin. Lonnie tightened his grip on the rifle, hardened his jaws, and tightened his finger across the trigger.

CHAPTER 15

"Lonnie?" Casey yelled as she emerged from the trees, riding her chestnut mare Miss Abigail.

Lonnie's heart was wrenched one quarter turn in his chest.

Ah, hell.

Casey stopped at the edge of the trees, on the far side of the small clearing in which the cabin sat. Lonnie stepped back inside the cabin door, lowering the rifle and drawing the blanket tighter around his shoulders, very aware that he wasn't wearing a stitch beneath it.

"What the hell're you doin' here?"

Casey looked around at Lonnie's clothes strewn between the creek and the cabin. Then she turned to Lonnie and gigged the mare into a trot, shaking her head. "I'm so sorry, Lonnie."

"Stow it."

Casey rode up to the cabin and dismounted, dropping Miss Abigail's reins. She paused to pick up Lonnie's longhandles, which she twisted in her hands, wringing them out, and then moved up to the cabin. She tossed the longhandles over the hitch rack and moved closer to Lonnie, her eyes large beneath the brim of her hat.

She raised her arms as though to hug him, but Lonnie stepped back.

"What're you doin' here, Casey? I'm just a boy from the mountains. A boy who gets in trouble a lot. Ain't you just so nice befriendin' such a troubled soul!"

Lonnie swung around, retreating inside the cabin, and sat down on the edge of the cot, keeping the blanket pulled close about him. He saw Casey's shadow slide across the cabin floor as she stopped inside the doorway.

"Lonnie, I'm just awful," Casey said. "If you want me to leave . . . if you don't want to see me ever again, I understand. I'll ride away right now. But I'd like to explain. I owe you that much."

Lonnie glowered at the floor. "So, who's the fancy Dan?"

"Niles Gilpin."

Lonnie glanced at her over his shoulder. "Gilpin? That's the banker's name."

Casey turned the corners of her mouth down, nodding. "Niles is George Gilpin's son. He was studying at a college back east. He graduated last fall and came home to help his father in the bank."

Lonnie chuckled without humor as he turned his head back forward. "Now it's all coming clear to me."

Casey moved into the cabin. She sat down on the cot beside Lonnie. She took one of his hands in her own. She was wearing riding gloves. She didn't say anything for a moment. Lonnie didn't look at her, but he could feel her gaze on his face.

"Lonnie, I think it's time we faced facts," Casey said finally.

Lonnie turned to her. His cheeks were warm with embarrassment, anger, and jealousy—a nasty concoction that neither the fire's warmth nor the whiskey could alleviate. He steeled himself to keep from crying as he said, "You told me . . . you told me you loved me."

For some reason, despite his need for Casey's love, the word "love" only aggravated his humiliation. He wasn't sure why it was such a wonderful and repelling word, but it was.

Casey squeezed his hand. "I know I did. And I always will, Lonnie. We've been through a lot together. We almost died together. But we have to face facts."

"What facts are those?" Lonnie said with sarcasm. "That you found yourself a fancy Dan? The banker's son. Hell, Casey, if money means so much to you, we had a whole passel of it last year. For a time, old Wilbur Calhoun had me convinced that we should keep Dupree's loot and head to Mexico—don't you remember? You're the one who convinced me to turn it in!"

"Because that was the right thing to do, Lonnie. That money didn't belong to us."

"What *is* the right thing to do? To go skulkin' around with some fancy Dan behind my back? I'm sorry you didn't take what you said to me as serious as I did, Casey."

"I did take it seriously. I still do. But we're young, Lonnie. Too young to be making commitments to each other. The fact is, I'm going broke. Every month I get farther and farther behind. Soon, the county is going to sell my house because I can't pay the taxes on it."

"Gettin' hitched to the banker would solve that problem, wouldn't it?"

"Yes, I'm not sorry to say, it would."

Lonnie glared at her, hardening his jaws, trying not to cry though he felt on the verge of it. "I didn't think you were like that, Casey."

"Like what? Not wanting to be put out on the street? Listen, Lonnie, you're a boy. You don't understand how frightening life on the frontier can be for a young woman with no prospects. When Pa was killed, he left with me about fifty dollars cash and the house. He was behind on both house payments and taxes. In less than a year, I'll be broke. Do you know what that means for a young woman to be broke on the frontier? *Do you?*"

Now, it was Casey who seemed angry. She squeezed Lonnie's hand harder, until it hurt a little. Lonnie felt his own anger subside. He hadn't been thinking about Casey's welfare. Only his own.

Only his love for the girl.

Lonnie did know what happened to homeless girls on the frontier. They usually ended up either working as fry cooks for miserable hours on end in some sweltering café kitchen, or in hurdy-gurdy houses until they either died in childbirth or some disease took their lives much too soon.

Casey said, "It was easy to commit to each other a year ago. We'd been through a lot together—almost killed by Dupree multiple times, almost eaten by a bear! But we persevered and we did the right thing in returning the loot to the deputy US marshal in Camp Collins. But now we're back home. It's day to day. It's real life. And I'm scared, Lonnie. Giles is a good man with a good job and a future. He's warm and gentle and he likes me. You and I—what would we have to look forward to, once you were old enough to marry me? You yourself told me that you and your mother barely made enough to feed yourselves. And now she has a baby, to boot!"

Lonnie stared at her, his lower jaw hanging. He wanted to respond to all that she'd said with a reasonable argument of his own.

But the fact was, Casey was right. Lonnie hadn't been able to see past his love for her, and her love for him, to face the hard, cold facts that he was just too young and poor to marry the girl. And she, being two years older and on the verge of going broke and losing her house, couldn't wait around for him to get his ducks in a row.

Besides, Casey was a town girl. She'd probably never take to living on a remote mountain ranch even if Lonnie had enough money to build them their own cabin, which he did not. He'd need help and materials, not to mention time, to build that cabin.

Really, that cabin was merely a castle in the sky . . .

He just stared at her, unable to say anything. Finally, he closed his mouth, turned his head back forward, and stared at the flames leaping behind the stove's open door.

Very softly, Casey said, "I'm sorry, Lonnie." Then she kissed his cheek, gave his hand another squeeze, rose from the cot and went outside. When she didn't leave right away, he glanced through the window behind him to see her gathering his clothes between the cabin and the creek.

When she'd gathered them all, she brought them in and hung them to dry from wall pegs and over chair backs.

"You don't have to do that," Lonnie told her, his throat tight with emotion.

Casey swung the chair, over which his denim trousers hung, closer to the stove. Then she turned to Lonnie, her gaze somber, her eyes veiled with tears. She brushed a hand across her cheek, cleared her throat, and said, "I wanted to."

Then she strode out of the cabin, drew the door closed behind her, mounted her horse, and rode away.

Lonnie leaned forward, gnashed his teeth, and ground his knuckles against his temples.

CHAPTER 16

Late that night, lying on the cot in the line shack, Lonnie opened his eyes.

Something had awakened him.

What?

Outside, the General whickered.

More accustomed to danger than most young men his age, Lonnie grabbed his rifle from where it leaned against the wall near his cot, and scrambled out of bed. Clad in longhandles and socks, he sidled up to the window.

The half-moon was kiting high above the clearing, shedding a milky light that sparkled off the frost-rimed grass. Lonnie looked around, but he couldn't see anything.

Again, the General whickered. The horse's hooves thudded as the General moved nervously around the corral connected to the stable.

The General might have only winded a skunk or a coyote, but Lonnie had to check it out. Could be a mountain lion, even a grizzly. Or, worse, it could be two-legged prey . . .

Lonnie dressed quickly, pulled on his boots, pumped a cartridge into his Winchester's chamber, and went out, closing the door quietly and then stepping to his left, around the cabin's left-front corner and out of the moonlight. Pressing his back against the cabin's log wall, Lonnie dropped to a crouch and edged a look back around the front of the cabin and into the clearing beyond.

He glanced over to where the General stood, staring over the corral gate toward where the trail led up out of the trees. The General was nervously switching his tail.

Lonnie dropped to a knee and held still as he stared out toward the trail and the moon-silvered forest. There wasn't a breath of wind. The night was still and silent. It was darker over there at the edge of the clearing, down low where the trees shielded the moonlight from the clearing floor.

It was over there, however, that Lonnie saw a shadow move.

He pulled his head back a little closer to the cabin corner. He held his breath when he saw a man-shaped shadow run out from the trees and into the moonlight. The man was crouched low, his breath pluming in the chill air. The moonlight reflected off something shiny that he was holding down low in his right hand.

A gun.

Lonnie's heart skipped, fluttered.

He licked his dry lips and watched the man take cover behind a boulder where the trail curved up out of the forest and angled toward the cabin.

As Lonnie stared at the boulder, he spied another flicker of movement in the corner of his right eye. He swung his head around to catch a glimpse of what appeared another man-shaped, pearl-limned shadow run out of the forest. Frost-stiff grass crunched softly under the runner's boots. The man ran at an angle toward the back of the cabin, and out of Lonnie's field of vision.

Lonnie's heartbeat increased. The mountain air was cold, but his hands were sweating as he squeezed the Winchester. The hair on the back of his neck pricked with the fear that the second man might circle the cabin and move up behind him.

Lonnie looked toward the boulder behind which the first man had taken cover. The man's hatted head slid out slightly from behind the boulder. The man raised a hand to his mouth. He made what sounded like a soft birdcall though it really didn't sound much like any night bird Lonnie had ever heard.

The second man returned the call with another call that sounded more like an owl. An owl that had smoked too many cigarettes.

Something told Lonnie that the man behind the boulder was going to stay put and let the second man make the first move on the cabin. What they wanted, Lonnie had no idea, but a voice whispered the warning in his head that these two might be from the same pack that had ambushed him yesterday and had set his life spiraling into the hell he now found himself in.

Lonnie pulled back away from the cabin's front corner, swung around, and stole quietly back to the rear. He edged a look around the back of the cabin.

The second man was walking through the moonlight toward Lonnie. He was maybe forty yards away and moving slowly on the balls of his feet, almost hopping. He wasn't wearing spurs, or Lonnie would have heard them trilling. He appeared a big man wearing a bullet-crowned black hat and fur jacket.

He held a rifle in both hands up high across his chest.

Obviously, neither of these men was up to any good.

Lonnie stepped out away from the cabin, raising his rifle to his shoulder and taking aim at the big man walking toward him. "Stop right there."

The man stopped, jerking back with a start. He froze for a second then snapped up his rifle and fired, the explosion cleaving the silent night, red flames lapping from the rifle's barrel. The bullet screeched over Lonnie's right shoulder and hammered the cabin wall behind him.

Jerking back, Lonnie fired his Winchester. He was surprised to hear the big man yelp, for Lonnie had been moving when he'd fired and he hadn't expected to hit the man. Lonnie fell back against the cabin wall, got his feet beneath him again, and saw the big man lying on the ground, writhing, clutching his left thigh.

"Walleye!" the other man yelled. "Walleye, you hit?"

The wounded man twisted around and shouted with hoarse exasperation, "That loco kid just shot me!"

Pressing his back against the cabin's rear wall, Lonnie muttered, *"Walleye?"*

Inside the boy's head, another voice said, "Oh, no! Oh, no! Oh, no!"

Lonnie Gentry, you just shot another lawman!

Chick Bohannon shouted, "Kid, you hold your fire, now, you hear? You done just shot Walleye Miller! *Deputy Sheriff* Walleye Miller!"

Lonnie slid his gaze around the cabin corner, gazing toward the boulder that the moonlight touched and behind which he could see the head of his other stalker.

"What the hell are you two doin' skulkin' around out here, Bohannon?"

"You step out here where I can see you and put your rifle down, Gentry!"

Lonnie needed only two seconds to think about that. A year ago, he might have followed this lawman's order. But he'd grown a lot in a year. He'd learned a lot about men including lawmen. "So you can shoot me?"

"You're in big trouble, kid!"

"Walleye fired first!"

"He's a deputy sheriff!"

"Get over here and haul him away or I'll shoot him again!" Lonnie shouted, anger beginning to burn brighter than his fear. "Get over here and take him away, or so help me, I'll shoot him again!"

Gritting his teeth in fury, remembering the "swim" he'd taken in the stock trough for all to see in Arapaho Creek, Lonnie swung his rifle toward Walleye, who lay writhing and clutching his leg. He'd lost his hat and his long hair was spread across his shoulders.

"Bohannon!" Walleye shouted, voice pinched with pain. "I'm gonna need a doctor. *Bad!*"

"Kid, I'm comin' over. Don't shoot!"

"Raise your rifle above your head!" Lonnie shouted, suddenly enjoying the power he found himself wielding.

Slowly, Bohannon emerged from the behind the boulder. He raised his rifle in his right hand above his head. He moved slowly out away from the boulder and moved toward where Walleye was writhing and cursing through gritted teeth.

Lonnie kept his rifle leveled on Bohannon, but he kept an eye skinned on Walleye, as well.

The big deputy jerked his enraged, moonlit eyes toward Lonnie. "Kid, if I die, I'm gonna haunt you to your last livin' day—you hear me? I'm gonna come back and I'm gonna watch you *hang!*"

"Talk's cheap," Lonnie said, feeling calmer now, knowing he had the upper hand. "What the hell are you two doin' out here, anyways?"

"We come to have us a little chat about that man you said you found in Skull Canyon," said Bohannon, approaching Walleye.

Lonnie frowned. "What about him?"

"He wasn't there!" Walleye shouted. "You sent us on a wild-goose chase, you lyin' little devil!"

CHAPTER 17

Lonnie stared at the two deputies, incredulous. "What're you talkin' about? What wild-goose chase?"

"You know what wild-goose chase, you little fang-toothed snot!" barked Walleye, throwing his head back in pain. "Ah, god—it *hurts*. This little boardwalk cur *shot* me!"

Bohannon glared at Lonnie as he said, "Yeah, well, you ain't the first lawman he shot, neither!"

"He wasn't in the cave where I left him?"

The two deputies were ignoring Lonnie.

"Can you stand, Walleye? I'll help you back to your horse," Bohannon said, crouching over his partner.

While Bohannon draped one of Walleye's arms around his neck and helped him rise, Walleye said, "I gotta get to a sawbones, get this bullet dug out of my leg." He looked at Lonnie and snarled, "If I don't bleed out first!"

Lonnie's mind was with Cade McLory. "I left him in a cave. Did you see a cave?"

"We seen a cave, all right," Bohannon yelled as he helped the badly limping Walleye back toward the trees where they must have tied their horses. "The cave was there—the only cave around that part of the canyon. But there wasn't no dead man there. But you know that, don't you? If you think you're gonna make fools of me an' Walleye, you got another think comin', kid!"

Walleye whipped his head toward Lonnie once more. "I'll be

back to show you how smart you are, you little cur. You can bet the seed bull on that!"

Lonnie stared at the two as they shuffled off into the darkness of the trees then lowered his rifle and drifted back to the front of the cabin, pondering what the two deputies had told him. How could McLory not have been in the cave?

That wasn't possible. Unless some predator had dragged him out. But if that had happened the deputies would have seen some sign of him. They'd have known a dead man had been there. No predator would have dragged him off intact.

The only explanation Lonnie could figure as he moved back into the line shack and closed the door was that the cork-headed fools, Bohannon and Walleye, had investigated another cave. Apparently, there were at least two caves in that part of the canyon, though Lonnie had only seen one.

That had to be the explanation.

What other explanation could there be?

As Lonnie lay back down on his cot and got himself slowly settled down enough that he thought he might still squeeze a couple more hours of shut-eye out of the night, he decided he'd just have to return to Skull Canyon and see about the situation himself.

Lonnie was up at the first blush of dawn the next morning.

He packed his gear, saddled the General, and rode away from the line shack.

It took him well over an hour of hard riding to reach the entrance to Skull Canyon. When he did, he sat there at the gap in the ridge wall, staring up the brushy ravine that rose steadily and twisted around behind a bulging belly of bald granite and sandstone.

Very faintly, Lonnie could hear that tooth-gnashing whine of the wind funneling through the skull-like formation on the canyon's far end and which gave the canyon its name.

Was the canyon really cursed?

Was that why Bohannon and Walleye hadn't been able to find McLory's body? Was Lonnie now cursed because he'd spent a night in the canyon, and was that why his luck had suddenly gone south? Maybe the reason McLory had met a premature end was because of the canyon's curse . . .

If so, did Lonnie really want to ride into the canyon again?

No, he sure as hell did not. But the way he figured it, he could probably only be cursed once. So what more harm would another half hour in the canyon do? He wouldn't linger around till sundown again—that was for sure.

Still, the hair under his shirt collar pricked as he gigged the General ahead through the natural gate. He rode up the curving, rocky floor of the ravine and then swung the General west. The buckskin splashed across Ingrid Creek, and five minutes later Lonnie dismounted at the base of the western ridge wall.

He climbed the steep slope that led up to the boulders and wound his way behind the rocks until he found the long, egg-shaped opening in the ridge. Lonnie paused. His neck hairs were standing up even straighter. He wasn't sure what he was more afraid of—finding McLory here or not finding McLory here.

Lonnie crouched to peer into the cave. His lower jaw dropped.

McLory wasn't here. In fact, *nothing* was here. The cave was as empty as it had been when Lonnie had first come upon it the day before.

"Well . . . I'll be a monkey's uncle," Lonnie heard himself mutter as he dropped to his knees and stared at the place on the cave floor where he'd left McLory, near the fire he'd built and of which no evidence remained!

Lonnie moved on into the cave and looked around in awe.

There were no ashes on the cave floor. Not even a handful.

No unburned wood. No charred dirt. No blood from McLory. Not a scrap of anything remaining from last night.

It was as though Lonnie and McLory had never been here.

Which must be exactly what someone wanted someone else to believe.

On both counts—*who?*

Who would have taken such pains to scour the area of all sign of the dead man?

Why?

Where was McLory?

Below the cave, the General whickered warningly. Lonnie whipped around to stare out of the brightly sunlit cave opening, his blood whining in his ears. Faintly, he heard men's voices.

Lonnie dashed out of the cave and scrambled down to where he'd left the General. The horse stood between two boulders, making him visible from the canyon floor.

Placing a hand over the buckskin's snout to keep him quiet, Lonnie backed the horse behind the larger of the two boulders, so he wouldn't be seen. Keeping a hand over the General's snout, Lonnie turned to peer through the gap between the boulders, toward the canyon floor beyond the slender, meandering creek.

Men's voices grew louder.

A horse snorted. The clacking of hooves on rock rose to Lonnie's pricked ears.

The young man drew a slow, shallow breath as he watched four horseback riders enter the canyon. He drew back behind the boulder with a startled grunt when he saw that they were the same four men who'd try to run him down and kill him the day before.

CHAPTER 18

Lonnie edged another look around the boulder.

The horses the men were riding told him that these four men now moving up the canyon were the same men who'd tried to kill him. He recognized the brown-and-white pinto of the man who'd scrambled up the outcropping after him, as well as a broad-chested cinnamon dun.

He also recognized the man who'd chased him on foot. He was riding third in the pack, behind two who rode abreast and ahead of the fourth rider, who wore a cream slicker and had long, almost white hair hanging straight down to his shoulders. In profile, Lonnie could see he was a fair-skinned man, and his face was badly sunburned, his long nose almost glowing red. The flaps of his duster were drawn back so that Lonnie could see a big, pearl-gripped, silver-chased pistol jutting from a holster on his left hip.

Lonnie had remembered catching a glimpse of that rider, too, during a brief look behind when the four were bearing down on him.

The first two riders were conversing in low tones as the group rode on past Lonnie, walking their horses up the canyon.

When they'd passed, Lonnie stepped up into the gap between the two boulders, and watched them ride away from him, gradually tracing a curve in the west wall of the canyon and disappearing from sight.

Still, Lonnie stared after them, wondering who they were and why they'd been so determined to kill him.

Had they been the ones who'd removed McLory from the cave?

Why?

More questions reeled through the young man's head to the accompaniment of a low hum of dread in his ears. Obviously, something strange and out of sorts was happening in Skull Canyon. Lonnie's curiosity somehow pushed through his fear. He wanted to ride out of the canyon and forget everything that he'd seen here. He even wanted to forget about the men who'd almost killed him.

But the strong pull of his curiosity wouldn't let him.

He dropped the General's reins, said, "Stay here, boy," then shucked his Winchester from the saddle boot and stole down the steep slope to the canyon floor. He crossed the creek, only dampening his boots, and then jogged along the rocky floor of the canyon littered with apples from one of the passing horses.

He felt a pressing need to find out where the four men were heading and what was in the canyon that had compelled them to kill McLory and to try killing him, Lonnie. They must be holding stolen cattle somewhere in the canyon. What else would compel them to commit murder? If so, some of those cows might be Lonnie's.

Lonnie jogged until he reached a bend in the canyon wall, then cat footed around it, not wanting to run up on the group in case they'd stopped. Once around the bend, he saw the backs of the four riders as they continued riding in the opposite direc-tion—sixty yards away and gradually broadening the gap between themselves and Lonnie.

Just ahead, the canyon narrowed to not more than maybe a hundred feet, with the creek running along the base of the left side wall, with a spring-fed freshet running across the floor from the opposite wall, forming a boggy area. Lonnie tramped on through the soft, muddy ground, and began jogging again, not wanting to get so close to the four that their horses might wind him, but not wanting to lose them, either.

Skull Canyon was a large, deep chasm with several branches. Because of its dark legend, Lonnie had spent as little time in the canyon as possible, but he'd heard from other cowboys who'd grazed cattle in the canyon that it covered a vast, rugged area. Lonnie had also heard that many prospectors had once worked the canyon for gold and silver. Some still might, though he didn't know of any. He thought the legend, widely known throughout the area, probably kept most people out.

Lonnie continued to make his way along the canyon floor, which widened dramatically beyond the bottleneck. As he moved, wishing he'd thought to leave his spurs with the General, it occurred to Lonnie that the four men ahead of him might not be rustlers, after all. They might have discovered gold or silver somewhere in the canyon, and were shooting those they thought might be trying to jump their claim.

McLory didn't seem like the claim-jumping type to Lonnie, but he had hardly known the man.

Whatever they were doing was obviously illegal. And whatever they were doing, Lonnie had no idea what he was going to do about it. He wasn't exactly chomping at the bit to pay another visit to Sheriff Halliday. In fact, Halliday might be paying Lonnie a visit soon to talk about the deputy Lonnie had shot.

Lonnie jogged ahead now, trying to gain some ground on the four riders, who had disappeared around another right bend in the canyon floor. The canyon widened even more just ahead, and aspens and birches grew to both sides of the rocky center of the canyon down which a rushing, snowmelt river flowed every spring. Large, clay-colored boulders that had fallen from the steep ridge wall shone among the trees.

As the four riders appeared before Lonnie again, still riding away from him, he jerked with a start at what sounded like a large tree branch snapping. One of the four riders jerked back in his saddle.

The man's horse turned sharply to one side, giving a shrill whinny.

One of the other riders shouted, "What in the—?"

The shouted question was cut abruptly off as the rider who'd been shot fell backward down the side of his saddle to hit the canyon floor in a twisted pile.

Another gun popped among the trees and boulders so that now two rifles were cracking wildly. Lonnie jerked with each shot, as though the bullets were tearing into his own body.

Smoke puffed and gun flames shone in the trees and rocks to each side of the trail. The four riders screamed and bellowed curses as they were blown out of their saddles. They hit the ground and rolled as the rifles continued to crack and belch, gun smoke wafting in the tree branches.

Lonnie stood staring in wide-eyed, hang-jawed shock at the four men rolling on the ground, writhing in pain only to be shot again by the two ambushers. Amidst the belching of the gunfire, Lonnie could hear the quick rasping of the rifles' cocking levers. The four riderless horses galloped, whinnying shrilly, on up the canyon, the last one buck-kicking and stomping on its reins as it fled.

Lonnie stood frozen, as though his boots were stuck to the canyon floor. His eyes were riveted on the four men, all of whom now lay twisted and unmoving on the floor of the canyon, under a large, drifting gunsmoke haze.

When he saw two men moving down out of the trees and boulders to each side of the trail, Lonnie swung around and took off running back the way he'd come, breathless fear overpowering his curiosity.

CHAPTER 19

Lonnie scrambled up the steep slope to where the General waited, staring at Lonnie through the gap between the boulders. Breathing hard, casting cautious glances back in the direction of the slaughter of the four riders, Lonnie slid his Winchester back into its sheath and swung up onto the buckskin's back.

"Let's split the wind, General!" Lonnie said, whipping his rein ends against the General's hip.

The stallion had heard the shooting. He did not hesitate to oblige his rider. The sure-footed buckskin dropped down the steep incline in two long strides then galloped the rest of the way to the canyon floor. He leaped the creek, bulled through some berry bramble, and swung toward the canyon's yawning mouth.

Lonnie cast another anxious glance behind him and was relieved to see that no one had followed him. He put his head down as the General galloped on through the gate and down the gradual slope through the pines, following the old horse trail along Ingrid Creek.

Lonnie gave the General his head. The horse knew where home was, and that was where Lonnie wanted to get as quickly as possible. He didn't care if he never saw the entrance to Skull Canyon again in this life. In fact, he didn't even want to think about the possibility of his cows straying into the canyon so that he'd have to track them down.

The way he felt about it now, if any of his beef-on-the-hoof strayed into Skull Canyon, they could find their own damn way out!

As the General galloped along the creek that wended its way down the gradual mountain slope, Lonnie kept seeing and hearing the killing of the four riders in his mind's eye. The shooting had sounded like firecrackers popping at a Fourth of July celebration, like the one they had with horse races every year in Arapaho Creek. Only, what Lonnie had just heard and seen had been no celebration.

It had been a slaughter.

Not that he really cared about the four men who'd almost done the same thing to him, but watching their violent demise had Lonnie feeling so shaken that his entire body quivered. He felt so sick to his stomach he thought he might throw up what little he had in his stomach.

Fortunately, it wasn't much.

He was too shaken to think about Skull Canyon right now, or about who might have gunned down the four riders or about who might have taken Cade McLory's body out of the cave.

Lonnie just wanted to get home to the peace, quiet, and safety of his and his mother's ranch headquarters. He just wanted to sit down to a good meal with his mother and then tend his barn chores and then hit the sack for a long, badly needed night's rest in his own bed.

He hoped little Jeremiah would let him sleep and not spend half the night crying for May Gentry's attention. If the latter, Lonnie would go out and sleep in the side shed off the barn, which Lonnie had outfitted with a cot and wool blankets. That's where he slept when Shannon Dupree spent the night with Lonnie's mother in the cabin.

A little over an hour after leaving the canyon, Lonnie rode northeast along the floor of the broad valley in which his ranch lay, at the base of a rise of forested, spruce-green peeks. Lonnie trotted the General through the wooden portal straddling the trail.

The Circle G brand had been proudly burned into the high, wooden crossbar by his father when Calvin Gentry had finished building the barn and cabin from the timber growing along the slopes and mountains flanking the ranch, back when Lonnie had been only two years old and they were all living in a small, temporary shack, waiting for the main cabin to be finished.

Lonnie rode into the finely churned dust of the yard fronting the large, low-slung, shake-roofed log cabin, heading for the stock trough below the windmill whose wooden blades churned lazily in the late-afternoon breeze. As he did, he frowned at the two strange horses standing in the corral attached to the barn's side shed.

One horse was a blue roan, the other a steeldust with a black mane and black head except for a long, crooked white stripe running down its snout. The mounts stood forward of the four horses from Lonnie's rough string, which he used mostly to give the General a break during busy spring and autumn roundups.

The two unfamiliar horses stood staring toward the cabin. Their tack straddled the top rail of the corral, to the left of the gate. Two Winchester carbines leaned against a corral post.

Deep lines cut across Lonnie's forehead in a frustrated scowl. Visitors.

He hadn't figured on that. They rarely had visitors way out here. At least, not since Dupree had bit the dust. Why did they have to have visitors tonight of all nights?

As Lonnie dismounted the General by the windmill and slipped the horse's bit, so he could drink freely, Lonnie surveyed the cabin. The west-angling light reflected off the sashed windows. Smoke from a supper fire plumed from the stovepipe.

As Lonnie hauled his gear over to the corral, his mother's

muffled laughter rose from inside the cabin. A man's laughter followed. Lonnie glanced over his shoulder at the lodge, and grimaced.

"Oh, no," he said under his breath. "Please, no . . . not again."

May Gentry was understandably lonely, living way out here without a husband. But that loneliness had led to trouble in the past. Lonnie hoped that kind of trouble hadn't come calling again . . .

When Lonnie had rubbed the General down, grained, and stabled him, Lonnie crossed the yard to the cabin, slapping his hat against his thighs, causing trail dust to billow. He could hear two men talking with his mother inside the cabin.

He didn't care for the lighthearted tone, but, then again, he was glad there was no trouble.

Lonnie climbed the front porch and saw a pitcher of fresh water sitting on the second shelf of the washstand, beneath the top shelf that held the tin washbasin. A fresh towel hung from the nail beside the mirror hanging slightly askew from the cabin's front wall. Using the cake of lye soap provided, Lonnie scrubbed his face, neck and ears, and used a small bristle brush to scrub the dirt and grime out from beneath his fingernails.

As he washed he could hear his mother chatting amiably with the men inside the cabin. Hearing the buoyant happiness and faint coquettishness in his mother's voice rubbed him the wrong way though he supposed it shouldn't. She had the right to enjoy the company of men.

The problem was, May Gentry was a nice-looking woman, but she wasn't very discriminating. She'd drawn more than a few rogue male eyes her way, including the eyes of the roguish outlaw, Shannon Dupree.

Lonnie toweled himself dry, combed his damp, close-cropped, light-brown hair in the mirror, ignoring the cowlick, and then flipped the latch of the front door. As the hinges squawked—he had to oil them one of these days—the conversation inside the cabin stopped. Two men sat at the halved-log dining table in the kitchen part of the cabin, straight out from the front door. One man sat at the table's far end, the other adjacent to him, his back to the front wall.

Lonnie's mother stood with her back to the range, rocking the tightly wrapped blanket of Lonnie's little half brother, Jeremiah, in her arms. The baby was fussing, and May was flushed from the effort of trying to calm him.

"Oh, there you are, honey!" May Gentry intoned. "I've been worried about you, Lonnie. Won't you come in and meet our two supper guests—Bill Brocius and George Madsen? I've offered to let them stay in the bunkhouse out back for a few nights . . . if they don't mind a few spiders, that is, as the bunkhouse hasn't been used in a month of Sundays!" Beaming, Mrs. Gentry glanced at the two visitors, and said, "Bill, George—this is my son, Lonnie, Jeremiah's big brother."

Brocius was the one sitting at the table's far end. Madsen sat adjacent to Bill, facing Lonnie's mother. Lonnie shook Madsen's hand first and then reached across the far corner of the table to shake Bill Brocius's hand.

"Pleased to meet you," Lonnie said, unable to work up much enthusiasm for the introduction.

"The pleasure's all ours, boy," Madsen said. "Your mother told us a lot about you." He was fair-skinned with dark-brown hair, a dark-brown beard, and bulbous red nose. Brocius was a compact, clean-shaven man with a high forehead and thin, sandy hair combed so that a lock swept down over his right, pale blue eye. Both appeared in their thirties.

The men had washed recently. They had freshly scrubbed looks, and their hair, like Lonnie's, was damp and combed. Lonnie thought he smelled the sweet, cloying odor of pomade on one of them, or maybe both.

Brocius seemed to study Lonnie with a faintly sheepish, devious air, though he kept a smile on his small, thin-lipped mouth. Or maybe Lonnie just imagined the devious gaze, being suspicious of men who got along too well with his mother, especially when they hardly knew her.

Madsen was smiling, too, but he had dark, deep-set eyes that gave him a menacing look.

"Bill and George work for a mining company," May Gentry told Lonnie, rocking the sleeping Jeremiah in her arms. "They're . . . they're . . . what did you fellas call it?"

"Geologists," Brocius said. "We're scoutin' around, lookin' at rocks an' such, tryin' to find evidence of any gold or silver in the area."

"I see," Lonnie said, unable to feign interest.

His mind was still up at Skull Canyon, and all he wanted was to shove some vittles into his gullet and then get about his barn chores. He wasn't in the mood for socializing. He had livestock to tend before he could roll into the mattress sack, and he felt deeply fatigued—both mentally and physically.

He looked at his mother. "When's supper, Momma? I feel as empty as a dead man's boot."

"Lonnie Gentry, what a way to talk in front of our new friends!" May scolded. "Why, Bill and George are going to think I didn't raise you to talk proper!"

"Not at all, not all, May," Brocius assured her, chuckling as he sat back in his chair and began rolling a cigarette from the makings sack on the table before him. "I was raised in the country myself. I know what it's like."

Lonnie noticed that Madsen had his head turned to one side, scrutinizing Lonnie. He was trying to look subtle about it, but Lonnie could tell when he was being sized up. Madsen made Lonnie feel uncomfortable. But when he looked at Brocius, he realized Brocius made him feel uncomfortable, too.

"So, Momma," Lonnie said, peering around his mother and noting an iron pot steaming on the range, "when's supper?"

"As soon as the rolls are done, Mister Scowly Face. Look at you. You're in one of your moods again, Lonnie Gentry. Here— why don't you take little Jeremiah outside for a spell. Walk him from one end of the yard to the other while I visit some more with our supper guests. He's been so fussy since you've been gone." To her guests, she said, "Lonnie's so much better at getting the baby settled down—isn't that peculiar?"

To Lonnie again: "By the time you get back, I imagine the rolls will be done, and we can dish up . . . but only after you've said grace, Mister Scowls. So while you're out there with your little brother, you think up a nice, sweet table prayer and show these gentleman that you have better language than that you use around the cattle!"

May Gentry had handed over the tightly wrapped bundle of little Jeremiah to Lonnie. The baby's little, red, pinched-up face was turning redder now as the child started to fuss harder.

Lonnie silently cursed as he took the baby in his arms.

He walked outside, silently, bitterly fuming. He kicked a rock and then he turned toward the cabin to see Madsen watching him from the window right of the door. Madsen had that same, dark, speculative look as before.

What did that look mean?

"One thing after another," Lonnie said, as he started walking his squawking brother around the yard, hearing his mother's and her visitors' laughter rise again from inside the cabin. "When will it ever end?"

CHAPTER 20

Jeremiah didn't squawk long after he and Lonnie started walking out toward the ranch portal. Lonnie often took care of the baby, only three months old, when his mother was in one of her nervous states and needed a few minutes alone, or was down with the "vapors."

Lonnie had found he'd had a calming effect on the baby. He wasn't sure why, but when Lonnie held Jeremiah, the baby usually stopped crying within a minute or two. Then Jeremiah would either drift to sleep or lie staring up at his big brother as though in fascination, sort of gurgling and sighing contentedly deep in his little chest.

Lonnie walked toward the ranch portal, jostling the baby gently. Though he'd never admitted as much to his mother, and maybe not even to himself, he liked having the kid around. When it had been just Lonnie and May, they'd seemed less like a family than they did now.

The problem was that when staring into the baby's deep-blue eyes, Lonnie often saw the eyes of Shannon Dupree staring back at him. The baby didn't look anything like Dupree now, but Jeremiah would likely take on some of his father's aspects when he grew older.

Lonnie often wondered how he himself would feel about that, reminded constantly that Jeremiah was the son of a man whom Lonnie, his brother, had killed. He also wondered how Jeremiah would feel about that, when he eventually was told.

Would he hold the killing of his father against Lonnie?

Lonnie didn't feel guilty about having killed Shannon Dupree. Dupree had been going to kill Lonnie and Casey. Besides, if there was ever a man who needed killing, that man was Dupree. No, Lonnie didn't feel guilty about killing him.

He felt guilty about having killed.

Humming gently as he rocked his brother in his arms, Lonnie turned away from the ranch portal and started back toward the cabin. He hoped his mother had done enough chinning with her supper guests, because Lonnie was damn hungry.

He'd hoped to be able to talk to May alone this evening, but that didn't look like it was going to happen. Judging by the air of revelry inside the cabin, he'd likely turn in long before his mother and Brocius and Madsen did. He'd wanted to tell his mother about all that had happened to him during the past twenty-four hours, to get it off his chest.

But, then again, maybe it was just as well May didn't know. She was not a strong woman. Lonnie had learned that the hard way. If she knew about the men who'd tried to run down and kill her son, and about Cade McLory and the four riders whom Lonnie had seen shot off their horses—who knew what she'd do?

Merely reflecting on it nearly had Lonnie panicking and wanting to run far, far away from here. The only problem was, there was nowhere to go.

He'd just started wondering about the two strangers in his house, when May Gentry opened the cabin door and called him to supper. Lonnie went in, handed the baby over to his mother, who took him into her bedroom to feed him, and then sat down at the opposite end of the table from Bill Brocius.

May had told them to get started, so Lonnie dug into the rabbit stew and fresh bread, grateful that May had apparently forgotten about grace. Brocius and Madsen had apparently forgotten about it, too. Lonnie doubted that either man was in the habit of saying table prayers. They both had a hard, trail-savvy look about them.

If they were really working as geologists for a mining company, he was a monkey's uncle.

He didn't know who they really were or what they were do-ing here, but he didn't like them. He'd seen too many strangers in the Never Summers over the past two days. And too many of those strangers had tried to kill him. Not only that, but he didn't like the way these two strangers looked at his mother.

Lonnie and his mother's guests ate in silence for a time, all three too involved in padding their bellies to waste time with conversation. That was fine with Lonnie. He had nothing to say to these men—at least, nothing he could say without getting in trouble with his mother.

Then Brocius gave a snort as he set his fork down on his nearly empty plate, brushed a fist across his nose, and split a roll in two. He glanced at Madsen and then turned to Lonnie: "So, sport, you've lived here all your life, I reckon."

Lonnie was buttering his own roll. "That's right."

"You probably know every nook and cranny of these moun-tains, strapping lad like yourself."

Lonnie hiked a shoulder as he set his knife down and dipped his roll into the remaining stew on his plate. He bit into the succulent, gravy-soaked, buttery bread.

Madsen looked over his coffee cup at Lonnie. "You probably know a lot of the folks who live in these mountains, too."

Again, Lonnie only shrugged as he continued to shovel stew into his mouth while swabbing the gravy off his plate with his roll. He could tell by their fishing that these men wanted something from him. Well, let them want. Let them fish. Through their questions, Lonnie might learn something about *them*.

"You know anything about a stolen army payroll shipment that might have been buried up in these mountains, several years back?" asked Brocius.

Lonnie looked at Brocius who held his steady, penetrating gaze on him. Now that the man had mentioned it, Lonnie had heard about such a shipment.

Lonnie had dismissed the story about the stolen army payroll as just another legend. There were as many legends in these mountains as there were people who lived and *had* lived in and around the Never Summers.

When Lonnie didn't say anything but only returned Brocius's curious gaze, Madsen leaned forward and, keeping his voice down as though to make sure no one else overheard the conversation, said, "You have heard about it, haven't you, boy? Tell us what you know."

Lonnie knew little. But he enjoyed the power he suddenly found himself holding over these two grown-up strangers. "What do you wanna know about it?"

"Has anyone ever found it?" Brocius asked.

Again, Lonnie merely shrugged.

Brocius glanced at Madsen, gave a baleful grin, and returned his cunning gaze to Lonnie. "Come on, kid. Tell us what you know."

"First, tell me what you know about it," Lonnie said, casually helping himself to more stew.

CHAPTER 21

Brocius gave a dry chuckle.

Madsen stared at Lonnie with silent menace.

Lonnie ate his stew, trying not to look at Madsen. Both these men made him nervous, but Madsen more than Brocius. He didn't want either one to see how he felt, however.

"What we know," Brocius said, "was that a strongbox containing an army payroll was stolen down in Arizona about seventeen years ago. The gang that stole it was going to powder the trail to Mexico, but their route was cut off by a contingent of cavalry out of Fort Bowie. So the gang swung north instead.

"They evaded the cavalry but telegraphs were sent to local lawmen and some deputy US marshals in New Mexico, and these men formed a posse. They chased the gang up into Colorado. Supposedly, they were heading for the Hole in the Wall in Wyoming. They didn't make it.

"Their gang was whittled down by the posse as they headed north, until only two men was left. Both of those men were wounded, one badly. He and the other man made it into the Never Summers, where, as the story goes, they hid the strongbox. Then one of the men died. The sole survivor left the Never Summers to get medical attention for himself, and was captured by the posse that was still on the scout for him."

Brocius picked up the blue-speckled coffeepot sitting on the table, and refilled his stone mug. As he set the pot back down, he said through the steam wafting up from his cup, "That sole surviving thief never did tell the law where he and the other man had hid the strongbox. But it's long been believed that they hid it somewhere in the Never Summers. Now, some are saying it must be in or somewhere around Skull Canyon."

Lonnie had known that part of the story was coming since Brocius had been about halfway through his tale. Still, he literally almost fell off his chair. His shock must have shown in his features, because Madsen, who'd been staring at him with those flat, deep-set brown eyes gave a wry snort.

"Is that where it is, boy?"

Lonnie composed himself, cleared his throat. "Couldn't tell ya."

Brocius dipped his chin and pinned Lonnie with a direct, threatening look. "Can't? Or won't?"

"Can't," Lonnie said quickly, realizing the trouble he was in.

These men were after what all those other men including probably Cade McLory had been after—stolen army loot! Which means that they were likely as kill-crazy desperate as all the others. Again, in his mind's eye, Lonnie watched the four riders get shot out of their saddles.

"Can't," Lonnie repeated with more urgency this time. "I heard sometime back about the loot maybe bein' cached somewhere in the Never Summers. But I never knew where. That right there is everything I know on the subject."

It was as though Madsen hadn't heard what Lonnie had just said. "Has someone found it? Or is it still out there somewhere?"

Brocius said, "We don't want to waste our time on a wild-goose chase."

"I have no idea," Lonnie said.

Madsen narrowed a suspicious eye at him. "You do know—don't you boy? You're a lone wolf, wily as a coyote. Most boys like you got their ears to the ground, so to speak. They move around. They're savvy as Apaches. That's you—ain't it, kid? You know more about that loot than you're lettin' on."

"Hell, no!"

"Lonnie Gentry, did I just hear you cuss in front of our guests?"

May Gentry had just stepped out of her bedroom which opened off the parlor part of the cabin. As she quietly latched the bedroom door so as not to awaken little Jeremiah, she came toward the kitchen, frowning.

"Uh . . . sorry, Momma," Lonnie said. "I don't know what happened. I reckon it just slipped out."

"Oh, we don't mind," Madsen said, leaning over to tussle Lonnie's hair. "He's a green one, this younker. That's all right— the best colts got some pitch in 'em."

May Gentry refilled Madsen's coffee cup, saying, "Lonnie's problem is that he has an ornery streak. Gets a little too full of himself from time to time. I reckon that's my fault. I'm too soft on him." She shook her head and filled her own cup. "A boy needs a man's touch. Lonnie hasn't had that since his father died . . . God rest his soul."

May Gentry sighed as she sat down near Brocius and across from Madsen. Holding her steaming cup in her hands, she regarded Lonnie with sadness, shaking her head.

Lonnie pushed his plate away and rose from the table. Anger burned in him, but he tried to keep it on a leash. "Thanks for supper, Momma," he muttered, wiping his mouth with his napkin. "I'd best get to my night chores and turn in."

Lonnie felt all eyes on him as he grabbed his hat off a wall peg, opened the door, and went out. He stood at the top of the porch steps, a mix of emotions roiling within him—fear, confusion, and anger. He had to admit that he was also curious about the stolen army payroll loot.

He'd hoped he'd seen his first and last cache of stolen money when he and Casey had delivered the Golden bank loot to the deputy US marshal in Camp Collins.

He'd been wrong.

And now he couldn't help wondering how much loot there was in that army strongbox, and if the loot really was hidden somewhere in Skull Canyon. If so, judging by the number of men looking for it, it hadn't been found.

It must be a sizeable amount to have attracted so many treasure hunters.

As Lonnie's eyes scanned the forested western ridges standing tall and dark before him, the very last of the setting sun's rays gilding the tops of the highest pines and firs, he entertained a brief fantasy of finding that cache himself. He wouldn't take it, because it didn't belong to him. But he'd bet aces against navy beans that after all these years the army was offering a sizeable reward for the return of that strongbox.

He fantasized about cashing that reward note and of riding a long, long ways away from here.

Of leaving this place of so much misery and heartache behind him.

Lonnie heard his mother and Brocius and Madsen talking and laughing in the cabin behind him. He moved down off the porch steps and headed for the barn.

CHAPTER 22

As the last light bled out of the sky and the cool mountain night descended on the valley, Lonnie bedded down in the lean-to side shed off the barn.

He was surprised to hear the laughing and obviously pie-eyed Brocius and Madsen leave the cabin only about an hour or so later. Either they'd brought a bottle or Lonnie's mother had broken out the brandy she occasionally uncorked when she couldn't sleep.

Lonnie had thought that they and May, who hadn't had any visitors except for the occasional traveling tinker or drummer in a month of Sundays, would sit up half the night. He'd also been worried one of the men might not leave the cabin till morning.

Lonnie was pleasantly surprised.

Still, he couldn't sleep. Too much was racing through his mind. He kept seeing those blindly staring eyes of Cade McLory as well as the four riders being shot out of their saddles while guns smoked and sparked in the surrounding trees and boulders.

He could hear the screams of those men as they'd died.

Also, he couldn't help imagining digging up that stolen loot himself. Even if there was only a small reward on that payroll cache, it would likely be enough money to give a young man a decent start somewhere he'd have half a chance.

Lonnie had the cold, brittle feeling that he'd run out of chances here in the Never Summers.

Finally, sick of all the unwanted thoughts and images assaulting him, he threw his covers back, drew on his boots and his hat, and left the side shed clad in his longhandles and holding a blanket over his shoulders. He found the night's chill pleasantly uncomfortable, distracting him from the barrage of unwanted worries. He sat on a hay rake parked near the corral's front corner and studied the stars that were dimmed by the rising moon.

After a while, a sound drew his attention toward the cabin.

A shadow moved out around the cabin's left-front corner. The shadow slid up to the front of the porch. It mounted the porch, and then Lonnie could hear the light taps of boots on the porch's wooden floorboards.

A light was turned up inside the cabin, causing the kitchen window right of the front door to glow wanly through the gingham curtains. The door opened, and the man-shaped shadow, topped with a Stetson, stooped as he passed through the lit opening.

The door click closed. The light in the window died.

Lonnie wondered which one it was—Madsen or Brocius.

He wasn't surprised that his mother was entertaining one of the men. In fact, it plowed through all of his worries to make him feel dull and numb. That was a pleasant feeling after the sharp pangs of anxiety that had been assaulting him only moments ago.

Even if the reward was only a hundred dollars, a hundred dollars would take him far. He could maybe get a job in Denver, say, swamping out saloons or livery barns. He could possibly land a cowboying job if he could convince a ranch owner that he had all the skills, and sometimes more, of cowpunchers twice his age, though that might be a feat.

Few folks thought a boy his age was good for much of anything than lying to him and shooting at him, and—he was thinking of Casey now—of betraying him.

Lonnie eyelids grew heavy. He felt as withered as an old, dried-up cornstalk. He could probably sleep now.

He went back into the side shed, rolled into his blankets, causing the cot to squawk beneath him. He punched his pillow, laid his head back on it, took a deep breath, and fell asleep . . . until a sound woke him.

He lifted his head, blinking groggily. He'd been in a deep sleep. Something glinted in the moonlight angling through the side shed windows, in the air before his head. There was a ratcheting sound that he instantly recognized as a gun hammer being cocked.

Then he saw a figure take foggy shape in the moonlight before him.

His heart hiccupped, and he was about to reach for his rifle when the cold, round maw of the revolver was pressed up taut against his forehead.

"One move, and I'll drill you, kid."

Madsen's voice.

Lonnie froze. He squeezed his eyes closed, waiting for the bullet.

"What . . . what do you want?"

"Just to finish up the conversation from earlier."

"I told you," Lonnie said, his heart racing now, "I don't know anything about that payroll."

"I got a feelin' you do."

"That's just cause I was actin' cocky at first. I tend to do that. Like Ma says, I tend to get full of myself. But . . . please believe me . . . all I ever heard about that loot was that it might have been buried in the Never Summers somewhere. That's it. If it's in Skull Canyon, it's news to me."

Madsen didn't say anything for nearly a minute. He kept the revolver pressed up close to Lonnie's head. It was cold and hard and unforgiving, and Lonnie vaguely wondered if he'd feel the bullet before it blew his brains out, or if he wouldn't feel anything but just pass into Heaven or Hell or wherever it was he was headed.

The gun clicked quietly as Madsen depressed the hammer, let it fall benignly against the firing pin. He pulled the barrel away from Lonnie's head. Lonnie drew a deep, relieved breath and opened his eyes.

Madsen let the gun fall straight down against his right side.

"Kid," he said, "I can't tell if you're really, really smart or really, really stupid."

Lonnie cleared his dry throat. "That makes two of us."

Madsen holstered the big revolver and then drew up the ladderback chair from the small, plankboard eating table near the sheet-iron stove. He slacked into the chair with a weary sigh, doffed his hat, and leaned forward, turning the hat in his hands. He was a dark, man-shaped silhouette against the two moonlit windows behind him. His round, bearded face with deep-set eyes now filled with shadows looked especially sinister in the shadowy moonlight.

Lonnie was glad the man had holstered the pistol, but he wouldn't rest until Madsen had left. Again, Madsen didn't say anything for a time, likely knowing that his silence was causing Lonnie a great deal of anxiety, and likely enjoying it.

"We're Pinkerton agents."

Lonnie blinked, studied the man in the darkness. "What's that?"

"Me an' Brocius," Madsen said. "We're Pinkerton detectives."

CHAPTER 23

Again, Lonnie blinked at the menacing visage of Madsen sitting before him. "I don't understand."

"You ever hear of the Pinkerton Detective Agency?"

"Yeah."

Lonnie had never been to school, for the nearest school was too far away even if he hadn't been too busy at the ranch to attend. But he'd been bound and determined to not have to "make his mark" with an X every time he needed to sign his name, like so many of the old-timers did.

To that end, he'd acquired a rudimentary, mostly self-taught knowledge of reading and writing. When he rode to town every couple of months for supplies, he scrounged around in trash heaps and privies for newspapers, usually returning to the ranch with a few local papers as well as several issues of the *Rocky Mountain News* out of Denver.

During his reading, he'd stumbled upon stories about the famous Pinkerton Agency founded by Allen Pinkerton and based in Chicago.

But he'd certainly never figured on meeting two detectives from that illustrious company. Especially not out here, at his own ranch . . .

Madsen said, "The army hired the Pinkertons to find the stolen loot. That's what me an' Brocius are doing here. The Pinkertons have been looking for that strongbox ever since it was stolen, but the detectives working the case—there've been several over the years—always came up cold. The company sort of put the case on the back burner . . . until the outlaw who rode with the gang who stole the gold in the first place broke out of prison three or four weeks ago."

Lonnie remembered the name that Deputy Marshal Appleyard had mentioned. "Crawford Kinch?"

Even in the darkness, Lonnie saw a puzzled frown slice across Madsen's forehead. "How did you . . . ?"

"Like Brocius said, I'm savvy."

"That's the name, all right. You seen him, kid?"

"Nope. And I reckon I don't want to, neither. Or so I've been told."

"That would be right." Madsen paused, sighed, and then leaned a little farther forward. "Look, I've laid my cards on the table. It's time for you to tell me everything you know about that loot."

"I've already done that, Mister Madsen." Anger flared in Lonnie suddenly, and he sat up a little in bed. "Do the famous Pinkertons make a habit of holding cocked guns to boys' heads?"

"Not officially," Madsen said, sitting back in his chair. "But we do whatever's necessary to get the job done. Pull your horns in, kid. That arguably nasty little tactic worked in your favor."

"How so?"

"I believe that you don't know where the loot is."

"Why didn't you just tell us who you were in the first place?"

"Folks aren't as willing to talk to detectives as they are, say, geologists. And there's men out looking for that gold who would kill others to keep them from finding it first."

Don't I know! Lonnie wanted to say but didn't.

"I got a proposition for you."

"Look, I can read and write *a little,* but could you chew that up a little finer and spit it out slower? What's a 'proposition'?"

"I got an offer for you. You show me an' Brocius the way to

Skull Canyon, and we'll pay you five dollars."

Lonnie shook his head. "I don't want nothin' more to do with that canyon."

"Nothin' more? What do you mean?"

"Nothin'."

"All right, ten dollars."

Lonnie considered it. Ten dollars was a lot of money. "Forget it. I wouldn't do it for twice that much. I don't like the way you came in here, lyin' to me and my ma about who you are. I don't like Brocius bein' in our cabin right now. I don't like havin' a gun pressed to my head."

Madsen quirked a wry, menacing half-smile. "I could do it again."

Lonnie grabbed his rifle from where it leaned against the wall behind him. He cocked the Winchester, aimed it at Madsen's chest. "You've worn out your welcome, Mister Madsen. You'd best leave."

Madsen stared at Lonnie, his shoulders rising and falling slowly as he breathed. "All right, all right. You win, sonny."

Madsen walked to the door then glanced over his shoulder at Lonnie. "For now, you win. You an' me—we'll be talkin' about this later."

"I'll be lookin' forward to it."

Chuckling, Madsen went out.

Still holding the Winchester, Lonnie went to the door, opened it, and watched Madsen retreating in the moonlight, his footsteps sounding crisp and clear in the heavy night silence but dwindling quickly.

Lonnie closed the door and slipped the nail through its hasp, locking the door. He leaned his rifle against the wall and lay back down on the cot with a heavy, weary sigh . . . only to be awakened again by hoof thuds outside the barn.

Lonnie lifted his head with a frustrated sigh. Fatigue hung

heavy on him. He didn't know how long he'd slept.

What now?

He grabbed his rifle, stepped into his boots, and donned his hat. He cracked the door and poked his head out. A horse and rider had just trotted past the barn to stop before the corral to his left. It was still dark, but he recognized the horse as well as the blonde hair tumbling down from the rider's gray felt hat to spill across slender shoulders clad in a short leather jacket.

"Casey?"

Lonnie had kept his voice down. Now as the girl swung down from her saddle, she jerked around with a start.

"Lonnie?" she said, also speaking softly. "You startled me! What're you doing out here?"

He wasn't too bothered about Casey seeing him in his longhandles. She'd seen him in his longhandles before, when they were making their run over the mountains together. Besides, she'd seen him in only a blanket just yesterday at the line shack.

"Long story." Lonnie frowned. He still felt more than a little bitter. His heart was still broken though he had even more pressing matters on his mind now. "What're *you* doing out here?"

Holding the reins of her chestnut mare, Casey walked over to him, glanced at the cabin, as though making sure they were alone, and said, "Lonnie, you're in trouble. Big trouble!" Her breath frosted in the air around Casey's head.

"If you rode all the way out here just to tell me that, you wasted a trip."

"Sheriff Halliday is getting a warrant for your arrest."

"Huh? *What?* Because I shot Walleye?"

"What do you *think*? You can't go around shooting sheriff's deputies without it eventually coming back to bite you, Lonnie!"

"Walleye shot first! Just like last time with Willie, I was only trying to protect myself."

119

"Walleye and Bohannon said you ambushed them."

Lonnie shook his head. He looked around for a rock, and kicked it. "I reckon that doesn't surprise me."

"The sheriff and Bohannon are riding out here to arrest you later this morning, Lonnie. I heard them talking out front of the courthouse yesterday evening."

Lonnie laced his hands behind his head and looked toward town, as though he might see the two county lawmen riding toward him out of the early-morning darkness. "Well, that tears it!"

Frustration bit him hard. As he'd figured he would, he found himself between a rock and a hard place.

Casey said, "What're you going to do?"

"How the hell should I know?"

"Here's what I think you should do, Lonnie. I think you should save the sheriff a trip."

Lonnie swung around in shock. *"What?"*

"It's the only way to take some of the bite out of what's about to happen. Maybe if you ride to town and tell Halliday what you just told me, he'll believe you. At least the judge might be lenient."

Lonnie cocked his head a little and narrowed a suspicious eye at her. "Do *you* believe me, Casey?"

She stared at him for a long moment. Then she moved toward him and stopped just inches away from him, gazing at him levelly. "I know you wouldn't ambush anybody, Lonnie. But I also know you're prone to trouble."

"Prone to trouble, huh?"

"Don't act like it's such a surprise."

Lonnie could give only a caustic chuckle at that.

"Will you please do as I say? Ride to town and try to defuse the situation before it explodes. Tell Halliday what happened. He knows Walleye's own penchant for trouble. He'll probably believe you."

Lonnie swung around again. This time he stared toward the high western peaks standing dark against the fading stars. False dawn was starting. Birds were starting to sing.

Slowly, Lonnie shook his head. "I can't do it, Casey. Last time I was hauled into jail, I was dragged out into the mountains and nearly killed. You remember. Heck, you were the one who saved my bacon."

"Lonnie, I don't see what choice you have."

"I do. You'd best get on back to town."

Lonnie swung around and started back into the barn.

"Not so fast, bucko!" Casey grabbed his arm and turned him back around. "What have you got on your devious mind, Lonnie Gentry?"

"*Devious?* Now, ain't that the pot callin' the kettle black!"

Lonnie jerked his arm loose of the girl's grip and went on into the side shed. Casey stomped in behind him. "I know you're mad at me, Lonnie, but I can't help that. Whatever you might think of me, I still . . . I still care about you. I don't want you to do anything you're going to be sorry for later on."

"Thanks for your concern," Lonnie said as he kicked out of his boots and reached for his pants.

Casey walked to the table and lit the hurricane lamp, turning up the wick and causing shadows to scuttle like rats into the corners. "What're you going to do?"

"I rode to town earlier to tell Halliday about a dead man in Skull Canyon. He and the deputies think I lied. They think I sent 'em on a wild-goose chase to make fools of 'em. I reckon they think I'm so bored up here, with nothin' else to do, that I need a laugh bad enough to go to all that trouble."

Lonnie chuffed and shook his head in exasperation. "Maybe *they're* bored, but *I* sure ain't!"

"Lonnie, please don't," Casey urged. "Please ride back to

town with me."

Lonnie was stepping into his denims, moving fast and shaking his head. "I need to ride up there and see if I can't find poor McLory. If the sheriff realizes I wasn't lying about him bein' in the canyon, maybe he'll realize I'm not lyin' about Walleye and Bohannon scuttlin' like Apaches up to the line shack in the middle of the dang night!"

"Oh, Lonnie." Casey turned around and opened the door.

"Yeah, you get on back to town," Lonnie said.

"I'm not going back to town," Casey said, glancing back at him. "I'm going with you. Maybe . . . just maybe . . . I can keep you from getting yourself killed!"

CHAPTER 24

Lonnie quickly saddled the General and led him out of the barn. As he did, Casey led Miss Abigail up from where she'd been watering the mare at the windmill.

Lonnie glanced at the cabin and felt an urgent need to leave the yard before his mother awakened. Lonnie knew he should tell her where he was going, but she'd only try to stop him. She wouldn't be able to understand what was happening to her son. She'd only think he was up to no good, like everyone else in this neck of the Never Summers.

If he rode out now, May Gentry would think he'd headed back to their summer pastures higher in the mountains. That was just as well. She had her hands full with her overnight "guest" and little Jeremiah.

Lonnie turned to Casey. She was studying him as though reading his mind. She looked a little sad.

Lonnie swung up onto the General's back and, keeping his voice low, said, "You'd best not follow me, Casey. It's too dangerous. You don't know the half of what's been goin' on."

Casey stepped into her saddle and neck-reined the mare around. "Tell me," she said, touching spurs to Miss Abigail's flanks, heading west.

Lonnie rode after her. When they'd passed beneath the ranch portal and were a good distance from the cabin, heading for the main trail, Lonnie rode up beside Casey and started to tell her about the past forty-eight hours.

By the time he was finished filling her in on all that had happened, they were rising through the pine forest high above the ranch, and the big, lemon sun was on the rise behind them, heating the air and stirring the tang of pine resin. Lonnie shrugged out of his denim jacket and wrapped it over his blanket roll.

Riding ahead of Casey, leading the way, Lonnie glanced back over his shoulder at her. She stared straight past him, her eyes wide beneath the brim of her hat, her cheeks pale.

"You all right, Casey?"

Dully, as though she'd suffered a blow to the head, Casey turned to him but it took her several seconds to find her tongue. "My god, Lonnie—all that happened over *the past two days?*"

"Sure as tootin'."

Lonnie swung the General back to face Casey, who halted Miss Abigail. "*Now* are you ready to head back to Arapaho Creek?" Lonnie asked her.

Casey glanced around cautiously, looking a tad frightened. Then she stared past Lonnie, toward the high ridge of craggy peaks where Skull Canyon lay. Her cheeks turned even a little whiter.

"You wouldn't be chicken," Lonnie assured her. "You'd be smart. I oughta stay away, too, but I don't see as I have many options other than to try to find McLory and haul him to Arapaho Creek."

Casey sighed. "Well, you're gonna need help, Lonnie. If you do find him"—she gave a little shudder of revulsion as she no doubt imagined hefting the body of a dead man onto a horse—"you're gonna need help getting him back to town."

"I can find another way," Lonnie said. "I can rig a travois. It'll just take me a little time, that's all."

Casey appeared to consider this. Lonnie thought she was likely imagining the four riders getting shot out of their saddles, as he himself couldn't help replaying inside his head. Finally, Casey shook her hair back behind her shoulders and gigged Miss Abigail up and around Lonnie. "Someone's gotta save you from yourself. Looks like I drew the short straw!"

"What about the mercantile?" Lonnie called after her.

Casey glanced behind as she and the mare trotted up the trail. "Since I pulled double duty for him, Mister Hendrickson gave me the day off. Come on, Lonnie. What is it you always say? We're burnin' daylight!"

Lonnie watched her wavy hair bounce across her slender back as she rode up into the shade of the pines. The sunlight flashed in those blonde tresses like nuggets of pure gold. He didn't want her here, because he knew how dangerous it was.

On the other hand, he wanted her here, close by his side, so badly that he could feel the need in every fiber.

"All right," he said, concealing his great happiness as he spurred the General ahead, "but don't blame me if we get into the same sort of trouble we got into a year ago!"

"Riding with you, Lonnie Gentry, there's *always* going to be trouble!" Casey yelled behind her.

Lonnie couldn't help snickering a little at that as he galloped the General up the mountain.

"That's it," Lonnie said later, when they'd reached the canyon. "That's the cave where I left McLory."

Lonnie scrambled up the steep slope behind the boulders. When he'd reached the small shelf fronting the egg-shaped cavern, he threw his hand out for Casey making her way up the slope behind him. Casey took Lonnie's hand, and he gave her a tug.

Together, they crouched to stare into the cavern. Direct sunlight reached about five feet beyond the opening, but there was enough indirect light that they could see all the way to the stone wall at the back.

"See—no sign of him," Lonnie said.

"No, there sure isn't." Casey turned to Lonnie. "You sure this was the cave?"

"It's the only cave around."

"You built a fire in there?"

"Yep. Whoever took McLory, wiped the cave clear of all the fire ash, too."

Casey pondered this as she stared into the cave. "So . . . whoever took McLory out of the cave wanted to make sure that whoever you told about him wouldn't find a lick of any sign of either of you. So they wouldn't believe you about McLory."

"That's about the size of it."

Casey turned to Lonnie. "Why?"

"The only way I can figure it is they didn't want the law snoopin' around and possibly finding out that they—whoever killed McLory—was out here lookin' for the stolen army payroll. Whoever 'they' are—they probably killed those four riders I told you about, too. And likely hid their bodies. They don't want the law sniffin' around."

"Who could 'they' be?"

"Search me. But they're most likely wanted. That's why they didn't want the law around. Or *were* wanted, at least—if it was one of the four men I saw shot off their horses who shot McLory. I got a hunch there's a couple of different groups searching for that gold. One might even be led up by Crawford Kinch himself."

Casey straightened and looked around. "Let's find McLory and get out of here, Lonnie. It isn't safe here."

"You can say that again." Lonnie looked around, too, scouring the terrain around the cave with his eyes. "What would they have done with him?"

"Finding a dead man around here is going to be like looking

for a needle in a haystack. There's all *kinds* of places they could have hid him, Lonnie." Casey looked at him. "I'm starting to think this idea of yours is even crazier than I thought it was *before* we reached the canyon. I think we oughta go back to town."

"Yeah, I'll go back to town so Halliday can arrest me, and Walleye can shoot me tryin' to escape." Lonnie chuckled dryly. "No, thanks. I'll take my chances lookin' for McLory."

Lonnie looked around again. "I'm thinkin' they wouldn't have taken him far. No one wants to be haulin' a dead man around for longer than is absolutely necessary. They might have dragged him somewhere nearby, and tossed some brush or rocks on him."

Lonnie continued to move on along the base of the ridge, behind the boulders shielding him from the canyon floor.

"You're wasting your time, Lonnie."

"Maybe so, but at least I still *have* time. In town, I'd be livin' on borrowed ti—*oh, crap!*"

"Lonnie!" Casey screamed.

Lonnie had tripped over a boot-sized rock. Trying to maintain his balance, he'd stepped onto a downward slope covered with talus. That foot slid out from under him. Lonnie hit the ground on his belly and rolled down the slope. It was so steep that there was nothing he could do to stop or even ease his descent.

Fortunately, the slope was only about a twenty-foot drop. There was a boulder at the base of it. Lonnie slammed against the base of the boulder with a dull *smack!*

He grunted.

He found himself lying belly down against the boulder's base, in a small area that rainwater had likely eroded away to form a dip. When Lonnie turned over on his back, groaning at the pain in his limbs and head, he snapped his eyes wide, and gasped.

A pale hand hovered over his face, the dusty fingers curled

toward the palm.

"Lonnie!" Casey yelled from atop the slope. "Are you all right?"

Lonnie stared in horror at the stiff hand. Then he eased himself out from under it, gazing at the limb in shock.

"Yeah," Lonnie said dully. "Yeah, I'm all right. But I, uh . . . I think I found McLory!"

CHAPTER 25

Wincing, Lonnie gained his feet and stared down at the arm he'd partially uncovered when he'd rolled up against and sort of under the boulder, where erosion had dug out a crevice beneath it.

Apparently, whoever had found McLory in the cave had shoved him into the crevice and kicked slide rock down on top of him, covering the body. Lonnie saw bits of ash and charred wood, as well. This is also where they'd deposited the remains of the fire.

Casey dropped to her butt and slid down the steep slope behind Lonnie. When she gained the bottom, she crumpled her face as she pointed. "Is . . . that . . . what . . . I think it is?"

"McLory's hand."

"Oh, my gosh."

Lonnie looked at her. "You squeamish?"

Casey nodded. "When it comes to baiting my own fishhook, no. When it comes to handling dead men, yes."

"I'm gonna need help getting him out of here, Casey."

Still staring down at the uncovered hand and part of an arm, Casey flopped her hands against her thighs and said blandly, "Well, that's what I came here for."

Reluctantly, Lonnie dropped to his knees and began carefully removing debris from over McLory's body. His heart fluttered as he worked. He felt his innards recoil as he revealed more and more of the dead young man's body. Finally, he removed the last rock and chunk of charred firewood from over the young man's pale, dusty face.

Dust clung to McLory's hair. It was like a thin cap pulled tightly over his head.

Casey removed more debris from over McLory's legs.

She and Lonnie sat back on their heels, regarding the body now fully uncovered before them, a dark stain of blood showing through the remaining dirt and sand.

"Well, at least you weren't hallucinating, Lonnie," Casey said. "I was beginning to wonder."

"Yeah, so was I."

"How're we gonna get him out of that crevice? He looks pretty snug in there."

"Good question."

Lonnie leaned forward and, making a face as he put his hands on Cade McLory's stiff, lifeless body, he tried to pry the man out of the crevice. The body moved a little but didn't budge from the crevice.

"Good question," Lonnie repeated, sitting back on his heels once more.

"Maybe if we dig the dirt out from under him," Casey said.

"Might as well give it a try."

Lonnie and Casey used their gloved hands to scoop the coarse red dirt and gravel out from under McLory. When they'd dug a trench about ten inches wide and roughly as long as McLory himself, Casey tugged on the dead man's boots while Lonnie hunkered low beneath the boulder, hooking an arm around the man's neck, and tugged on his upper body.

After much straining and grunting and groaning, they managed to pry McLory up to the edge of the trench.

Now, he was at least free of the crevice beneath the boulder. But they still had to find a way to get him down off this steep slope and onto the General's back.

Lonnie and Casey discussed it. Then Lonnie scrambled along the shoulder of the slope to where the stallion waited patiently with Miss Abigail. Lonnie removed his lariat from where it hung coiled over his saddle horn, dallied one end around the horn and the other end around Cade McLory's ankles.

As he worked, Casey said, "This is sure some way to treat a dead man."

"I know," Lonnie said, sheepish. "But I figure since he's dead, he doesn't know what's happening to him. And me doin' this will help me not end up in his same condition. We sort of got to know each other the other night. I got a feelin' he wouldn't mind helpin' me out."

"He doesn't look very old," Casey remarked, staring pensively down at McLory's waxen, dusty features. "Maybe only a couple of years older than me. Now he's dead when he had a whole long life ahead of him not all that long ago."

"Ain't that the way it goes, though," Lonnie said, straightening. He looked down at Casey kneeling beside McLory. "Will you help guide him around the boulder when I start leadin' the General down the slope?"

Casey nodded.

Lonnie scrambled back over to the General. He turned the buckskin around and started leading him downslope. As he did, the rope drew taut. McLory's body lurched straight out away from the boulder, feet first. It sort of fishtailed around another, smaller boulder around which Lonnie had snaked the rope.

When it got hung up on the boulder and Casey couldn't free the body herself, Lonnie went over and helped her. Once free of the smaller boulder, Casey gave a clipped scream as McLory rolled down the steep slope toward where the General waited, halfway down the incline toward the canyon floor.

McLory rolled on past the General before piling up, belly down, a few yards beyond the startled stallion, who switched his tail edgily, whickering at the smell of a dead man.

Dust roiled in the body's wake.

"Oh, Jesus," Lonnie said.

"Well, that was one way to get him down off this bluff."

Lonnie and Casey glanced at each other then laughter exploded from them both at the same time. It wasn't that there was anything funny about what they'd done to poor McLory. It was a mutual acknowledgment of the situation's gruesomeness and of their haplessness in effecting the maneuver.

When their brief burst of laughter had died, Lonnie shook his head and started down the slope toward where the General was lowering his head to sniff the dead man. Lonnie rolled the corpse over onto its back. Casey moved down the steep bluff, grabbing large rocks to break her fall. Breathless, she came up to stand beside Lonnie.

"Now, to get him up on the General's back," Lonnie said, joyless at the prospect.

"Yeah, that should be fun."

Lonnie fetched the tarpaulin that he'd strapped beneath his bedroll before he'd left the ranch. He unrolled the tarp and wrapped McLory's body in it, tying the canvas closed with several lengths of rope. It took him and Casey at least ten minutes and several tries to hoist the body up onto the General's back. They dropped poor McLory several times, but Lonnie kept reminding himself that the man was dead and couldn't feel it.

Still, he felt ashamed for the way he and Casey were treating the body. But it wasn't like they intended to be disrespectful. Lonnie soothed his battered conscience by silently assuring McLory that he'd make sure he was respectfully laid to a peaceful rest in a proper grave in Arapaho Creek.

When McLory's wrapped body was lying belly down over the General's back, behind the saddle, Lonnie and Casey took a breather and long drinks from Lonnie's canteen. Using more rope, Lonnie secured the body to the General's back while Casey fetched Miss Abigail. They mounted their horses, splashed across the creek, and headed for the canyon mouth that seemed to beckon warmly to Lonnie though he secretly couldn't keep his mind off the stolen army loot and the possible reward being offered for it.

It was pointless to think about it, however. What he had to concentrate on was convincing Sheriff Halliday not to arrest him for shooting Walleye. Now that he had McLory's body, which proved he hadn't lied about that, anyway, he likely had a good chance of convincing Halliday that he'd only shot Walleye in self-defense *before* he'd known whom he'd been shooting at.

As Lonnie and Casey rode out of the canyon mouth, Lonnie felt his shoulders loosen in relief. Then they tightened again. He reined the General to a sudden stop.

"What is it?" Casey said, stopping her chestnut beside him.

Lonnie stared straight out from the canyon mouth, where he could see three shadows moving in the trees on the far side of Ingrid Creek, about a hundred yards away and moving in Lonnie and Casey's direction.

"Quick!" Lonnie reined the General around and, as much as he didn't want to, he yelled, "Back to the canyon!"

CHAPTER 26

Lonnie rode the General back through the canyon mouth, glancing back over his shoulder at Casey, who was galloping after him. "Did you see 'em?" he asked.

Casey nodded. "You suppose they're headed for the canyon?"

"Looked that way."

When they'd ridden around a slight bulge in the eastern ridge wall, Lonnie stopped the General and swung down from his saddle. Casey moved on ahead and then reined the mare in, as well. Lonnie tossed his reins to her.

"Wait here—I'm gonna check it out."

Lonnie stepped back around the bulge in the ridge wall, and stopped. He dropped to his haunches as he stared toward the canyon mouth gaping out on a small, grassy meadow through which the creek ran, and the pine forest beyond.

He could see the three riders crossing the creek, coming on slowly, one trailing a packhorse. Lonnie had been afraid that they might have seen him and Casey, but it didn't look that way. They were moving at a leisurely pace, spread out about ten feet apart. They were too far away for Lonnie to make out much about them except that one was riding a big Palomino and was wearing a black opera hat, very much out of place out here.

Lonnie waited, worrying a stone in his hand, as he gazed at the three riders who continued to move toward him. When they did not swerve to either side but rode on into the canyon, Lonnie stepped back behind the bulge in the ridge wall and turned to where Casey sat her mare, gazing toward him with a worried expression.

"They're comin', all right." Lonnie held his hand up for his reins, which Casey tossed to him. "We'd best ride on."

"Deeper into the canyon?"

"Where else we gonna go? Those men might or might not be the fellas who shot those four riders off their horses, but they're likely looking for the loot. I for one don't cotton to the idea of hanging around here to find out if they're friendly. We'd best hole up somewhere out of sight, and try to sneak out around them."

Lonnie had just turned out his left stirrup and was about to poke his boot through it, when he heard the thuds of galloping horses growing louder. He frowned and stared back in the direction of the canyon mouth, crickets of apprehension playing hopscotch along his spine.

He glanced at Casey and then walked back to the bulge in the ridge wall. He eased a cautious glance out around it.

The three riders were now galloping toward him.

The man in the top hat snapped a rifle to his shoulder. The carbine belched loudly. The slug screeched toward Lonnie and hammered the ridge wall only a few feet from his face.

Lonnie lurched backward, heart racing.

"Lonnie!" Casey yelled.

"Go!" Lonnie got his boot tangled up as he twisted around and started to run. He dropped hard on his belly, then lifted his head to yell louder, "Go, Casey! *Ride!*"

Casey neck-reined the mare around, and rammed her heels into the horse's flanks, lurching into an instant gallop. Hearing more shooting behind him as well as the smashing of the slugs into the ridge wall only a few feet away, Lonnie scrambled to his feet and up onto the General's back.

The stallion required no urging to flee. Even before Lonnie

was set, the stallion broke into a ground-swallowing run, nearly throwing Lonnie. When the boy had recovered, he hunkered low in the saddle and followed Casey and the mare along the gradually rising canyon floor. The ridge walls widened around them, and Ingrid Creek slid away on Lonnie's left. They crossed a clearing and then entered a mix of conifers and aspens.

Lonnie ground his molars as the reports of rifles echoed behind him.

He glanced back and drew a sharp, shallow breath. The three riders were galloping hell-for-leather after him and Casey, the one trailing a packhorse lagging a ways behind the other two.

Their bullets plumed dirt and spanged off rocks wickedly close to the General's scissoring hooves. That was the encouragement the General needed to run even faster. Lonnie could feel the horse lunging ahead, chewing up the ground and overtaking Casey.

Lonnie glanced back at the girl and said, "Follow me!"

Just then he swerved the General hard left. Casey followed. As they bulled through a stand of aspens, Lonnie glanced back the way they'd come. He couldn't see their pursuers, as they were back behind a bend in the canyon wall. Lonnie steered the General through a corridor between cabin-sized boulders, across Ingrid Creek and up a steep, grassy incline along a belly of shouldering granite.

Lonnie had recognized the gap in the boulders because he'd found a stray calf up this way only a year ago, mired in the creek. Hoping that their pursuers wouldn't see their tracks swerving off the main canyon floor, Lonnie put his head down and pressed his thighs tight to the General's back, to keep from being thrown off as the big buckskin lunged up the steep slope.

He glanced behind, worried that Casey wouldn't make it. But the girl had as much saddle savvy as Lonnie did. She wasn't having any trouble staying seated on the sure-footed Miss Abigail who seemed to almost be racing the General up the steep incline.

When the hill leveled off slightly, Lonnie turned the General to the right and onto the crest of the granite outcropping. He kept climbing into some pines, and then hauled back on the General's reins. As Casey moved through the low-hanging pine boughs behind him, Lonnie dropped out of the saddle, tossed his reins over a cedar sapling, shucked his rifle from its scabbard, and moved back down to the top of the outcropping.

He dropped to his knees and crawled to the edge of the cliff. He lay belly down and removed his hat, making less of him to see from below.

From here he could see the canyon floor from over the tops of the aspens and boulders lining both sides of it. No sign of the riders, but Lonnie could hear the distance-muffled clacking of their galloping horses moving farther up canyon.

Casey crawled up beside Lonnie and lay belly down. Taking his lead, she also removed her hat.

"Did we lose 'em?"

"For now."

"When they realize we're no longer ahead of them, they'll double back and likely see where we left the main trail."

"Maybe." Lonnie sleeved sweat from his brow. "The canyon floor's all rock, though. They'd have to be some mighty good trackers to see where we left it. They'd have to track as good as Injuns."

"What if they can?"

Lonnie pushed himself to his feet. "That's why we have to keep movin'."

"Why don't we head back down and ride on out of the canyon before they double back?"

Lonnie grabbed his reins off the cedar sapling and slid his rifle back into its boot. "And risk meetin' up with 'em again when they double back?" He gave a wry laugh. "No, thanks. Some of that lead they were slingin' was comin' mighty close. Those fellas are used to shootin' . . . and killin'."

Casey looked around, lines of apprehension cut deep across her forehead. "Where we gonna go?"

"I don't know. I haven't been much deeper in the canyon than where we are now." Lonnie looked up through the pines though he couldn't see much for the trees. "I reckon we go higher, try to put as much distance between us and them curly wolves as we can."

"Yeah, it looks like they're a bit proprietary about that loot." Casey gained her feet and, looking around cautiously, walked up to grab Miss Abigail's reins. "So . . . this is Skull Canyon."

Lonnie swung up into the saddle and glanced at her. "Yeah." He paused as she toed a stirrup and stepped into her saddle. "You scared?"

She looked at him, incredulous. "It's Skull Canyon. Aren't you?"

Lonnie grumbled a reluctant "I reckon . . . a little," and then gigged the General on up through the pines.

CHAPTER 27

Lonnie had no idea where he was leading Casey. All he knew was that he wanted to get as much separation between himself and the three gun-crazy riders as possible. Following a game path up higher into the forest, he kept swinging cautious looks behind him and occasionally stopping the General to look around and listen.

When he and Casey had crossed a pass and dropped down into what Lonnie assumed was a separate arm of the canyon—separate from the one in which they'd left the shooters—he paused to let the General drink at a small spring gurgling over a bed of polished stones.

Casey rode up beside him and let Miss Abigail lower her head and draw water from a small, dark pool glimmering as the sunlight filtered through breeze-jostled pine boughs. "Lonnie, if we keep riding blind like this, we're going to get lost. This canyon will make slow, painful work of us."

"Better'n goin' out so full of bullets we'll rattle when we walk."

"I say we start back."

Lonnie was looking toward a rocky crag rising straight ahead of him, several thousand feet above the rolling, spruce-green forest. The crag resembled a giant pipe organ jutting its arrow-shaped pipes against the flawless cobalt blue of the sky.

"I heard the canyon has two entrances," he told Casey. "Or exits—however you want to look at it. The other way out is near the base of the crag that's shaped like a skull. I think one of them peaks over yonder is the skull."

"How do you know?"

Lonnie hiked a shoulder. "Workin' with old punchers every spring and fall, you hear stuff."

"How far away do you think those cliffs are?"

"Hard to say. Five, maybe six miles. Once we make it out, we can circle around the canyon and make our way back to Arapaho Creek. It'll take some time, but I don't see as we have much choice."

Casey gave him a skeptical glance. "Lonnie, if you get us hopelessly lost or eaten by a bear . . . like the one that almost ate us last year around this time . . . I'll never forgive you."

Lonnie looked off. A pang of jealousy inspired him to mutter with sarcasm, "I suppose the counter jumper in the fancy suit will be expecting to see you this evenin'. Probably plans to buy you a fried-chicken supper at the Colorado House. Sorry about that."

Casey didn't say anything for a few seconds. Then: "Lonnie, you're not takin' me on a wild-goose chase on purpose, are you? Just to keep me away from that 'counter jumper,' as you so indelicately call Niles, who is no shopkeeper but a *bookkeeper*?"

Lonnie turned his head to her, annoyed. "Heck, no! If you done made up your mind about Mister Fancy Dan, I got nothin' more to say to you. Now, let's ride. Maybe we can make them crags before sundown. I for one would not like to spend another night in this canyon . . . especially with a girl with such poor taste in suitors!"

Lonnie urged the General across the creek and on up the game trail he was following. If he would have looked behind him, which he did not, he would have seen Casey smiling fondly at him as she put her horse across the creek and followed him.

As they rode, the crags grew larger before them. The pines

thinned out, the grass grew short and green, and ferns and evergreen shrubs grew shaggy along several creeks that now threaded this leg of the canyon. The air grew cool and the wind began making that eerie moaning sound as it blew around and over the tall, gray cliffs that stood at the canyon's far end.

Lonnie didn't see that a lake lay at the base of the crags until he was only a hundred or so yards away from it, following the canyon's grassy floor up a steep rise. The lake was pancake flat and the color of iron, with only a few breezy ripples marring its otherwise placid surface. The towering crags were reflected in it.

It was on the surface of the lake that Lonnie first saw the skull grinning up at him. He jerked his gaze toward the cliffs with a slight gasp.

"Hey . . . see it?" he said to Casey riding up behind him. He pointed. "You see the skull?"

Casey stopped Miss Abigail and lifted her gaze toward the cliffs. "Oh, my . . . yeah."

The formation indeed looked like a human skull devoid of skin and hair. It sat between two arrow-shaped pinnacles, on its own towering precipice—light gray in color and bearing two roughly circular indentations for the eye sockets, a long crooked crack for the nose, and a black crevice curved into the shape of a grinning mouth though one corner of the mouth was decidedly higher than the other.

A leering, menacing smile.

The wind whistled through the irregular gaps around the skull, sometimes making a high whistling sound while sometimes making what sounded like an elk's mournful, bugling cry.

Something sat atop the skull. A bird of some kind. Just then, as though to reveal itself to the newcomers, the bird flew up from the skull and vaulted in a long, smooth, downward arc toward Lonnie and Casey. It grew larger and larger. It looked like a large, brown rag with flapping wings. As it grew closer,

Lonnie saw the curved talons and the hooked beak.

When the raptor was maybe fifty feet above the lake it swooped upward and gave an eagle's ratcheting, echoing shriek as it sailed off on the southerly wind down canyon, in the direction from which Lonnie and Casey had come.

The skull moaned. The moan echoed over and over only to be followed by another one.

The echoes sounded like an angry giant bellowing through a bullhorn.

Lonnie felt an eerie chill. To distract himself as well as Casey, he swung around, following the bird with his gaze, calling, "Hey, if you see those three tough nuts who tried cleaning our clocks, drop a load on 'em for me, Lonnie Gentry!"

He grinned, satisfied with himself, at Casey.

Casey had swung down from Miss Abigail's back. She stood beside the mare, arms crossed on her chest, regarding Lonnie dubiously. "What if that bird was trying to tell us something?"

"What could that have been?" Lonnie asked, though he thought he knew what Casey was going to say.

"That we shouldn't be here."

Lonnie ignored the cold fingers of apprehension again raking his spine, and hiked a shoulder with phony nonchalance. "I reckon it's a little late for that." He glanced at the western ridges. "Sun's gonna set soon. We'd best find a place to camp for the night. We'll get an early start in the morning."

As he began leading the General to a stand of shaggy pines to his left, he pointed across the lake. "Looks like there's a break in the cliff wall there. I bet that's the way out of the canyon."

"Why don't we head for it now, Lonnie?"

Lonnie kept walking. "We'd never make it before dark. It's farther away than it looks."

"Is there anything you don't know, Lonnie Gentry?"

Lonnie stopped walking and tossed her a meaningful look.

"Yeah, there's a few things I don't know about."

His look was direct enough, his tone level enough, that she didn't have to guess what he'd meant.

CHAPTER 28

Lonnie found a place well back from the clearing at the point of the lake in which to camp. He found a dense stand of trees with a well-concealed open area inside them roughly as large around as an Indian tepee.

The first job was to pull McLory down off the General's back, which proved to be far easier than had getting him up there. Lonnie didn't relish the idea of wrestling him back up there again in the morning.

When he and Casey had picketed their horses to a line strung between two trees, they gathered wood and built a small fire. Knowing that when riding into the mountains you had to be prepared for anything, Casey had packed a bedroll, warm clothes, and a couple of ham sandwiches she hadn't yet gotten around to eating.

She and Lonnie arranged their bedrolls and other gear around the snapping flames of their fire. Lonnie hung a pot of coffee on his iron tripod.

He found his food pouch and was happy to discover a bit of deer jerky and two stale biscuits inside. He knew there were likely fish in the lake, but it was getting too dark to make his way back out into the clearing. It no doubt got so dark up here before the moon rose that he wouldn't be able to see his hand in front of his face.

The upside of that was no one else was likely to see him, either.

Still, the canyon gave him the willies. He decided to stay close to the fire as well as to Casey though he was still miffed at the girl, and his heart still ached, knowing she'd set her hat for another. He understood why she'd done it, but he didn't know how he was ever going to stop thinking about it.

He was glad she was with him now, though. At least they had what would probably be their last night together. He hoped it wouldn't be their last night, period, on this side of the sod.

As he gathered and deposited one more load of firewood, the low, windy moaning sounded again from out in the darkness. It sounded louder and more menacing now after night had come down and the last light had bled out of the sky.

"Lonnie, good lord—is that the skull speaking to us again?" Casey asked, kneeling by the fire, a leather swatch for the coffeepot in her hand. She stared off beyond where the glimmering firelight reached.

"If you look at it that way—or hear it that way," Lonnie said, "you're gonna get the fantods. Just hear it like it is—the wind blowing around that big rock up there. That's all."

"Are we going to have contend with that all night long?"

"I don't know. You want to go on up there and have a chat with the rock, see if you can get it to pipe down a little?" Lonnie chuckled as he sat back against his bedroll and tipped his hat back off his forehead.

"All right, Mister Smarty," Casey said as she handed over a smoking cup to him, "have a cup of coffee. I don't know why I feel so generous, but you can have one of my ham sandwiches, too. Made 'em both last night from the hog my neighbor butchered just last week." She extended a sandwich wrapped in waxed paper.

"You keep it," Lonnie said. "You'll need it for breakfast. You got a long trip back to Arapaho Creek, prob'ly take you half the day. Me—I can set some snares, and I might see if there's any red-throated trout in the lake yonder."

Casey sat back against her own saddle, about four feet to Lonnie's right, and looked at him through the firelit steam of her coffee. "What're you saying, Lonnie? You're not going to stay around here, are you?"

"I might poke around a little."

"Poke around a little for the strongbox?"

"Why not? There's likely a sizeable reward on that much money."

"What about the curse on this place? What about McLory?"

"He'll keep another day. It's cool up here. Then I'll build a travois. I can throw one together right quick. As far as the curse goes . . ." Lonnie sipped his coffee and looked around, wary. "I reckon if we get through this night there's no reason I won't get through the next night. Besides, I heard there's an old Mexican sheepherder's stone hut around here somewhere. That might be the place where old Crawford Kinch hid the money."

"What about the men who shot at us?"

"I'll lay low. Now that I know they're here, I'll be extra cautious." Lonnie shook his head slowly as he stared pensively out into the darkness. "I could sure use that reward money. What if it's five hundred dollars?" He gave a soft whistle through his bottom teeth. "That's a heckuva stake."

"A stake for what?"

"A stake for getting out of here." Lonnie dug a trench in the dirt with his right boot heel. "I think I done let too much grass grow under my feet up here in these mountains. Time to move on."

Casey slowly unwrapped her sandwich, staring at Lonnie and frowning. "Because of me?"

Lonnie glanced at her, hiked a shoulder, and sipped his coffee. "Heck, I don't blame you for takin' up with that counter jumper."

"He's a *bookkeeper,* Lonnie."

"I don't blame you for takin' up with that *bookkeeper,* then. What could I give you? Close quarters with my half-crazy ma and my screamin' half brother—an outlaw's son."

Lonnie gave a caustic chuff. "We'd struggle every day of our lives, just like Ma and I do now. That's no way for you to live. You been through a lot in this life, losin' both parents. You didn't deserve any of that. You're a purty girl, a good person. You deserve to have a happy life without worryin' every day about puttin' food on the table. I'd like to know a little of that myself. Heck, Ma will move to town and find a counter jumper of her own to support her and little Jeremiah. That'd be a better, more fittin' life for her. I'm just in her way."

When Casey didn't say anything, Lonnie glanced at her. He was surprised to see her staring at him through a veil of tears shimmering in her eyes. Then the veil broke. Tears spilled down her cheeks. They were honey-colored in the firelight.

Casey started to scuttle over to him, extending her arms as if to hug him. Lonnie moved back away from her, and rose, tossing the dregs of his coffee into the brush.

"I'm gonna check the horses, gather a little more wood," he said, setting his cup down next to his saddlebags, grabbing his rifle, and walking away from the fire.

There it was, he thought. In his mind he'd broken from her. His words had sealed the deal.

He felt better now. Lighter. Freer. His heart didn't hurt quite so much.

It still hurt. Just not quite so much.

He checked to make sure both horses were well tied to the picket rope. He didn't want either wandering off in the night, frightened by the distant scent of a mountain lion or prowling grizzly. He and Casey had tethered them close to a freshet running through the trees and now winking in the starlight.

Lonnie started to gather more blowdown branches, when he jerked his head up to stare out through the trees toward the lake. He'd heard something. It had to have been the wind because the bullhorn-like roar of the skull was nearly constant now though sometimes louder than at other times.

Now he heard it again—what he'd heard before. It was different, separate from the moaning. It seemed to be coming from not too far away, in the direction of the lake.

Lonnie picked up his rifle from where he'd leaned it against a tree. He took two heavy, faltering steps toward the sound then stopped abruptly, his blood running cold. He heard the sound again.

It was a man's high, mournful voice calling, "Innnngggggg . . . griiiiddddddddd . . . Oh, Innnnnggggg . . . griiiddddd!"

It mixed with the moaning to form a truly horrifying, low wailing sound that stabbed Lonnie deep in his loins.

The boy's heart thudded.

"Ingrid," Lonnie muttered to himself, cold sweat breaking out on his forehead. "Oh . . . oh, Jesus!"

Then, beneath the wind's moaning rose a man's cackling laugh.

That, too, stabbed Lonnie deep in his loins. Even deeper.

But the assault to his nerves was far from over.

Behind Lonnie, Casey's sudden, ear-rattling scream caused the boy to jump nearly a foot straight up in the air.

CHAPTER 29

"Casey!" Lonnie shouted as he ran back toward the fire shimmering straight ahead in the darkness.

He tripped over a deadfall and fell, dropping his rifle. He grabbed his rifle and got up and kept running. Casey's screams had died by the time he reached the outer edge of the firelight. Breathing hard, Lonnie stopped and stared across the fire, where a broad-shouldered man in a battered brown Stetson stood behind Casey, holding a big bowie knife tight against her throat.

Challenge flashed in his eyes as he glared across the fire at Lonnie. He curled one side of his upper lip, showing badly rotted and tobacco-encrusted teeth. "Stand down, boy. Drop the rifle."

Lonnie held the Winchester up high across his chest. He squeezed it in his gloved hands. He looked at Casey. The girl's face was blanched, her eyes wide with fear. Her throat moved as she swallowed. She winced when her throat moved against the bowie's sharp blade.

Lonnie tossed the rifle away.

"Let her go!" Lonnie shouted, balling his fists at his sides. "Or so help me, I'll—!"

Something hard slammed against the back of Lonnie's head, throwing him forward. He stumbled, hit the ground near the fire, and rolled close to the stones forming a ring around the crackling flames.

"Lonnie!" Casey cried.

The man with the bowie knife released her. She ran around the fire and dropped to a knee beside Lonnie, who lay groaning and clutching the back of his head with both hands.

In the corner of his left eye, Lonnie saw a man stoop down to pick up his rifle. He was a tall man in a long wool coat with long, grizzled hair curling down behind his ears, and a three- or four-day beard stubble carpeting his craggy cheeks.

He had large, light-blue eyes, which glinted in the firelight as he grinned after inspecting Lonnie's rifle. "Kid comes well-armed. An eighteen sixty-six Winchester repeater. Yellowboy."

"Tough one, huh?"

Lonnie turned his head in the other direction to see the man who'd been holding the bowie knife on Casey standing over him, glowering down at him. He wore a quilted deerskin coat and deerskin gloves. He had a round, meaty face and deep-set, cold gray eyes. He, too, had had several days worth of stubble on his sunburned cheeks.

"Boys got mouths on 'em these days," he grumbled down at Lonnie. "It weren't like that before I went in. Boys talked respectful like to their elders. My, how things change."

"Are you okay, Lonnie?" Casey asked, leaning down to regard the boy worriedly.

Lonnie nodded and looked up at the broad-shouldered gent standing over him. He was about to ask the man who he was but cut himself off when he saw a tattoo peeking out from under his upraised coat collar.

The man grinned and jerked his collar down, revealing the tattoo of a naked lady raising her knees as though she were perched coquettishly on a saloon table, batting her long eyelashes at the men surrounding her.

"You like it, kid? She's some faded—I got her in New Orleans just after the war—but she's still a looker, ain't she?"

"That's disgusting," Casey snarled. "Who are you?"

Lonnie said in a voice hushed with awe, "Crawford Kinch."

Kinch stared at him, vaguely puzzled. Then he smiled, showing his rotten teeth again. "You have me at a disadvantage, boy . . . even though I'm the one holdin' the bowie knife and Engstrom back there has your rifle."

"Lonnie Gentry," Lonnie said, rocking back on his heels. "This is Casey."

"She's some purty," Kinch said, glancing lustily down at Casey. "But I'm an old man who knows his manners."

"Me? I'm an old man but I don't know my manners," said the man whom Kinch had called Engstrom, ogling Casey. "And you're right . . . she's some purty."

"Stay away from me," Casey said. "Either one of you comes near me, I'll bash your head in!"

Kinch and Engstrom laughed.

"A polecat, that one!" said Engstrom.

Kinch sheathed his bowie knife and thrust his hand out toward Engstrom, who tossed him Lonnie's Winchester. "Tie 'em up, Dutch," he told his partner. "Good and tight."

"Tie 'em up?" said Engstrom, incredulous. "We're gonna have to kill 'em, Craw. Ain't no two ways about it. The kid knows who you are. Now, they both do. And they're after our gold!"

"We're not after your gold," Lonnie said. His words had fallen on deaf ears.

"Don't make no difference," Kinch said. "I ain't up to killin' kids tonight. I'm old and tired and I got contrary ways about me. You know that, Dutch. Killin' grown men after my gold's one thing." He shook his head as he switched his gaze from Lonnie to Casey and back again. "But two young folk with their lives ahead of 'em is another thing altogether. Saddens me, it does."

He gave a coyote-like, menacing grin at his partner. "We'll do it in the mornin'. Throw 'em both in the lake, see how good they float!"

He laughed at that.

Lonnie and Casey shared a wide-eyed glance of terror.

"You oughta thank us," Kinch told Lonnie. "We got them three curly wolves back there off your trail—didn't we, Dutch?"

Engstrom smiled.

"Huh?" Lonnie said.

"Sure, sure," Kinch said, winking at his partner. "You won't have to run from them no more. And me an' Dutch won't have to worry about 'em, neither."

"This canyon's fillin' up fast with dead men—ain't that right, Craw?"

"Sure is. It's time fer us to pull foot soon," Kinch said. "Before the law starts sniffin' around, finds our blood trail." Kinch cocked Lonnie's Winchester and aimed at the pair straight out from his right hip. "Either of you two move, you're be flappin' your golden wings tonight instead of tomorrow. No use rushin' things. You can live a good long time over the course of a few hours. I spent eighteen years in the territorial pen." His expression turned dark. "I know how long a single hour can be, let alone eighteen years when you're spendin' every minute of it thinkin' about a stash of hidden gold."

"Aren't you the philosopher," Casey said. "You're the convict who stole the payroll money. Lonnie told me all about you. Wicked!"

Staring at the rifle aimed at him, Lonnie said, "Easy, Casey. Pull your horns in—will ya? I for one don't wanna be flappin' golden wings tonight!"

CHAPTER 30

"Yeah, pull your horns in, girl," warned Engstrom, grabbing Lonnie's coiled lariat from where it lay by his saddle. He tossed his head to indicate behind him as he crouched down by Lonnie. "Who's the dead fella laid out back there?"

"One of the men you shot," Lonnie said. "You might not have given him a chance to introduce himself. His name was McLory. Cade McLory."

"Don't know who're talkin' about, kid," Engstrom said, tying Lonnie and Casey's wrists together, behind their backs. "All the men we shot of late we made sure were dead."

"Certain sure," said Kinch. He looked at Lonnie. "Your man was shot by someone else. There's two or three groups of bounty hunters hereabouts. Leastways, they *were* hereabouts," he added with a dark chuckle. "They're after me and my gold. They all want to be the first ones to reach the secret cache, hot on my heels, and they're shootin' each other for the privilege. Don't bother me none. Saves me an' Engstrom from havin' to kill every polecat powderin' our trail!"

He chuckled through his rotten teeth as he sank onto a log a ways away from Lonnie and Casey, holding Lonnie's rifle across his thighs. Engstrom was tying Casey's ankles.

"Fortunately," Kinch added, "there ain't enough lawmen to go around."

Lonnie said, "McLory was a bounty hunter?"

"Most likely. Part of a group huntin' another group. I swear,

153

I never seen the like in this canyon since the War of Northern Aggression. Little battles breakin' out every whichaway! Word spread fast that I busted out of the territorial pen. Dutch an' me thought we wasn't followed, but we led one group right into the canyon, and another group must've been followin' the first group! I reckon eighteen years breakin' big rocks into little rocks made me lose my outlaw savvy," Kinch added, shaking his head in disgust. "I wasn't watchin' my back trail."

"The old legend don't seem to be keepin' the gold hunters away." Engstrom grinned at Lonnie. "I had you scared—didn't I boy?" He threw his head back and gave a lower, quieter version of his call for Ingrid. "Why, you 'bout jumped out of your boots when you heard that. Not to worry, though. Just a legend prob'ly concocted by some prospector to keep folks out of the canyon and away from his diggin's."

"Don't laugh, Engstrom—it probably helped keep anyone from tryin' overly hard over the past eighteen years to find that strongbox. Just a coincidence I came to bury the loot here. A fortunate one, though. A haunted canyon—yessir. Just what the doctor ordered!"

Lonnie glanced over his shoulder at Engstrom. "Were you one of the gang that robbed the payroll, too?"

"Me? Nah." Engstrom stood and hitched his baggy canvas breeches up higher on his bony hips. "Me an' Craw met up in prison. I was in for murderin' the liveryman I caught . . . uh . . . I caught in a *compromising situation,* you might say. With my dear wife, Bertha." He threw his head back and sniffed the night air. "Ahh . . . sure is nice bein' free, though, ain't it, Craw?"

"Sure 'nough," Kinch said. "Why don't you fetch the horses, Dutch? We'll be beddin' down here at the fire of our new friends. You two don't mind—do you?"

"Would it do any good if we did?" Casey asked in her snooty, haughty way.

Engstrom chuckled as he walked off into the trees. "I don't mind a sassy girl as long as she's purty."

Lonnie looked at Kinch who was helping himself to Lonnie's cup of coffee. "You really gonna kill us tomorrow?"

"Don't have much choice, kid," Kinch said, sipping the coffee and looking at the cup with approval. "That's good. But, then, I ain't tasted a good cup of coffee since me an' Engstrom jumped the wall. They don't serve coffee in the pen, you see. Only water. And it ain't much good—the water—neither."

He took another sip of the coffee and shook his head as he looked around. "I'm never goin' back there. Never. I'd die first. That's why we can't leave anyone behind to tell where we been. As soon as we dig up that loot, we're hightailin' it to Mexico."

"No need to tell us that," Lonnie said.

"Why not?" Kinch grinned devilishly over the rim of the cup. "You'll be givin' up the ghost tomorrow. After you done helped us with the gold, that is."

Casey fired another of her raw glares at him. "What're you talking about?"

"I buried the strongbox deep—in what I suspect was an exploration hole dug by some prospector long before me and Bentley came along. Bentley was the fella who made it into the canyon with me. All shot up, Bentley was. I put him out of his misery." Kinch aimed Lonnie's rifle at the ground and said, "Pop! Pop! Two shots to the head." Then he grinned his wolfish grin again.

"You probably killed him to keep from having to share the loot with him," Casey said with a snort. "Or so he couldn't tell anyone else where it was."

Kinch arched his brows at the girl. "You know, I always heard that brains and beauty didn't mix. After meetin' you, sweetheart, I might have to rethink that old saw."

"You're awful," Casey said. "And you smell bad. How long

has it been since you've had a bath?"

Kinch sniffed under his left arm. "Pshaw! I'm sweet as a spring lily." He chuckled. "But to answer your question—oh, say, about eighteen years."

He laughed louder.

"What's so funny?" Engstrom said as he led two horses toward the camp.

The General and Miss Abigail both snorted around and whickered at the smell of the strange mounts.

"The sweet little flower says I smell bad."

"You do smell bad, Craw—that's what I been tryin' to tell ya," Engstrom said, stopping the horses at the edge of the firelight. "You an' me need us a good long bath in a fancy hotel just as soon as we dig up that loot of yours."

"I reckon you're right," Kinch said, grunting as he rose from the log. "Good to have such a smart fella with such winnin' ideas backin' my play."

"Aren't you two just two peas in a pod?" Casey said. "Why haven't you dug up the gold yet?"

Kinch set his coffee cup down and walked over to tend his horse.

"And lead all the jaspers doggin' our heels straight to it?" said the old outlaw, walking stiffly, hunched a little forward, as though his lower back ached.

As Engstrom tossed his saddle onto the ground near the fire, he said, "We decided to hang low and let 'em all kill each other, or at least cull their own herds, before we dug it up and lit out with it."

"No point in leadin' 'em right to it," Kinch said, "so they could just shoot us and take the strongbox for themselves."

"How did you find us?" Lonnie said. "Way over here at the far end of the canyon."

Engstrom squatted down in front of the boy, his eyes fairly

glowing as he said, "Why, because the gold is right nearby, my boy. So close I can smell all that gold blowin' on the southern breeze."

He closed his eyes and drew a long, slow breath, his horsey face fairly blossoming as he took in what he believed to be the smell of gold coins on the eerily moaning wind.

Later, when they'd eaten and had their fill of coffee, the two men rolled up in their blankets and rested their heads against their saddles on either side of the fire. They pulled their hat brims down over their eyes.

Kinch started snoring almost immediately.

Engstrom was looking as though he, too, was drifting off, when Lonnie turned toward Casey to whisper, "These two jaspers are crazier'n a tree full of owls."

"Yep," Casey agreed, nodding. "And we'd best try to work our way out of these ropes before sunrise, or we'll be flyin' off on golden wings before noon."

CHAPTER 31

"I think I'm starting to work mine loose," Lonnie whispered when he and Casey had been working at the ropes binding their wrists for over an hour. "He tied 'em good, but I'm getting some slack."

"Good," Casey said.

Lonnie could feel her shoulders rubbing against his as she worked to loosen her own bindings. Lonnie glanced toward the shadowy lumps of their two captors, one on either side of the fire that had burned down to dully glowing coals. Both men were snoring loudly beneath their hats, bellies rising and falling deeply.

Crawford Kinch whistled faintly with each snoring exhalation.

Lonnie kept working at the ropes, turning his wrists from side to side and clawing at the ropes with his fingertips. He got enough slack in the rope around his right wrist that he thought he could pull his hand through the loop.

Again, he glanced at the two men. They were still asleep, snoring peacefully. They must have been relatively certain that none of the other men hunting the gold had picked up their trail.

Lonnie winced against the pain of the rope scraping his skin as he pulled his hand slowly through the loop. He pulled hard, grinding his molars against the burning pain of badly chafed skin. Feeling the slickness of blood oozing from a cut, he groaned softly, bit down on his lower lip, and pulled his right wrist free.

"Got it!" he said, unable to control his glee despite the skin he'd scraped off.

"*Shhh!*" Casey admonished.

They both looked at Kinch. The old outlaw had stopped snoring.

Lonnie cursed under his breath.

"Stay asleep, you old codger," he said inside himself. "Please, please, please—*keep sleepin'!*"

Kinch grunted, sighed, ran a hand across his mouth then turned onto his side. His hat tumbled off his shoulder. Soon, he resumed snoring.

Casey turned her head toward Lonnie, wide-eyed with anger. So quietly that the boy could barely hear her, she said, "Idiot!"

This time, Lonnie had to agree with her.

Quickly, he used his free hand to free his other hand. As he did, he glanced toward Kinch and then toward Engstrom, who lay as he had before, hat over his eyes, snoring deeply.

When Lonnie was free, he turned to Casey and began untying the ropes binding her wrists. It didn't take him long. Lonnie stood and then helped Casey to her feet. She looked at him as though to say, "What now?"

Lonnie glanced to where his rifle leaned against the log near where Engstrom was lying. The Winchester was on the other side of the man, ten feet from Lonnie.

The boy strode around behind the log, moving nearly silently on the balls of his boots. He looked at his rifle barrel glistening in the moonlight. Slowly, he reached for the jutting barrel, which was about two feet to the right of Engstrom. His hand was a foot away from the barrel when Engstrom rolled over, grabbed the rifle, cocked it, and aimed it from his knees at Lonnie.

"Uh-uh," Engstrom said, grinning winningly, thoroughly

satisfied with himself. "I think I'll hang onto it a while longer."

He glanced from Lonnie to Casey, who stood frozen in horror, and laughed.

"What is it? What is it?" Kinch said, grabbing his own rifle and cocking it.

He looked around wildly.

"Oh, nothin'," Engstrom said, holding his rifle on Lonnie, who stood with his hands raised to his shoulders. "Just these two younkers keepin' us two old curly wolves on our toes—that's all."

He gave Lonnie a mocking wink.

Lonnie glanced at Casey, who returned the glance, crestfallen.

Disappointment was a heavy stone inside him. He cursed to himself.

Kinch and his friend Dutch Engstrom not only retied Lonnie and Casey, they tied their hands behind their backs and their ankles behind their backs, as well. Their wrist ropes were connected to their ankle ropes by a foot-long length of hemp. They lay on their sides, facing each other on the ground, like two hogs bound for tomorrow's slaughter.

Not long after the two outlaws had rolled back up in their bedrolls, their snoring resumed.

Lonnie looked over at Casey lying three feet away from him. He couldn't see her clearly, as the moon was waning, but he thought she lay with her eyes open, staring hopelessly at the ground.

Lonnie doubted that either of them would get much sleep for the remainder of the night. Their positions were far too uncomfortable for slumber.

"Casey?" Lonnie whispered.

She rolled her sad eyes up to him.

"You all right?"

"Do I look all right?"

Lonnie sighed and winced at the tension that the deep breath added to his strained arms and shoulders. "No, I reckon not. Sorry about all this. I reckon we should have lit out of the canyon back when you said we should."

Casey didn't respond to that. She just went back to staring at the ground.

Keeping his voice low, Lonnie said, "I reckon you were right to throw in with the counter jumper."

"He's a bookkeeper, Lonnie."

"I meant you were right to throw in with that bookkeeper." Lonnie paused. "I reckon Niles or Giles or whatever his name is wouldn't have gotten you in half as much trouble as this."

Casey stared at the ground.

After a few seconds, she made a snorting sound.

Lonnie frowned curiously, staring at her. Then he saw her shoulders jerking, and he realized that she was laughing.

Her shoulders lurched more violently and she made a strangling sound as she laughed louder, blowing dirt and pine needles into her face. Then Lonnie found himself snorting, as well. His snorts grew into uncontrollable laughter as he, too, saw the dark humor in their situation.

Kinch and Engstrom stopped snoring.

Kinch lifted his head from his saddle. "Good night, children!" he ordered.

Lonnie and Casey pressed their faces to the ground to squelch their laughter but it took their shoulders a long time to stop jerking.

Even though Lonnie knew tomorrow would likely be his last day on earth, morning couldn't come fast enough. The chill mountain air of the long night aggravated the aches and pains in his strained joints. The two old outlaws didn't start rolling and snorting out of their bedrolls until well after dawn, however. They continued snorting and coughing and spitting phlegm for close to a half hour before they came over and cut Casey and Lonnie free so they could limp off into the woods and relieve themselves.

Kinch said, "Either one of you gets the urge to make a run for it, just remember I was a sharpshooter back during the War of Northern Greed and Criminal Aggression, and I can shoot the eye out of a junebug at two hundred yards."

Kinch and Engstrom laughed at the exaggeration.

Even if Lonnie had had the urge to run, he doubted he could have run—not after being trussed up like the proverbial fatted calf for half the night. Besides, he wouldn't have left Casey. He doubted she was in any better condition to run than he was.

When he finished his business, he glanced back toward the camp. Kinch was down on one knee, coaxing last night's fire back to life. He had Lonnie's rifle near. Engstrom was off in the trees on the far side of the camp, tending their horses. Kinch glanced up occasionally at Lonnie, making sure the boy didn't run off.

Casey walked up out of the trees behind Lonnie. Her hair was badly mussed. She looked pale and tired out and frightened. Lonnie's heart ached at seeing her so beaten down. He grabbed her arm, glanced toward Kinch who was blowing on the mounded ashes, and leaned in close to the girl.

"As soon as your horse is saddled," Lonnie said, "you climb up on Miss Abigail and hightail it back to town. You understand?"

Casey scowled at him, as though he'd said something ludicrous. "I won't leave you alone with those men, Lonnie."

"There's no point in us both dyin', Casey."

Casey gazed into his eyes for a moment, her eyes soft. "If you're going to die, Lonnie, I'm dying with you."

"Hey, you two lovebirds," Kinch called, "get over here *now!*"

Lonnie stared back at Casey, shocked by what she'd said. She was a puzzle, this girl.

His throat felt thick and tight. He cleared it and said, "If I don't have to worry about you, I'll find a way out from under them. You know I can do it. That's how I am. So, first chance you get—and you probably won't get one, but *in case you do*— you ride like Miss Abigail's tail's on fire!"

Kinch straightened now and shouted, "What'd I just tell you two? If you ain't back here in three seconds, your end is gonna come sooner rather than later!" He picked up Lonnie's rifle and cocked it loudly.

"We're comin'!" Lonnie called.

He jerked his desperate, beseeching gaze back to Casey. "Got it?"

Dully, turning her mouth corners down, Casey nodded. She strode past him, brushing her hand against his, and headed back to the fire.

"What were you two talkin' about over there?" Kinch wanted to know.

"None of your business," Casey snapped at him.

"If you two try anything, you're wolf bait—understand?"

Lonnie said, "Wolf bait ain't gonna dig up that gold for you."

Kinch glowered at him, his eyes dark beneath the brim of his battered hat. "Stop your sassin' and gather wood for the fire, but don't you leave my sight, boy. The girl's gonna be here, makin' coffee and corn cakes. If you run, she'll pay. Now, get to work—both of ya. You got you a job of work ahead!"

CHAPTER 32

When they'd all padded out their bellies and had their fill of coffee, Kinch and Engstrom led Lonnie and Casey by gunpoint out to where the horses were picketed.

"Saddle up and be quick about it, children," Kinch ordered. "As soon as you're in the saddle, your wrists will be tied to the horn. We're gonna tie her horse to your buckskin's tail, and Dutch will be leadin' your buckskin by the reins. So don't even think you're gonna get a chance to run off—understand?"

He stared pointedly, suspiciously at Lonnie.

Lonnie shook his head as though in grim defeat. "You two got it all figured out, don't you?"

"Let's just say this ain't our first rodeo," Engstrom said. "Is it, Kinch?" he called over the mule's back.

"No, it sure ain't," Kinch said.

Lonnie glanced at Casey, nodding at her to be prepared for a chance to run, then picked up his saddle blanket and tossed it over the General's back. He took his time rigging the General. He wanted Casey to have her mare saddled ahead of him. When the two outlaws had their own mounts saddled and ready to go, Lonnie was taking his time inspecting the General's right rear hoof.

"He's a slow mover, that one," Engstrom said, indicating Lonnie. "You watch him like a hawk, Kinch. He looks like he couldn't toe up a horse apple from a frozen barnyard, but he's sly as a three-legged coyote."

He gave Lonnie a sharp look.

"I'll walk out a ways and make sure we're alone out here. If anyone camped nearby, I'll likely smell their smoke."

"Don't worry," Kinch said. "The kid knows if he tries anything, the girl's gonna pay."

Kinch narrowed an eye at Casey. Lonnie turned to Casey, and his heart immediately started tattooing a frenzied rhythm against his breastbone.

Casey had her mare saddled and ready to go. She'd seen her chance. With one quick, anxious look at Lonnie, she stepped fleetly up onto Miss Abigail's back, and shot a haughty glance at Kinch, who merely stared up at her dully, slow to comprehend what she was fixing to do.

The outlaw had thought that Lonnie was the one he had to keep the closest watch on. He'd been wrong.

Casey said, "Yeah, but what if the girl hornswoggles you, you cork-headed fool, and tries something herself?"

Cheeks flushed with desperation, the girl neck-reined the mare around on a dime and batted her heels against the chestnut's flanks. With a single lunge off her hindquarters, Miss Abigail was off and running through the trees.

Kinch grabbed his rifle and raised it, cocking it and yelling, "Why that—!"

As the man aimed at Casey, Lonnie threw himself against Kinch, shoving the rifle up as the outlaw triggered it. The rifle thundered as Kinch fell on his back, Lonnie landing on top of him and struggling to wrench the rifle out of the outlaw's hand.

"Lonnie!" Casey yelled in the distance.

Lonnie turned his head and shouted, "I'm all right! Keep goin', Casey! *Ride!*"

He'd just gotten that last shout out before Kinch slammed the butt of his rifle against Lonnie's head. It was a glancing blow, but it threw Lonnie onto his back, where he lay staring up at the sky while little, golden butterflies danced in front of his eyes. Beneath the ringing in his ears, he heard Casey's hoof thuds dwindle quickly into the distance.

"I'll go after her!" Engstrom said, running up to his saddled horse.

"Let her go," Kinch said, pushing up off a knee and heaving himself to his feet, breathing hard, cheeks flushed.

He glared down at Lonnie. "We still got this one here. He'll dig up the gold for us. Then we'll kill the hydrophobic mongrel and be shed of this canyon once and for all. By the time she can bring the law, we'll be halfway to Denver and points south."

Lonnie's head ached, and the rough ride around the lake and up a low ridge wasn't doing it any good. He rode with his wrists tied to his saddle horn. Engstrom was leading the General by his bridle reins. Kinch led the way up the steep slope around outcroppings of jagged rock resembling the backbones of dinosaurs.

Tall pines and firs loomed over and around them.

Lonnie had lost his bearings, but he thought they were somewhere near the canyon's far northern end, though he couldn't see the craggy peaks around the skull from this low angle. He could hear the hoarse, raspy breathing of the wind around the giant skull, however.

The two outlaws stopped frequently to study their back trail, to make sure no one was following. Then Kinch would collapse his spyglass, mount his sorrel, and continue riding.

"You sure you remember where you buried the strongbox?" Engstrom called to Kinch around midday, the blazing sun burning down from straight overhead.

"Well, it's been eighteen years," Kinch said, looking around carefully and also a little anxiously, Lonnie thought. "Excuse me if I don't ride right up to it, Dutch!"

"I'm just askin'," Engstrom said, throwing his hands up in supplication. "Just askin', that's all . . ."

Kinch started to look around more and more anxiously. By the set of his shoulders, Lonnie thought the old outlaw was beginning to panic, thinking he might not have remembered the route to the gold as well as he'd thought he had. He'd probably gone over the map in his head hundreds if not thousands of times, all those years he'd spent behind bars.

Only to discover, in the end, that the years had fogged the trail . . .

That was all right with Lonnie. The sooner they got to the gold, the sooner he'd be dead. He was still waiting for a chance to skin out away from these two old bandits. After losing Casey, however, they were being more careful. They'd tied Lonnie's wrists tight to his saddle horn, and Engstrom looked back often to make sure Lonnie hadn't worked himself loose.

Kinch hauled back suddenly on his sorrel's reins. He sat studying a black granite ridge wall down which a small spring trickled over a glistening path of blue-green moss. At the bottom of the ridge the water had formed a slight pool ringed with deep grass. The water flowed over the lip of the pool and down across the trail in a rivulet that murmured like delicate wind chimes.

"What is it?" Engstrom asked Kinch.

Kinch worked his nose like a dog. "That smell. I know that smell. I remember that smell!"

"I reckon my sniffer's done been fouled by too many full privies and slop pails not to mention that rotten prison food they was always feedin' us. Rotten potatoes and man sweat is about all I can smell anymore."

Lonnie could smell what Kinch was smelling. The smell of green growth and wet rock and mushrooms and the slightly cloying smell of moss and mold. He could tell from the way

167

Kinch was now looking around, sniffing, that those smells were reaching up from the past to tickle his memory.

"There!" Kinch said, pointing on up the slope a ways, toward the base of the granite ridge wall. "That's it right there, or I'll be hanged!"

Kinch galloped the sorrel on up the ridge and stopped near a depression at the base of the stone wall. Wildflowers grew in the high grass over and around the depression. So did honeysuckle shrubs and even a few gnarled cedars and pine saplings.

Kinch swung heavily down from his horse and stood staring at the depression, fists on his hips.

He turned toward Engstrom after a time and grinned. He pointed at the depression. "That's it. We laid up here, making sure we were shed of the posse. The old digging we found is that low spot right there. We slid the strongbox off our mule and into the hole, and caved it in. That brush has done grown up in the eighteen years since. No one's messed with that hole. I can tell they haven't. The gold is still down there, Engstrom!"

He looked around, and then pointed upslope toward several humps of black granite about the size of large ranch wagons. "Beyond them rocks up there—that's where I buried Bentley, so's no one would ever find him."

He looked again at Engstrom, who'd remained on his horse.

"Come on, come on!" Kinch said, beckoning. "Bring the mongrel." He grinned at Lonnie. "And a shovel!"

CHAPTER 33

Lonnie rammed the folding shovel into the dense, tangled roots at the base of a shrub, and glanced at the two men sitting in the grass about ten feet away from him. Both held their rifles across their thighs, watching him eagerly.

Sweat ran down Lonnie's cheeks. It burned in his eyes.

He'd dug two feet down into the hole and was still coming up against large rocks and shrub roots, which required prying and twisting and heaving away, so that he could continue digging deeper into the hole.

"Come on, come on," Kinch said. "You're young and strong, boy. Keep diggin'!"

"I'm thirsty," Lonnie said, dabbing sweat from his eyes with his neckerchief. "Toss me my canteen, will ya?"

His canteen lay in the grass near where the two old bandits lounged like church deacons at a Sunday afternoon picnic. They were passing a small, flat bottle of whiskey back and forth between them.

"No more water till you're done," Kinch growled.

"The faster you dig down to the strongbox," Engstrom said, "the faster you can have a drink of water—ain't that right, Kinch."

"There you have it, kid. Dig!"

Lonnie started digging again with an angry snort. His head hurt from the braining that Kinch had given him. His shirt and longhandle top were sweat-basted to his chest and back.

After another ten minutes of digging, he stopped, breathless, and turned to the two old reprobates still passing the bottle, their eyes growing more and more glassy. "This would go a heckuva lot faster if one of you would take a turn and give me a breather," Lonnie said. "It's hot, and, like I said, I'm thirsty. And who knows how far down that box is."

Kinch wrinkled his nostrils and narrowed his eyes. "Who raised you to talk down to your elders?"

"I'm just sayin'—"

"What you're doin' is sassin' your elders *and* your betters," Engstrom said, pointing an angry finger at Lonnie. "Now, you get to work or I'm gonna come over there and box your ears."

"Keep it up, kid," Kinch put in, "and I'm gonna drill a bullet into each of your knees. How would you like that?"

"How would that help?" Lonnie said, exasperated.

Kinch merely jutted his jaw at him, glaring.

Lonnie sighed and continued digging.

He pried up another rock and dug a few more shovelfuls of gravel. The shovel met something that had no give to it. Lonnie rammed the shovel down against whatever it was, probing, then turned to the outlaws. "Hey, I think I got it!"

He was relieved that his work might soon be over, even though it meant his life would likely soon be over, as well. He was so hot, tired, and hungry that he no longer cared if he lived or died.

The outlaws scrambled drunkenly to their feet, keeping their rifles on Lonnie, and hurried over to the hole.

"Well, keep diggin'!" Kinch ordered. "Keep diggin'!"

Lonnie kept digging until he'd uncovered the top of the stout wooden, two-feet-by-one-foot strongbox. There was a rusted metal hasp but no lock. The lock had likely been shot away by the outlaws some eighteen years ago.

"Sure as tootin'," Kinch said, running an eager hand across

his mouth. "There she is, Dutch!"

Engstrom whistled.

"Come on, kid—put your back into it," he ordered. "Haul it on out of there!"

Lonnie went back to work, digging along all sides of the box. When he'd gotten a gap dug all around it, he got down on his hands and knees, grabbed one exposed handle, and tried pulling the box out of the ground.

It was still stuck solid.

"It's not moving an inch," Lonnie said, sitting back on his heels. "If you two want that box out of there, you're gonna have to help me lift it instead of just standin' there blowin' your horns!"

Engstrom glowered at Lonnie. He started toward him, making a fist. "By god, I'm gonna—!"

"Hold it right there!"

The strange voice stopped both men in their tracks.

They and Lonnie swung around to see Sheriff Frank Halliday hunkered down atop a boulder about fifty feet away, aiming his Winchester, which he now loudly cocked. "I got you covered! Drop those rifles and do it now or I'll blow you out of your boots!"

Lonnie might have been ready to die a few minutes ago, but a wave of relief washed over him like a fragrant spring breeze. Despite the trouble he was in for having shot Walleye, he felt as though a yoke had suddenly been lifted from his shoulders.

Kinch stared, shaking his head in awe. "I can't believe it. I just can't believe it."

Engstrom turned to him, his lower jaw hanging in shock. "How can it be, Kinch? How can this be? We was watchin' our back trail so close!"

"Drop the rifles!" Halliday repeated.

The old outlaws cursed and tossed their rifles away.

Engstrom took his face in his hands and sobbed. Kinch just stared, bleach-faced. Lonnie sank back onto the edge of the hole, and dropped his shovel. He heaved a long, ragged sigh of relief, and sleeved sweat from his forehead.

"Appleyard!" Halliday yelled.

Presently, Deputy US Marshal John Appleyard strode out from behind some shrubs to Lonnie's left, spurs chinging, red neckerchief blowing in the breeze. The federal lawman aimed a Spencer carbine straight out from his right shoulder as he moved toward the two outlaws, squinting down the Spencer's barrel.

"You all right, kid?" Appleyard asked.

"I'll live," Lonnie said.

He stopped seven feet from Kinch and Engstrom, keeping his rifle aimed at them. "On your bellies. *Now!*"

The old outlaws got down on their bellies. While Halliday kept them covered from atop the boulder, Appleyard tossed their rifles away and then handcuffed them each behind their backs.

"All right—it's clear!" the federal lawman called to the sheriff.

Appleyard glanced at Lonnie. "Sure you're all right, boy? That's a nice-sized goose egg you have on your head there."

Lonnie was surprised by the federal lawman's concern. He wasn't accustomed to such concern, especially from a lawman.

"I'm all right—thanks," Lonnie said.

He went over and picked up his canteen. As he did, Halliday walked out from behind the boulder. He moved past Lonnie without so much as glancing at the boy. That was fine with Lonnie. Halliday seemed more concerned about the strongbox, which Appleyard was now kneeling over.

The federal lawman grunted and groaned as he tried to pry up the lid. He'd leaned his rifle against a sapling near the top of the hole. "It's on there tight," Appleyard said, and tried again, wedging his fingers down along the edge of the lid.

The lid slid up out of the box, its ancient hinges squawking. As the lid fell back, Appleyard and Halliday stared down at the burlap pouches mounded inside. The pouches were obviously old. They were threadbare, and the "US ARMY" stamped on their sides in black was badly faded.

Appleyard plucked one of the pouches out of the box. Hefting it in his hand, he grinned up at Halliday standing over him, at the edge of the hole. Halliday held his rifle down low in his right hand. He held out his left.

"Toss one."

Appleyard tossed him a bag, which clinked when Halliday grabbed it.

"There's said to be fifty thousand dollars here," Appleyard said.

Halliday whistled as, cradling his rifle in his arms, he opened the pouch and dipped his hand inside. He pulled out a handful of gold coins. They flashed brightly when the sun caught them. The sheriff dribbled them back into the bag.

They made joyful clinking sounds.

Lonnie felt himself salivating at the sound of all that wealth.

Kinch, who'd risen to his knees, looked up at Halliday. "What do you say we split it four ways?"

Engstrom was rising to his knees now, as well. "That's a helluva lot more money than you'll ever make as a sheriff! You, too, there, Marshal!"

Appleyard shook his head. "That money's goin' back to where it came from—the US Army."

"No, it's not."

Appleyard frowned at Halliday. Lonnie jerked his own startled gaze to the sheriff, too. Halliday was smiling down at Appleyard. Halliday was hefting the money pouch in his left hand. He raised his Winchester in his right hand, aiming the barrel at Appleyard's chest.

"Wait, now," Appleyard said, straightening. "Hold on, now, Halliday!"

As he lunged for his rifle, Halliday fired.

Appleyard grunted as the bullet punched into his chest and blew him backward off his feet. He fell back in the hole and rolled sideways. He lay half over the open strongbox.

Lonnie stared in shock, his ears ringing from the rifle report, as Halliday turned to Kinch. The old outlaws regarded the sheriff with loose-lipped disbelief.

"Wait, now, Sheriff," Kinch said, leaning back on his heels. "Wait now. Hold on!"

Halliday shot him.

Engstrom screamed as Halliday shot him, too.

Lonnie jerked violently with each loud, echoing rifle report.

His heart dropped like a cold stone in his belly when Halliday turned toward him and aimed the rifle at his head.

CHAPTER 34

"Bury it," Halliday ordered Lonnie.

The boy stared at the smoking barrel of the sheriff's rifle aimed at his head. The smoke smelled like rotten eggs in the air around him. Lonnie stood frozen, shocked. He glanced around at the dead men.

"Go ahead, kid—bury the loot."

"Wha . . . huh . . . ?" Lonnie said. "You want me to . . . *bury* it?"

"That's right."

Keeping his rifle aimed at Lonnie, the sheriff stepped down into the hole. He picked up one of Appleyard's ankles and dragged the man's body out of the hole. He deposited the dead federal lawman beside Kinch and Engstrom.

Then he took his rifle in both hands again.

"I got no use for the gold. Not now, anyway. If I took it now, folks would get suspicious. Several people in Arapaho Creek know that me an' Appleyard headed to the canyon, to look for Kinch. If I didn't come back, they'd figure I'd found the gold and lit out with it. I'd be hunted."

Lonnie stared at the lawman as Halliday glanced around at the dead men, chewing his bottom lip thoughtfully, anxiously. It was as though the sheriff was speaking to clarify his thoughts on the subject of the gold.

On the subject of his keeping it for himself.

Lonnie didn't like how the man was talking. At least, he didn't

175

like that the man was telling him all this . . . what he was going to do. It gave Lonnie a bad, bad feeling down deep in his loins. A moment ago, he'd thought he'd been saved. Now, he appeared as doomed as he'd been when Kinch and Engstrom had had him by the short hairs.

"True, folks might think that both me and Appleyard was killed . . . maybe by Kinch and his old prison buddy," Halliday continued. He stared at Lonnie but he seemed to be seeing right through the boy and into his own future. "Maybe by the bounty hunters who've been shootin' each other around here of late. But if I rebury the gold and leave it here, on the end of the canyon where no one's likely to look for it, I can wait a month, maybe two. No one else will look for it here. The only reason I knew to look for it at this end of the canyon was because I talked to one of the old posse riders, years ago. He followed Kinch and Bentley up this far, but he didn't tell nobody but me . . . when he was dyin' of cancer. I knew it was around here somewhere, and, sure enough—good ole Kinch escaped the pen an' led me right to it!

"Yeah, that's it. I'll wait a couple of months. I can give notice to the county that I decided to resign . . . and ride back out here for the gold and light out with it. That way, no one will hunt me, and I won't have to run to Mexico. Hell, no—I can go east or west. Always did want to live high on the hog in a place like Frisco!"

"What about Kinch?" Lonnie said. "What about . . . the marshal and Engstrom?" He wanted to ask about himself, too, but he was afraid of the answer.

"Appleyard died in the service of his country—killed by Kinch and his old prison pal. I, of course, killed the outlaws. I'll fetch them all back to town, bury 'em proper. I got no idea where the gold is. Kinch must've forgot where he buried it and was just ridin' in circles around the canyon, lookin' for it. Yeah, that's it. He was just ridin' in circles."

Halliday looked at Lonnie, grinning. "That sounds good, don't it?"

He actually seemed to be waiting for Lonnie's response.

When none came, he said, "With Kinch dead, the other gold hunters will give up the chase. Lookin' for the gold without Kinch to lead them to it would be like looking for a single pine needle in all the north-south stretch of the Rockies. Besides, I think most of 'em have done shot each other by now, anyways."

Halliday chuckled, in love with his plan.

"In a few months, the gold will go back to bein' nothin' more than a legend. Except for me." Halliday chuckled again, glancing around again at the dead men. "Except for me. I'll just ride in here, dig it up, and ride away—a very, very rich son of a gun!"

He jerked his rifle at the strongbox. "What're you waitin' for, kid? Get to coverin' up that box!"

Lonnie's mouth was dry. His tongue felt like a parched chunk of ancient leather. He ran it across his lower lip, and said, "What . . . what about me, Sheriff? What're you gonna do about me?"

"Good question!" Halliday was walking out a ways from the hole, looking carefully back the way he'd come as though making sure that no one had heard the gunfire and come to investigate.

That was doubtful, Lonnie knew. It was a big canyon. Halliday and Appleyard must have cut Kinch's trail up here by a mere twist of improbable fate. Maybe they'd heard the crack of Kinch's rifle earlier, when he'd fired at Casey.

"What do you think I should do with you?" Halliday asked when he returned to the hole, which Lonnie had halfheartedly started to fill in again. "Huh, kid? You think you can keep a secret?"

Halliday hitched up his pinstriped pants and sat on a rock

about six feet from the hole. He leaned his rifle against the rock and dug into his coat pocket for his makings sack.

"Yeah, I can keep a secret," Lonnie said with no real enthusiasm. He knew Halliday was just toying with him. The sheriff had killed three men as though it had been nothing more than shooting coyotes off a gut wagon. He'd have no qualm about shooting Lonnie . . . as soon as Lonnie had finished his chore, that was.

"Let me think on it," Halliday said, dribbling chopped tobacco onto the wheat paper he troughed between two fingers. "In the meantime, you just keep workin'. Come on, come on—put some effort into it, will ya?"

Lonnie took his time burying the strongbox. He was in no hurry to die. He'd gotten accustomed to the idea of his death several hours ago. Still, he wasn't going to urge it on any faster than he needed to.

Besides, a vague, deep-down part of him managed to keep hope alive that somehow he'd come up with a way to save himself. As he worked, he glanced several times over at Halliday sitting on the rock, smoking cigarettes, sipping whiskey from Kinch and Engstrom's bottle, and staring dreamily at the hole Lonnie was filling in, as though he were daydreaming about what he was going to do with all that gold.

While the sheriff daydreamed about his riches, Lonnie considered ways to save himself.

If he could get close enough to Halliday, he might be able to smash him in the head with the shovel, and lay him out cold . . .

But how was he going to get close enough to the man to do that?

"Sure is hot," Lonnie said, when he had the hole about three quarters filled in. "Would you mind handing me my canteen,

Sheriff? It's that one over there near Appleyard's feet."

"You're almost done. When you're finished covering the hole and makin' it look all natural-like, then you can have a drink, though I don't really see much point."

He chuckled darkly.

"I'd be able to work faster if I had a drink, Sheriff."

Halliday gave a disgusted chuff. Leaving the rifle leaning against the rock, holding his quirley in his left hand, he walked over and picked up Lonnie's canteen. The boy's heart quickened as Halliday turned toward him. Lonnie squeezed the shovel, getting ready to lift it quickly for a resolute swing.

But then Lonnie's gut fell with disappointment. Halliday only tossed him the canteen. The canteen hit Lonnie in the chest and fell to the ground.

"Nice catch," Halliday said, chuckling as he walked back over to his rock.

Lonnie felt like crying, but held himself in check. He set the shovel down, crouched to retrieve the canteen, unscrewed the cap, and took a drink.

When he'd had his fill, he tossed the canteen aside and resumed covering the hole. As he tossed the last few shovelfuls on the hole, Halliday walked into the brush and dragged back some blowdown branches.

The sheriff had his cigarette in his mouth. He'd left the rifle leaning against the rock. Lonnie stopped shoveling to stare at him, his heart quickening again.

Halliday shouldered Lonnie aside and dropped the branches over the hole, hiding it. Lonnie couldn't believe his luck when Halliday turned away from Lonnie, and crouched to pick up a limb that had broken off of the main branch.

His heart galloping like a stallion inside his chest, Lonnie squeezed the shovel. He raised it in a high arc. Halliday straightened and turned toward him, the cigarette smoldering between his lips, his eyes narrowed against the smoke. He tossed the branch down on the hole and widened his eyes as the shovel arced toward his head.

CHAPTER 35

Halliday started to raise his hands to deflect the shovel, but he didn't get them halfway to his chest before the shovel smacked his left temple with a resounding *clang!*

"Oh!" Eyes rolling back in his head, Halliday stumbled backward.

He managed to get both feet under him. He shook his head. Blood ran down from the deep gash high on his forehead. As he regained his balance, he dropped his hand to the Colt holstered on his right hip.

Again, Lonnie raised the shovel and swung it down with a grunt.

Clang!

Halliday's hand fell away from the revolver as he twisted around and went stumbling and falling into the brush on the other side of the hole. Lonnie stared at the man. Halliday lay belly down, unmoving. Throwing the shovel aside, Lonnie ran over to where General Sherman stood, ground-tied and nervously twitching his ears.

Lonnie grabbed the General's reins. He was breathing hard, heart racing, shaking with anxiety. He glanced back toward where Halliday lay where Lonnie had left him. He still didn't appear to be moving.

Lonnie turned his stirrup out, but he was so tired and stiff that he had to try three times before he managed to pull himself up by the horn and shove his left boot through the stirrup and swing up into the saddle. He turned the General around and touched spurs to the stallion's flanks.

The buckskin galloped around shrubs and large boulders and pines and then started down the gradual slope toward the canyon floor.

Lonnie hadn't paid much attention to the way they'd ridden up here. He'd been too crestfallen and still dazed by Kinch's assault on his head. There was no trail, only a twisting passage through boulders and pines down the hill that grew steeper until Lonnie had to hold the stallion to a trot or risk the horse stumbling on blowdowns and deadfalls as well as patches of dangerous slide rock.

He'd just gained the base of the slope and had started galloping toward the lake he could see shimmering beyond a stand of firs and pines, when something buzzed in the air behind him. The buzz grew louder. The bullet pinged off a boulder ahead and to Lonnie's right.

Rock dust puffed from the side of the boulder. A quarter second later, what felt like a giant, powerful fist slammed into Lonnie's left temple.

Lonnie heard the echoing crack of the distant rifle as he dropped the reins and was hurled out of his saddle. The ground came up to assault him without mercy. He passed out even before he stopped rolling.

Darkness enveloped him.

The pain was there inside him, radiating out from his head. But it was like a loud knock on a door at the far end of a very large house.

The knocking grew louder. Lonnie opened his eyes to see two familiar faces staring down at him. He had trouble placing them at first, because his brain was like a dark room draped with cobwebs. But then the names of his mother's "guests" came to him—the Pinkerton agents, Brocius and Madsen.

"Looks like he's comin' around," said Brocius, though his voice was muffled by the hammering clang in Lonnie's ears. "He killed Appleyard, you say?"

From even farther away rose another familiar voice: "Hard to believe, ain't it? A kid as young as that." Then Halliday walked into Lonnie's view. The sheriff's eyes were swollen, and dried blood formed a long, red river down over his nose and down his cheek. He held his rifle on his right shoulder.

He gingerly fingered his temple as he said, "Laid me out cold. Don't know why he didn't kill me. Had the drop on me. Maybe he figured he'd done enough killin' for one day."

The bearded Madsen was still crouching over Lonnie, who lay on the ground where he'd landed when he'd been knocked off the General's back by the ricocheting bullet. Madsen shook his head. "Well, given that he's got no pa and his mother don't seem to know what to do with him—I reckon it all adds up to a bad apple, all right."

"No!" Lonnie wanted to shout at the tops of his lungs. But it was like shouting in a dream. He couldn't seem to get the words out. It was as though a large, wet rag had been shoved into his mouth.

"Gonna take him back to town, Sheriff?" Brocius asked.

"Oh, yeah," Halliday said, scowling down at Lonnie, slowly nodding his head.

Lonnie glanced around. Kinch, Engstrom, and Marshal Appleyard lay belly down over the backs of their horses. The horses stood around Lonnie and the three men now. The General stood nearby, head down, staring at Lonnie skeptically, switching his tail nervously.

"Oh, yeah." Halliday shook his head. "I don't care how young he is. That feral pup is gonna stand trial for murder."

"If he lives," Madsen said, chuckling. "That's a nasty crease on his temple there." He raised his voice as he gazed down at

Lonnie. "Hey, kid, you hear me?"

Then all went dark again. When Lonnie awoke, he was riding slumped forward in his saddle. His wrists were tied to his saddle horn. His boots were tied to the stirrups. Halliday was leading the General by his bridle reins. The two Pinkertons rode to either side of the sheriff.

The men were talking and chuckling like old pals as they rode, easing down out of the mountains. Lonnie looked around to get a fix on where they were, but then a big, black hand closed over his face, and when he woke again, he was in a jail cell.

He lifted his head, wincing against the throbbing pain slicing deep into his skull from his temple and setting all his nerves on fire. The cell wobbled around him.

Though his vision was fuzzy, he recognized the sheriff's office in Arapaho Creek. He'd been in this very cell roughly a year ago, when he'd been arrested for the murder of one of the two deputies who'd mistaken him for one of Dupree's gang.

Well, here he was again . . .

He squinted his eyes to see a man sitting at the rolltop desk against the jailhouse's front stone wall, to the left of a window through which buttery mountain light angled. The man at the desk had his back to Lonnie. It was a broad back clad in a dark-brown wool vest over a pinstriped cream shirt. A white bandage was wrapped around the top of the man's head. Brown hair streaked with gray fell out from beneath it to curl onto his shirt collar.

Smoke curled up from the pipe the man was smoking as he crouched over the desk, writing on a notepad.

Lonnie looked more closely around his cell to see that a hide-bottom chair angled up beside his cot. A light, fawn-colored leather jacket hung from the back of the chair. He could smell a familiar, subtle, flowery fragrance. Casey was standing to his right, staring out the barred window. She was partly silhouetted against the bright sunlight, but her blonde hair sparkled like liquid gold.

She turned her head toward Lonnie and jerked with a little start.

"You're awake." Casey sat in the chair. She crouched forward, gazing at Lonnie, eyes bright with concern. "This is probably a silly question, but how do you feel?"

"Reckon I've felt some better," Lonnie said, pushing himself up a little higher on the cot, which hung out from the cell wall on iron chains.

There was a small, wooden table to his right. A basin sat on the table. Casey reached over to the basin, plucked a cloth out of the water, and wrung it out.

"That's a nasty cut on your head, Lonnie. You're lucky you didn't bleed to death. Doc Hagen said he got you stitched up just in time. He'll be around soon to change your bandage."

Hearing the two of them talking, Halliday turned in his chair. "Well, well," the sheriff said. "You're still kicking, huh, kid?"

Both his eyes were discolored and slightly swollen, the right one more than the left one.

"No thanks to you," Lonnie said. He'd spoken too loudly. The noise clanged inside his head, battering his tender brain plate.

"Lonnie, that's enough," Casey said, stretching the damp cloth across his forehead, which he now realized had a bandage wrapped around it, same as Halliday. "Don't you think you're in enough trouble?"

Halliday chuckled, shaking his head. His chair squawked as he turned back around to face his desk and his paperwork.

Lonnie had a feeling he knew the answer to the question, but he asked, anyway: "What kind of trouble am I in, Casey? What did Halliday say I did, exactly?"

Casey pressed the cloth against his forehead. She stared down at him sadly, lips pursed. "You just rest up, Lonnie. No need to hear about it just yet. Later, when you're stronger."

Lonnie placed his hand on hers. "Tell me."

Casey drew a deep breath. She glanced over her shoulder at Halliday, who had his back to them again. She turned to Lonnie.

"Well, Lonnie Gentry, you're really in the soup this time. You've been charged with the cold-blooded murder of three men, including a deputy United States marshal. Your trial is due to take place just as soon as you can walk."

CHAPTER 36

"Casey," Lonnie said, squeezing her wrist. "You gotta listen to me. You're the only one I can trust."

He glanced at the sheriff who was still hunkered over his paperwork, filling the office with the aromatic smell of pipe tobacco. The sheriff didn't appear to be listening to the conversation in the cell, but Lonnie knew he was. He was trying to catch every word.

That's why Lonnie kept his voice low.

"Casey, I didn't kill nobody," he whispered, staring at the girl with desperation. "It was him—Halliday. He shot Kinch and his old prison pal, Engstrom *after* he shot the marshal."

Casey glanced over her shoulder at Halliday. "Why would he *do* that, Lonnie?"

"Why do you think? Because he wanted to take the gold for himself. Kinch showed me where it was. I dug it up. But then Halliday and Marshal Appleyard rode up on us. That's when Halliday shot all three of 'em. He had me rebury the money. Now, if we can get someone to ride out to that canyon and . . ."

Lonnie stared at Casey, who regarded him with a weird expression. "Casey," he said, "you believe me, don't you?"

His head was suddenly aching even more than before.

His stomach felt tight and raw.

"Casey," he urged, squeezing her wrist. "Answer me."

"Sure, Lonnie," she said, regarding him as though he were a strange language she was trying to interpret. She pulled her wrist free of his grip and ran both hands down her face, shaking her hair back from her cheeks. "Of course, I do. It's just . . ."

"Just what?"

"It's just . . . that . . . why would Halliday think he could get away with taking all that gold? I mean, there are so many men after it. The US Army is after it! How far would he think he could get?"

"That's why he had me rebury it after I dug it up for Kinch," Lonnie said, leaning far toward her.

Keeping his voice low was a hard feat, for he desperately wanted . . . *needed* . . . to convince Casey of the truth.

"He wants to let some time pass before he goes after it. So no one gets suspicious. Now, with Kinch dead, everybody . . . includin' the army . . . will likely give up on that gold. It'll go back to bein' just one more legend in the Never Summers. Halliday intends to resign his job here in a few months and ride out and dig up the loot and live high on the hog in San Francisco!"

Casey just stared at him, confused.

"Casey, for god's sake—you have to believe me, of all people!"

The girl brushed befuddled fingers across her forehead. "Lonnie, I want to believe you. But you have to admit, that sounds a little far-fetched."

"Sure, it does. But that's the story. Halliday told me what he was going to do. Gold will make folks do desperate things."

"Yes, it will."

"What do you mean?"

Casey glanced once more at Halliday and then turned back to Lonnie, gazing at him with renewed gravity. "Lonnie, why did you really want to ride back to that canyon yesterday? Was it really to find the body of Cade McLory?"

Lonnie studied her. He felt the chinking in his own armor begin to grow brittle.

"Yes," he said, finally, after studying his hands for a time.

"Yes, it was. But I gotta admit I was sort of wanting to see about finding the gold my own self."

Casey pursed her lips, her cheeks dimpling.

"But I had no intention of keeping it for myself, Casey. I promise. I was only wanting the reward for turning it in!"

Tears began veiling Casey's eyes as she now began to study Lonnie with a vague sort of sadness. She canted her head to one side. And then, with a sharp stab of mental agony, he knew what she was thinking about.

Last year, during their trek over the mountains with Dupree's loot, they were helped by a cynical, old, ex-Confederate soldier, Wilbur Calhoun. Calhoun had lived alone with his dog in the mountains for years, having run away from the nearly destroyed South and his own dark past in the years after the war. For a brief time, Calhoun had half-convinced Lonnie that he and Casey should take the stolen money for themselves.

Casey was remembering that momentary weakening in Lonnie's character. He could see it in the girl's heartbroken gaze.

A single tear dribbled down her cheek.

Staring at Lonnie, she sniffed, brushed the tear from her cheek with the back of her hand, and said, "Sheriff Halliday, I think I'd like to go, now, please."

Halliday rose from his chair. He grabbed a key ring hanging from a ceiling support post, and unlocked the door. He regarded Casey with phony sympathy. "I don't blame you a bit, Miss Stoveville. Kind of hard to take, ain't it? Seein' a boy with his whole future ahead of him ruin everything out of plum meanness and greed . . ."

Casey slipped into her jacket. She turned once more to Lonnie, who stared at her in shock. How could she could believe Halliday? But, then, he supposed it was understandable, given that he'd actually entertained the notion of running off with the loot from the Golden bank. He had only himself to blame for that.

"Casey, don't believe him," Lonnie urged. "He's a killer. In two, three months, he'll leave town—you can bet the bank on that. He's gonna go dig up the gold and hightail it!"

Halliday opened the door. As Casey stepped out, sniffing, Halliday scowled at Lonnie, shaking his head in phony disappointment. "How he does go on. I'm sorry, Miss Stoveville." He closed the door, turned the key in the lock. "In the boy's defense, he grew up hard. Livin' out in them mountains will drive full-grown men crazy. Here, he's only fourteen. He lost his pa. Now he's livin' with his ma who is, as I reckon you know, less than . . . well, less than what you'd call a perfect mother. Raisin' that killer Dupree's child . . ."

"I know," Casey said quietly, closing her upper teeth over her bottom lip as she gazed up at the sheriff. "I did expect more from him, though. After all we'd been through together, I'd thought he'd grown, matured."

She turned her disenchanted gaze at Lonnie. It was like a cold, hard slap across Lonnie's face.

"But, like you said, he's had it tough out there." Casey returned her gaze to the sheriff. "Sheriff Halliday, what . . . what do you think will happen . . . if the judge finds him guilty, I mean? He's only fourteen years old. Surely his age must be considered."

"I don't know," Halliday said. "I for one am going to ask the judge to go as easy as he can on him. But . . . you know, there is the problem of his killing that deputy last year."

"That was in self-defense!" Lonnie yelled, sitting up now on the edge of his cot. He winced at the brutal assault his yell dealt his battered head. "And it was an accident besides!"

Quietly, reasonably, Casey said, "The judge must take into consideration that Lonnie was responsible for returning the stolen bank money to Golden."

"Oh, I'll make sure he knows all about that. The problem is, Miss Stoveville, we both probably know that if you, the sheriff's daughter, hadn't been such a good influence on him—well, who knows where he might have taken that money?"

Halliday turned his dark, accusing look at Lonnie. Anyone else would probably have only seen the dark side of that look. The phony side. But Lonnie saw the mockery deep in the man's eyes, as well, and it caused rage to boil up in him.

"You bastard, Halliday," Lonnie said. "You no-good rotten bastard!"

CHAPTER 37

"Lonnie," Casey said, stomping her foot down. "Cursing the sheriff isn't going to help your situation one bit!"

"Please, Miss Stoveville," Halliday said, taking the girl by her shoulders and steering her toward the office's front door. "You'd best go. You don't need to hear any more of what that criminal has to say. You're a fine young lady, and you shouldn't mix with the likes of that . . . that . . . kill—!"

Halliday cut himself off when a knock sounded on the door. The door opened and none other that Casey's fancy Dan poked his head into the office.

Seeing Casey, fancy Dan's eyes widened. He smiled and removed his hat. "Ah, Casey, there you are. Mister Hendrickson said I'd find you over here. I just stopped by to see if I could take you to lunch."

He glanced past Casey and the sheriff, and scowled at Lonnie, as though he were scrutinizing dog dung on his boots.

"That's sweet of you, Niles, thank you," Casey said, giving the fancy Dan a weak smile.

She glanced once more at Lonnie, a little sheepishly, and walked over to where her suitor waited by the door.

"You two kids have a good time, now!" Halliday called after them.

The fancy Dan, the banker's son, pinched his hat brim to the sheriff, glanced once more, distastefully, at Lonnie, and followed Casey out of the office. When he'd closed the door behind him, Halliday strode over to Lonnie, laughing, kicking his boots out happily, planting his fists on his hips.

"Now, see that—you're just a disappointment all the way around! Oh, well—don't worry about Miss Stoveville. Looks like the banker's son will keep her distracted." Halliday whistled. "That girl sure is purty—ain't she? A shame you made her so unhappy. Maybe she'll feel a little better about it all, once the judge decides to play cat's cradle with your head." The sheriff laughed.

A red haze of fury dropped down over Lonnie's eyes. He bounded up off the cot and ran to the cell door, wrapping his hands around the bars and bellowing, "I'm gonna kill you, Halliday! If it's the last thing I do, I'm gonna kill you!"

Just then the office door opened and a pudgy, little man in a slouch hat and cream-colored suit with a red foulard tie walked into the office. He scowled warily at Lonnie, tapping ashes from the dynamite-sized cigar he held in his pale, pudgy fist. He wore a gold ring on his little finger.

"Good lord—is that the little miscreant there?"

Halliday swung around to the man. He switched demeanors as quickly as changing hats. Turning his mouth corners down and wagging his head, he sighed and said, "Judge Peabody, meet Lonnie Gentry. Full of vim an' vinegar even with that notch I carved across his wooden head."

Gritting his teeth against the pain in his temple, Lonnie swung slowly around, more crestfallen than he'd ever been, and dropped back down on the edge of his cot. He leaned forward and took his head in his hands.

"Listen here, young man," Peabody said, striding up to the door of Lonnie's cell and glowering at the boy inside. "It would do you to be on your very best behavior. And I would not consider threatening the county sheriff before you're due to go on trial for murder very good behavior at all!"

Lonnie merely sighed and shook his head, staring at the floor.

The judge turned to Halliday. "I see he's conscious now, anyway."

"That he is, Judge. That he is. Oh, and, uh . . . just so you know—that *was* good behavior for him."

The judge shook his head.

"Why don't we go ahead and try him tomorrow, then? I have to be in Denver by the end of the week for a meeting with the governor." Peabody turned to Lonnie, and snarled like a bobcat caught in a leg trap. "The governor is making sure that we judges and law enforcement officers are tightening the reins on the criminal element all across this great territory of ours. We've had enough crime. We must bring civilization to the frontier. A peaceful, harmonious future is ours only if we haze the rats into their holes!"

He turned back to Halliday. "I'm having my gallows wheeled up to Arapaho Creek. Should be squawkin' through the mountains right now. They're pulling it up from Benson, where I hung three claim jumpers only yesterday."

Lonnie jerked his head up. "You can't hang me. I'm only fourteen years old!"

"They'll set it up out on Main Street," the judge continued to Halliday. He looked at Lonnie and poked his cigar into his mouth. "Just in case, mind you. Just in case . . ."

Lonnie was flabbergasted. "I'm only fourteen years old!"

"The kid has a point, Judge. He's only fourteen years old. You can't hang a boy so young!" The sheriff was a darn good actor. He sounded like he really meant it, though the boy also knew that the sheriff was resisting the tremendous urge to cast Lonnie a furtive wink. "Keep in mind his home life has been less than, well, stable. His mother is somewhat of, uh . . . Jane-about-the-mountains."

"Yes, I've heard about his home life," Peabody said, blowing more smoke. "Too bad, too bad. Of course, I'll take that into consideration."

"Thanks, Judge. There might be a chance of turning the little killer around . . . however slim," Halliday said.

Lonnie glared at the sheriff.

"I can only consider the evidence, Sheriff." Peabody gave a caustic chuff as he turned again to Lonnie. "In the meantime, I suggest you refrain from threatening the sheriff here with bodily harm. That is *not* a good testament to your character!"

The judge poked the cigar back into his little, round, pink mouth, and waddled out of the office.

When Peabody was gone, Halliday turned his wolfish gaze on his prisoner. "You might want to massage your neck muscles, kid. They don't call him Hang-'em-high Hank for nothin'!"

Halliday laughed.

Lonnie sagged back down on the cot. He rolled onto his side and choked back tears of fear, fury, and frustration. It was a hard-fought war, but he would not, could not, let himself break down in front of Halliday. If he allowed himself to succumb, the corrupt sheriff would know he'd broken Lonnie's spirit. Halliday would have won.

Somehow, Lonnie had to keep his emotions on a leash.

And, somehow, he had to figure a way out of this current mess he was in.

As he lay there, calming himself, he drifted off to sleep. He woke once when the doctor came into his cell to replace the bandage on his head. Then his fatigue, as well as the tea that the doctor gave him for the pain, caused him to drift back off into the land of blissful slumber.

He woke later in the afternoon and lay there on his cot, trying to pick his spirits up by thinking positive thoughts. But positive thoughts were few and far between. How could he think positively when he was due to be tried the very next day for three murders he had not committed by a judge known as Hang-'em-high Hank?

Not only that, but he was alone. He did not know if anyone had gotten word to his mother about his current predicament. He hadn't thought to ask Casey about that. Surely, Casey would have sent word out to May Gentry. But even if Lonnie's mother knew about what he was going through, she was tied down with little Jeremiah. She couldn't very well leave the baby to ride through the mountains to visit her jailed son.

Besides, what could she do to help?

She'd probably only become hysterical and cause Lonnie even more frustration, even more worry.

Lonnie rose with a wince, hardening his jaws against the thundering pain that the movement caused his battered head, and moved to the window. There was nothing to see out there but trash and stacked, split firewood and a two-hole privy flanked by pine trees. But it felt good to sniff the warm breeze, to smell the weeds and the creeks that meandered around the edges of the town.

Who knew when he'd be able to enjoy such smells again?

Who knew if, after tomorrow, he'd ever smell *anything* again?

Dead men didn't have much of anything to smell, most likely.

He gave a shiver at the thought of his own demise. Especially his own demise by hanging . . .

But surely the judge wouldn't hang a fourteen-year-old boy. He might say he would, but when it came right down to it, he'd most likely send Lonnie to some reform school in Denver. The possibility began to seem more and more likely the more Lonnie thought about it, for surely the good, law-abiding citizens of Arapaho Creek wouldn't let the judge and Halliday hang a boy.

No doubt about it. He'd likely be sent to Denver. He should be able to escape such a school for wayward boys fairly easily, given the cunning qualities he was so well known for.

When he managed to make his break, he'd find a way to prove his innocence as well as prove, once and for all, that Sheriff Frank Halliday himself was the one responsible for murdering Marshal Appleyard.

Somewhat relieved by the more optimistic train of his thoughts, Lonnie drifted back to sleep.

CHAPTER 38

Lonnie was awakened early that evening by Deputy Bohannon bringing him a bowl of thin stew and a chunk of dry bread from one of the town's lesser eateries. When he was nearly finished with the Spartan meal, Lonnie was paid a visit by the attorney whom the county had assigned to represent Lonnie in court the next day.

Vincent Briggs was a known drunk and whoremonger. His suit was too small for him, and his longhandles showed through several places in his threadbare pants. He smelled like a walking spittoon and a beer bucket.

Lonnie dutifully related his version of the tumultuous events to the man with no real passion. His audience seemed to have trouble staying awake and upright. Briggs kept blinking his eyes exaggeratedly, grunting and wetting his pencil's dull point on his tongue.

About all he said was: "Hmm. Uh-huh . . . hmmm."

Heck, if Lonnie's own girl, Casey Stoveville—at least, she'd once *been* his girl—didn't believe Lonnie's story, why should anyone else including a drunken, old, used-up attorney who couldn't have done Lonnie much good if he'd even believed his tale?

When the attorney left after penciling only a few brief notes in a yellowed pocket notepad, Lonnie lay back down for another badly needed nap.

A raucous clattering assaulted his ears and set his head burning afresh.

He sat up, wide-eyed. Instantly, his guts recoiled.

Randall "Walleye" Miller was raking a tin coffee cup across the bars of Lonnie's cell door. Miller lowered the cup and grinned, his wandering eye roving to the outside edge of its socket. He had a crutch under his left arm. His left thigh was thickly padded beneath his greasy denim trousers.

"Sorry, killer—didn't mean to wake ya!"

Miller chuckled. Judging by how glassy his eyes were, he had a few drinks under his belt.

"Just thought I'd let you know I got office duty tonight. I always got office duty, seein' as how I ain't gettin' around nearly as well as I once did."

The deputy's smile evaporated. He scowled at Lonnie, broad nostrils flaring angrily.

"The doc said I come close to losin' this leg."

"Yeah, well, you only got yourself to blame for that," Lonnie said.

Walleye scowled at him again through the bars. Then he swung around and hobbled over to the ceiling support post from which the iron key ring hung. Walleye removed the ring from the spike in the post, and returned to Lonnie's cell.

Lonnie's heart thudded.

"Say, now . . . ," the boy said, staring at the key in Walleye's hand.

Walleye smiled with one half of his mouth as he stuck the key in the lock. There was the metallic rasping, scraping sound of the locking bolt being slid back into the door. The bolt clicked. The door sang as it sagged in its frame.

Walleye pulled the key out of the lock.

"You wanna run, boy?" The deputy paused, eyes narrowed, malicious. "Here's your opportunity."

Walleye hobbled back to the support post. He returned the key ring to the spike then sat down in the swivel chair behind the rolltop desk. He turned the chair toward Lonnie's cell. Walleye removed his sawed-off, double-barrel shotgun from atop the desk, and set it across his lap.

"Go ahead, killer. Make a run for it." Walleye smiled again with challenge, one nostril flaring, a dark flush rising up behind his thick, curly beard. "I want you to."

He caressed the gut-shredder's rabbit-ear hammers with his thumb.

Lonnie looked at the shotgun's wicked double bores. He looked at Walleye's savage features.

Lonnie sagged back down on the cot and rested his arm on his forehead with a ragged sigh of defeat.

Lonnie lay on the cot for a long time, considering his situation.

While the events of the past several days, starting with his being nearly run down by the four horseback riders in the high mountains, galloped across his mind like a herd of wild horses heading for water, he found himself wondering if he really was as bad as everyone said he was.

Was he a wicked, no-account kid who'd been steered in the wrong direction by the early death of his father and his lonely, wayward mother? He supposed he was a headstrong boy. He had things he wanted to get done in this life. And he was bound and determined to make a good life for himself. Before the trouble outside Skull Canyon, he'd wanted to make a good life for himself *and* his mother and brother.

Only after the trouble had not only started but had risen like water in an arroyo during a flash flood, he'd decided to search for the stolen payroll money, collect the reward on it—if a reward was being offered, that was—and light out on his own.

That was probably where he'd gone wrong, he decided. After

the trouble with the four riders and then finding Cade McLory on death's doorstep and being nearly drowned in the stock trough by Walleye, not to mention discovering that Casey had set her hat for the fancy Dan, he should have forgotten about the loot. He'd told himself he'd gone back to Skull Canyon to fetch McLory back to town, to help prove his own innocence in shooting Walleye.

But that had been a fib he'd told himself as well as Casey.

He'd really gone back to the canyon because he'd been drawn to the attraction of the buried loot. He'd felt sorry for himself, for the way his life had turned out, for the abuse he'd taken from brutish men, for suffering the indignities of a wayward mother and other folks around him who didn't understand him—who mistook his independence and determination to be taken seriously for recklessness.

He'd intended on abandoning his mother and his baby brother.

Self-pity was what had drawn him back to the cursed canyon and the money. He'd wanted a chance to leave these mountains and start a new life for himself, believing wrongly that you could leave one life cold and start a whole new one without bringing the core of yourself along for the ride.

Self-pity.

That was his mistake.

Self-pity and believing that money could change your life in anything more than superficial ways.

If he got out of this tight spot alive—and that was starting to look more and more unlikely—he'd keep that in mind the next time he considered abandoning his responsibilities to ride off seeking greener pastures. His life was here in these mountains with his mother and his brother. He wished it could be with Casey, too, but that looked as unlikely as his living through tomorrow without having his neck stretched.

Still, he made a mental note to try to be better.

Then he heard Walleye snoring.

Lonnie looked up from his cot.

Sure enough, the big, bearded deputy sat in the chair facing Lonnie, his head dipped to his chest. His hands lay slack on the shotgun. Deep snores rose from his fluttering lips.

Lonnie looked at his unlocked cell door, and his heart gave a hard, anxious thud.

Chapter 39

Lonnie looked at Walleye again.

Was he pretending, or was he really asleep?

The big deputy's broad, lumpy chest rose and fell heavily as he snored. His lips continued to flutter with each exhalation.

He sure *looked* asleep.

Lonnie dropped one leg over the side of the cot. Then the other leg. He winced when the cot's chains jangled faintly. He rose slowly and moved just as slowly toward the door, walking on the balls of his boots.

He stopped at the door, looked once more at Walleye. If the man wasn't really asleep, if he was only faking it, as soon as Lonnie started to open the door, Walleye would likely lift the shotgun and blow Lonnie to Kingdom Come.

Lonnie's heart skipped a beat.

But, then again, what did it really matter? Tomorrow, there was a good chance he'd be hanged from the judge's famous gallows, which, constructed on a large, wheeled wagon bed, could be moved quite handily from town to town. He knew that hanging was a bad way to die. He'd heard the stories about men strangling slowly and soiling themselves as they danced bizarrely several feet from the ground, a gathered crowd cheering them on while eating popcorn and ham sandwiches.

A far better fate would be a quick death being blown into little pieces by Walleye Miller's barn blaster from a distance of ten feet.

Lonnie placed his right hand on a bar of the door. He gave it a slow, easy shove. The door opened, the hinges groaning very softly but still too loudly for Lonnie's comfort. He pushed the door more slowly, an inch at a time, gritting his teeth at the very low singing sound that the hinges made.

Lonnie's heart raced. The door was open two and a half feet. He could slip through the opening and be across the office to the front door in about three seconds.

Lonnie drew a deep breath. He glanced once more at Walleye. No doubt about it—the man was dead out.

Lonnie sidestepped through the opening. Keeping his eyes on the ugly shotgun resting across Walleye's broad thighs, he made his way across the room on the balls of his boots. He made it to the front door. He placed his hand on the knob and glanced once more at Walleye.

Suddenly, Walleye lifted his chin from his chest.

He threw his head back against the chair and opened his eyes. He stopped snoring.

Lonnie's blood turned to ice. He stared, ready for the hail of buckshot that would end his days.

Walleye's eyes rolled back in his head, showing the whites. His eyes closed and his chin dropped again to his chest without resistance. The deputy wagged his big, bearded head a couple of times, groaning and smacking his lips.

Then he became very still. Lonnie waited, his heart hammering in his ears. Soon, Walleye began snoring again, inhaling slowly, broadening his shoulders and then exhaling through his mouth, making a sawing sound, causing his lips to flutter.

Lonnie's own shoulders sagged with relief. He turned to the door in front of him and started to turn the knob. He stopped when a voice sounded outside the sheriff's office.

"All right, Gandy. I'll be around again in another hour or two. I'll check your back door!"

Deputy Bohannon was heading toward the jail office!

Lonnie jerked another look at Walleye, whose head was still down. But he'd stopped snoring. Outside, footsteps were growing louder. Lonnie swung around and beat a hasty, quiet retreat back to his cell. He drew the door closed behind him but did not latch it.

Footsteps thudded on the stoop fronting the sheriff's office. The front door opened.

His heart beating wildly, Lonnie sat down on his cot and took his head in his hands, rubbing his eyes and yawning, as though he'd just awakened.

Bohannon stopped just inside the open door through which the smells of the night came on a breath of cool mountain air. He looked at Lonnie and then turned to Miller.

"Walleye!"

The walleyed deputy jerked his head up with a start. He rose from his chair, widening his eyes, and aiming his shotgun at Lonnie's cell.

"Hold on! Hold on!" Lonnie yelled, throwing his hands up.

Bohannon scowled at the cell door. He moved forward, stopped just outside the cell, and looked at the gap between the door and the cell. He looked at Lonnie and gave a dry chuckle.

He looked at Walleye, slammed the cell door closed, and said, "Bad luck to cheat the hangman, fool!"

Lonnie had a miserable night's sleep.

He probably wouldn't have slept at all for anticipating his date with Hang-'em-high Hank the next day, but the head wound kept pulling him under into a harried race of dreams that included images of a shadowy gallows and of hang ropes and a laughing, cheering crowd. Lonnie's own death dreams were confused with images of Cade McLory wandering through a cave and calling for Lonnie to come and bury him.

On the heels of the McLory dream, Lonnie woke in a cold sweat. He'd been so preoccupied with saving his own neck that he'd forgotten about McLory's body, which lay where Kinch and Engstrom had invaded Lonnie and Casey's camp in the mountains. Thoughts of poor McLory being dined upon by mountain lions, coyotes, and wolves added a whole new, grisly dimension of horror to dreams of Lonnie's own demise.

He was almost glad when Walleye woke him by wickedly raking the tin cup across the bars of his cell, even though the sound was like a long, rusty nail being driven into the same place the bullet had cut a nasty furrow across his head. After he'd eaten a breakfast as Spartan as his supper, the doctor returned to clean the wound, apply a fresh smearing of arnica, and change Lonnie's bandage.

At ten a.m., both Walleye and Bohannon handcuffed and shackled the boy. They prodded him out of his cell and down the street to the courthouse, a two-story log building with a courtroom on the lower floor heated by a large, fieldstone hearth. The dozen or so spectator benches quickly filled with a milling crowd of townsfolk—men as well as women and even a few children—always eager for the spectacle of a trial and a possible hanging.

In fact, trials and hangings were more eagerly anticipated than the revelry that accompanied the Fourth of July.

The two Pinkerton detectives, Brocius and Madsen, were sitting on a bench in the front row. Lonnie wondered if they were still staying out at his ranch. Then he wondered if his mother might have made it to town for the trial—certainly she'd heard about it by now from the two Pinkertons if from no one else—but after sweeping the room with his gaze, he decided she hadn't.

May Gentry had her hands full with little Jeremiah.

As Lonnie's eyes swept the room, he found himself meeting Casey's concerned, worried gaze. The girl sat on a bench in the middle of the room. She wore a small, straw hat trimmed with fake flowers. Lonnie tried to send her a smile, but then he remembered her skepticism regarding his story, and fancy Dan.

Lonnie's cheeks turned to stone. He looked away from the girl.

The trial was delayed when a young collie dog followed its owner into the courtroom and then didn't want to leave when its owner ordered it back outside. Instead, the pup sought refuge behind the judge's bench sitting up high at the front of the room. Enflamed by the crowd and the judge's raucous gaveling, the young dog ran barking around the room while its owner and Sheriff Halliday and Deputies Walleye and Bohannon chased the creature through the laughing crowd and back out the double front doors into the street.

Only after the dog was gone and the doors were closed did someone notice that Lonnie's attorney, Vincent Briggs, was not sitting with his client at the defendant's table before the judge's bench and to the right of where the grim, straight-backed prosecuting attorney, Archibald Fleischman, sat trimming his nails with a clasp knife.

Bohannon was ordered to locate Briggs, who came in ten minutes later smelling as he always did but more so—like a spittoon and a beer bucket. Bread crumbs no doubt from a free saloon lunch counter clung to his necktie and ratty wool vest.

"Please forgive me, your honor," the attorney said as the crowd settled down. "I was taking notes for the trial while I ate a sandwich, and the time simply got away from me."

Lonnie could tell the man was slurring some of his words as he nervously brushed crumbs and a few chunks of ham that clung to his gold watch chain sagging from his vest.

"The perils of such dedication—eh, Vince?" Judge Peabody said from his bench, giving a caustic snort.

He rapped his gavel down hard on his sound block. The

laughing crowd fell silent.

The judge gave Lonnie a grave glance and then swept his businesslike gaze across the small sea of fidgeting onlookers. "Now, let's get down to brass tacks, and maybe we can get out of here by noon!"

CHAPTER 40

"The first and . . . um . . . the *only* witness I'd like to call today is none other than Sheriff Frank Halliday himself," announced the tall, gray prosecutor, Archibald Fleischman, gripping the lapels of his claw hammer frock coat as though he were afraid the coat would blow away if he didn't hold it down.

As the sheriff rose and started toward the witness chair beneath the judge's bench, Halliday stopped and turned to Lonnie. He wore a fresh bandage around the top of his head, as did Lonnie himself. Halliday's bandage sported a small bloodstain where Lonnie had beaned the man with the shovel. As he stared at Lonnie, the sheriff turned his mouth corners down, gave a grim wag of his head, then continued walking over to the witness chair.

He took a seat, fingering the bandage gently, making a show of the injury.

Again, he shook his head, as though the tale he were about to tell was a grim one indeed, and not an easy one to relate.

Lonnie snorted at that.

The boy was not shocked to hear the sheriff tell the same story he'd related to Lonnie—about Lonnie throwing in with Kinch and his prison pal for a cut of the gold, and then, getting the drop on both the unwitting and unsuspecting Halliday and Appleyard—"Who'd think a boy so young capable of such savagery!"—opening up with the Winchester he managed to snap up off the ground before laying Halliday out cold with a shovel.

The crowd of onlookers murmured and muttered as the sheriff told his tale. At one point, the judge had to interrupt Halliday and used his gavel to settle the crowd before nodding to the sheriff to continue.

When the sheriff punctuated his tale with another disbelieving wag of his head, Lonnie couldn't help but leaping to his feet and yelling, *"If I'm such a hard-hearted, cold-blooded killer, why didn't I cut you down with the rifle, too, Halliday, you fang-toothed liar?"*

Of course, that had been a grave misstep on Lonnie's part.

Everyone in the courtroom, including the six-man jury seated on the far side of the room, looked at him as though he were a lion on a dangerously long chain.

"You'll get a chance to tell your side of it, young man!" the judge scolded, hammering his gavel down on the sound block. "Till then, you hold your tongue or I'll have you bound and gagged!"

When the judge asked Briggs if he wanted to cross-examine the sheriff, Lonnie's so-called attorney merely shook his head. The man no doubt wanted to get back to the free lunch counter as quickly as he could, Lonnie thought with another inward chuff.

The prosecutor called Lonnie to the stand. The sheriff refused to remove the shackles on Lonnie's ankles.

"Can't take a chance on him making a run for it, your honor," Halliday said, shaking his head darkly.

One of the female onlookers gave a quiet gasp at the prospect of the crazed young killer running wild throughout the town.

The judge nodded his understanding to the sheriff.

Lonnie traversed the space between the defense table and the witness chair awkwardly, chains rattling, boots scuffing on the courthouse's worn puncheon floor. Prompted by the prosecutor, Lonnie told the true story of how Halliday shot Appleyard and then both of his prisoners, Kinch and Engstrom, while they lay handcuffed on the ground.

The crowd gave a collective, incredulous murmur as Lonnie related the grisly events. Halliday sat on a front-row bench, scowling and shaking his head in disgust at the low morals of one so young.

"Why didn't he shoot you, then, too?" the prosecutor wanted to know.

"Because he wanted me to bury the loot for him, so he could come back and dig it up later," Lonnie said. "He would have killed me after I'd gotten the job done, too, if I hadn't laid him out with the shovel!"

Halliday looked around the room, pointing to the bloodstained bandage on his head. Several women gasped and shook their heads at the evidence of such violence in one so young . . .

"I can prove my story is true, Judge," Lonnie said. "Take me up into them mountains, and I'll show you where the loot is buried, just waitin' for Halliday to come retrieve it after he's let things simmer down for a couple months."

"Why don't you just tell us where it is?" asked the prosecutor, fists on his lapels, a knowing grin tugging at his mouth corners.

"There's no way I can tell it," Lonnie said. "I can't remember that clear. But I can show you, sure enough!"

"Oh, certainly, certainly," the prosecutor said, broadening his knowing smile as he looked around at the riveted crowd. "You'd love to be given a saddled horse, wouldn't you? You'd love to be taken up into those mountains and given the opportunity to escape your grim fate . . . *wouldn't you, you cunning little devil?*"

The crowd erupted at that.

"Why, I've never seen the like of such a young criminal as that!" bellowed a jowly old woman with small, round steel glasses beneath a gray, lace-edged poke bonnet. She had a thick Southern accent, as did most of the folks in and around the Never Summers.

She'd lurched to her feet and was giving the judge a commanding glare. "We all know who his mother is. Why, she bore an outlaw's child! This critter's father was a no-good *Yankee*. And now he's killed three more men. When will it stop, I ask? *When will it stop?*"

"Sit down, sit down, Mrs. Harmony! If you erupt like that again, I'll have you escorted to the door!" Peabody slammed his gavel down several times, the reports echoing like pistol fire. "Pipe down! Pipe down!" he admonished the loudly milling crowd.

When the din had died, the judge turned to the prosecutor.

"Any more questions, Mister Fleischman?"

"None sir," the prosecutor said, strolling leisurely back to his table. "None whatsoever. I think we've all heard quite enough!"

"I know I have!" intoned Mrs. Harmony before giving the judge a sheepish glance.

The judge asked Briggs if he wanted to call any other witnesses. Briggs merely opened his hands and shrugged as though to say, "Who is left to call?"

It was Lonnie's word against Halliday's.

The judge asked the jury for a show of hands for guilty or innocent. Lonnie's wasn't surprised when all six hands went up for guilty.

Mrs. Harmony gave a quiet, satisfied chuff.

The crowd murmured its approval.

The judge turned to Lonnie, and said, "Young man, considering your youth and lack of adequate supervision as well as your heroic trek across the mountains last year to deliver stolen bank money to the deputy US marshal in Camp Collins, I'm going to show some mercy. Two years in the Long's House for Wayward Boys in Denver!"

The crowd erupted, shouting its approval.

Lonnie heard Casey cry, "But he's just a boy! You can't hang a boy, Judge! You *can't!*"

Then the girl broke down in tears.

Lonnie looked at her, befuddled. She sat holding a handkerchief to her nose, shoulders jerking as she cried.

"But, Casey," Lonnie said under his breath, "I'm not going to hang. Why, the judge said . . ."

He let his voice trail off when he realized that his mind had played a cruel trick on him. He'd only *imagined* the light sentence. What the judge had *really* said was, "Hang the boy and save havin' to hang the man later!"

And then he'd adjourned the trial and sat back in his chair, crossing his arms on his chest with satisfaction.

Chapter 41

Behind Lonnie, who remained sitting at the defendant's table, the courthouse crowd was eagerly, loudly filing out into the street to enjoy the festivities over at the judge's specially constructed, portable gallows.

"On your feet, boy," said Walleye Miller, aiming his twelve-gauge at Lonnie one-handed. His other arm was slung over his crutch. "You're about to be the guest of honor at a little necktie party!"

If he'd smiled any more brightly his eyes would have popped out of his head.

"Let's go, kid," said Bohannon, waving his pistol.

Lonnie rose to his shackled feet and looked at Sheriff Halliday, who was the only one in the courtroom still seated. He was staring at Lonnie, grinning around the cigar in his mouth, which he was puffing to life, the match flame flaring as he inhaled the smoke.

Lonnie was too numb to be able to conjure any anger. Last night he'd feared that if he was sentenced to hang he might make a fool of himself by peeing down his leg, or breaking down bawling, which he knew from reading the occasional copy of *Policeman's Gazette* was what often happened to even the most hardened outlaws in similar circumstances.

But he felt nothing at all. He was numb.

It was as though his body as well as his mind had turned to stone. Around him, everyone seemed to be moving very slowly.

All sounds seemed to be emanating from the bottom of a very deep well. He couldn't even work up any sadness or regret that he wouldn't be able to say good-bye to his mother or his little half brother.

He was going to die.

And it no longer meant anything to him.

"Look at him," said Bohannon as he and Walleye began leading him down the aisle toward the open double doors. "Cold as ice."

"Hang the boy," Halliday said, walking along behind them, "and save havin' to hang the man." He chuckled evilly at that.

But even for the man about to cause him to die for crimes he had not committed, at the hands of the man who *had* committed them, Lonnie could work up no anger. As he shuffled along, his hands cuffed before him, his ankles bound by shackles, he only wished they'd get to it sooner rather than later.

A preacher had materialized, and he was walking up beside Lonnie. Lonnie was not a churchgoer though he'd studied the Good Book some with his mother on long winter evenings when the snowbanks rose to the cabin's windows. He did not know the sky pilot, as men of the cloth were cynically called. He was reading what Lonnie recognized in a vague sort of way, with no actual interest, as the Twenty-Third Psalm.

The gallows lay at a wide spot in the main street of Arapaho Creek, on the far side of the narrow, twisting creek that ran almost directly down the street's center. A cottonwood shaded it from the brassy, high-altitude sun.

A crowd had gathered in a semicircle around the wheeled structure that sat on stout wagon wheels higher than Lonnie was tall. The upright from which the noose dangled, as well as a platform to which a total of eight steps led, was made to collapse into the wagon bed for easy traveling, when a team of two mules was hitched.

Every inch of the combination gallows and wagon was painted red, earning it the nickname Hang-'em-high Hank's Hell Wagon.

Now the red upright stood tall over the red platform, a stout noose dangling from the crossbeam.

The gallows was a frequent sight in mining camps around the mountains. Lonnie had always wondered how many men had died falling straight down through its single trapdoor. When he'd glimpsed the forbidding-looking structure being driven around the mountains by the judge's teamster who doubled as his hangman, Nestor Polk, a chill had rippled along his spine.

Now, he felt nothing. He might have been walking toward a simple, benign lumber dray parked before a mercantile, waiting to be loaded.

Lonnie was prodded up into the wagon by Deputy Bohannon while the other two lawmen and the preacher waited below. Nestor Polk stood waiting atop the platform, beside the noose dangling down over the trapdoor. Lonnie stopped beside the grim, gray-bearded Polk, who wore a long, black, claw hammer coat, a bullet-crowned black hat, and a thick, black four-in-hand tie. His long, curly side-whiskers blew in the wind.

The hangman was legendary in these mountains. He was known to be a strange, silent, humorless man with frosty blue eyes set beneath silky white brows. Lonnie had never been this close to the executioner before. The man smelled like mules, sweat, chewing tobacco, and whiskey.

The corked mouth of a brown bottle poked up out of a pocket of his black coat.

"Want a bag?" Polk asked, holding what appeared to be a black feed sack in his hand. He spoke in a raspy whisper.

Lonnie looked at the bag, puzzled. Then he remembered that men were often executed with bags over their heads.

Lonnie shook his head. He didn't want his last sight to be the darkness of a bag over his head.

"He's a cold one, Polk," Halliday said from the street below.

"Yeah, well, we'll see how cold he is when the trapdoor falls away beneath his boots." Polk looked at Bohannon and said loudly enough to be heard above the crowd's expectant din, "Remove the cuffs and shackles!"

Polk grinned, showing two slightly protruding, fang-like eye-teeth.

"Oh, right." Bohannon chuckled, and crouched to remove the shackles binding Lonnie's ankles. "Wanna give 'em their money's worth!"

As Polk tightened the noose around Lonnie's neck, the boy looked out over the crowd gathered before him. Men, women, children, and dogs had gathered for the occasion. Even a few cats rested on the second-story balcony rails of the brightly painted parlor houses. Scantily clad soiled doves milled on the balconies, smoking and staring toward the gallows. They likely appreciated a break in their work, which would likely start booming again in a few minutes.

Two old women were selling sandwiches from a wicker basket, and several of the shopkeepers, Lonnie noticed, had moved their wares outside onto their boardwalks to take advantage of the potential customers gathered in the street.

Lonnie peered around the crowd for Casey. He didn't see her anywhere. That was good. She didn't need to see this.

The fancy Dan—Niles or Giles or whatever his name was—stood beside his father, old Gilpin, the banker, on the boardwalk fronting their bank. The young dandy and his bald-headed, slightly stoop-shouldered old father stared grimly toward Lonnie.

The crowd quieted some as the preacher raised his voice to sermonize to the crowd. It was a long-winded speech and Lonnie was glad when Halliday broke in with: "All right, that's enough, Reverend. Save it for Sunday. We're gathered here for a hangin' not a church service!"

The crowd erupted.

Kids danced around, chasing each other with sticks.

Dogs barked.

"You got anything to say?" Polk asked Lonnie, blowing his sour breath in Lonnie's face.

"Nope."

As calm as he was, Lonnie tensed himself for the drop.

Polk's cheek twitched as he threw the wooden lever. There was a raspy bark as the trapdoor gave beneath Lonnie's boots. The boy fell straight down through the hole in the platform. There was a loud cracking sound, which must have been the breaking of his own neck as he continued to plunge down through the hole.

But, wait—the rope hadn't tightened yet.

Now it drew taut. Lonnie's body jerked upward. For a second, he thought the rope was going to rip his head off. His eyes bugged as he strangled, clawing at the rope and kicking.

The crowd was roaring.

Another cracking sound rose faintly beneath the cacophony. Lonnie's belly lurched straight up into his throat as he continued dropping straight down over the side of the wagon. The rope around his neck eased its pressure.

The clay-colored street darted toward Lonnie's boots.

He heard himself give a loud grunt of expelled air as his feet hit the dirt. He fell and rolled onto his side, stunned, automatically clawing at the noose that was pulled up around his jaws, raking his skin.

He looked around. The crowd was screaming, dispersing. Dogs barked wildly.

What the hell?

Someone gave a loud, raking Rebel yell. The sound was

strangely familiar to Lonnie's shocked, dull brain. Guns crackled.

Women screamed. Men shouted.

Hooves thundered as two horses bounded toward Lonnie from beyond the crowd. The crowd thinned as it dispersed, women and children screaming, men shouting, Halliday yelling, "What in the hell?"

The horses and one rider came racing through the quickly thinning crowd, the rider triggering a pistol above her blonde, tan-hatted head. One of the horses was the chestnut mare, Miss Abigail. The other was General Sherman.

"Lonnie!" Casey screamed as she ran her horse into the lawmen. "Hop on—let's fog it away from here!"

Miss Abigail pitched, front hooves coming down on Walleye Miller's wounded leg. The deputy screamed. Bohannon was already down, rolling in the dust.

Lonnie looked up at the rope dangling from the gallows. Its end was ragged. Something had sliced it.

The boy ripped the noose up over his head and tossed it away. His neck ached from that first, sudden jerk, but he'd live. As the General came up, dancing in place beside Lonnie and blocking the cursing Halliday, Lonnie threw himself at the horse. The General lunged off and Lonnie ran along beside him, pulling himself up by the saddle horn and hop-skipping as he tried to toe a stirrup.

A pistol cracked behind Lonnie. He didn't have to look back to know the shooter was the enraged Halliday.

Lonnie shoved a toe through the stirrup, and swung up into the leather. Casey tossed him his reins, which he caught, frowning at her, not quite believing what had happened.

Maybe he was still strangling beneath the gallows and his oxygen-starved brain was merely hallucinating all this?

He glanced behind as the crowd ran every which way. Halliday ran along the street behind Lonnie, aiming his revolver out in front of him. The dog that had run wild in the courthouse ran up behind the lawman, now, believing the man was playing with it. The dog grabbed the lawman's left pants cuff, and shook it.

The lawman's pistol spat smoke and flames, but the bullet sailed wild.

Lonnie turned his head forward. Casey rode just ahead and to his right. When she glanced over her left shoulder and gave him a wide-eyed, anxious smile but also a smile of relief, he realized it was true. He was free.

Somehow, the girl had saved him.

At least, for now.

But who had cut the rope?

He and Casey hit the outskirts of town and galloped into the country beyond, heading for the mountains.

CHAPTER 42

When they'd had to slow their horses after a quarter mile of hard riding, Casey said, "Let's hold up here."

"Why?" Lonnie said, pulling back on the General's reins.

As if in reply to his question, a wild, raking Rebel yell cut through the air behind them. It was the same yell Lonnie had heard before in town, when the excitement was starting. Now he saw a figure galloping toward them along the trail, silhouetted against the skyline.

The town was a small, dun-colored splotch low on the horizon, behind the horseback rider growing steadily larger.

As the rider approached, Lonnie could make out the gray Confederate campaign hat the rider was wearing. It was battered and weather-stained, the edge of its rim badly frayed. Barreling toward Lonnie on a cream stallion, the rider crouched low in the saddle, glancing quickly behind him then turning his head back forward, the wind pasting the front brim against the man's forehead.

When the man was fifty yards away and closing fast, Lonnie saw a shaggy, black-and-white collie dog running a ways behind the horse and rider, doing its best to keep up.

Wilbur Calhoun drew rein before Lonnie and Casey, the old ex-Confederate's dog loping up behind him, tongue hanging down over its lower jaw, tired. Calhoun poked his hat back off his forehead, and grinned at Lonnie. His weathered face was long and angular. It hadn't seen a razor's edge in several days.

Lonnie stared in disbelief at the old soldier turned mysterious mountain rider who'd saved his bacon from the fire more times last year than Lonnie wanted to count.

"Wilbur . . . *Calhoun?*"

"Helluva party they throwed for you, boy," Calhoun said, breathless. "Sorry I had to be the one to break it up. I was just startin' to have fun, too!" The ex-Confederate glanced behind him once more, squinting against the dust. "Come on, children," he said, turning back around. "A posse'll be after us soon!"

Calhoun galloped on up the trail, the shaggy collie dog loping along behind.

Lonnie gave Casey a curious glance. The girl hiked a shoulder then touched spurs to Miss Abigail's flanks. "I'll tell you later!"

Lonnie booted the General after Casey. They followed Calhoun on a winding course into the mountains. They'd ridden for nearly an hour, pacing their horses, before Calhoun led them up the side of a steep, rocky ridge stippled with firs and white-stemmed aspens.

Five minutes later, the three were lying belly down at the top of the ridge, staring down the other side toward the trail twisting up through the forest.

Soon, hooves thundered. The shadows of oncoming riders darted through the trees down the slope beneath the ridge.

The posse grew closer until Lonnie could make out Sheriff Halliday leading the dozen or so men, including Deputy Bohannon, who rode directly behind him, along the trail, passing their quarry from left to right and quickly disappearing back into the forest.

Lonnie had recognized several of the other men comprising the posse—mostly shopkeepers from town.

"Well, that tears it," Calhoun said. "Kid, they look awful disappointed you didn't get a stretched neck out of that deal back there. I reckon they're gonna keep after us, which means we'd best keep ridin'."

Calhoun climbed to his feet and moved on down the back side of the slope to where their three horses waited near a runout spring, grazing. The collie lay nearby, eyes riveted on its ex-Confederate master. Lonnie and Casey gained their feet. Casey gave Lonnie a brief, reassuring smile. She squeezed his hand, pecked his cheek, and then followed Calhoun down the slope.

Lonnie stared after her, bewildered by her and everything that had happened to him recently, including what had just happened under that gallows in town. He had so many questions that he didn't know where to start asking.

Anyway, this wasn't the time for questions. It was a time for trying to stay ahead of Halliday and the posse.

Lonnie moved on down the slope, mounted up, and rode.

The boy thought he knew every nook and granny of this side of the Never Summers, but he didn't recognize any of the landmarks around him. Calhoun obviously knew this part of the mountains better than Lonnie did. At least, Lonnie hoped that was so. He hoped the old Confederate wasn't just riding blindly to lose the posse.

That would be a good way to get lost, and no one wanted to get lost out here, in a range so vast. Lonnie himself had been lost, albeit briefly, and it had been a sick, panicked feeling that had filled him from head to toe. That's why he always took care to mind where he was and where he was heading, taking note of landmarks.

Even then, it was easy to get turned around and lose your sense of direction until the panic gripped you and you were assaulted with the belief you would die alone out here, where no one except wolves and mountain lions would ever find you. Of course, Lonnie usually had his horse and his rifle. If he kept his wits about him, he could live for a time off the land.

Still, the terror of finding himself lost and totally alone was a panic akin to being buried alive.

As he and Casey followed Calhoun through valleys and over ridges, Lonnie kept a sharp watch on their back trail for the posse. There was no sign of them. He didn't hear any distant hoof thuds or shouts, either. The only sounds were the birds, squirrels, burrowing critters, and the endless soughing of the wind.

Late in the day, Lonnie looked ahead, beyond Casey and Calhoun riding ahead of her, to see that they were climbing a steep rise toward what appeared to be the ruins of a stone cabin wedged between two large, pale granite escarpments sheathed in towering pines. Most of the cabin's brush roof was missing, but the half-ruined hovel was shielded by an overhanging lip of rock high above.

Lonnie hadn't seen Calhoun's dog, Cherokee, for a while, but now the shaggy, burr-laden collie came running down a slope on Lonnie's left, through patches of sunlight and shade.

The dog obviously knew this neck of the mountains so well it had even found shortcuts not traversable on horseback.

Calhoun stopped his cream stallion, which Lonnie remembered he called Stonewall after the Confederate general. The old soldier removed his battered gray hat and sleeved sweat from his forehead, floury white where the sun rarely reached it. The white was in stark contrast to the near-Indian red of the man's craggy lower face carpeted in dark-brown stubble threaded liberally with gray.

"Home sweet home," Calhoun said as he stuffed the hat back down on his head and began stripping his saddle from the cream's back.

"Home?" Lonnie said, swinging heavily down from his own saddle. "But your cabin's over to the north, near the base of Storm Peak Pass." Lonnie remembered the cabin from last year, when Lonnie and Casey had spent a night there, after they'd nearly been killed by not only Shannon Dupree but by a rogue grizzly bear, as well.

Lonnie gave an inward shudder as he remembered that time. But, then, he was now in circumstances nearly as dire . . .

"That's *one* of my cabins, all right." With a heavy grunt, Calhoun set his saddle down against the base of a pine. "This one here's another. I figure it was built by some old prospector or maybe a sheepherder or some such. I've seen tufts of old wool caught on branches around here, and patches of ancient sheep dung. Whoever built this place, it hadn't been lived in for many years till I came."

"What brought you here?" Casey asked Calhoun as she stripped her tack from Miss Abigail's back.

Calhoun looked at her, gave a vaguely sheepish grin, then started walking around the stony, needle-carpeted slope, gathering blowdown branches for firewood.

Casey glanced at Lonnie. "So much for indiscreet questions, I guess."

"I reckon," Lonnie said.

Calhoun had confessed last year to Lonnie and Casey that he'd accidentally killed his wife while purposefully trying to kill her lover back in Georgia, after he'd returned home from the war to find them together on Calhoun's own farm. Running from the law, he'd come west to start a new life. But what that new life had entailed, Calhoun hadn't said.

The lack of explanation in and of itself told Lonnie the man had probably gone outlaw. Why else would a man need more than one cabin in the most far-flung reaches of a far-flung mountain range?

Possibly, Calhoun was just a loner who lived off the land. Maybe his secrecy was due to prospecting, as most prospectors held their cards close to their chest. Or, maybe after all he'd been through both during and after the war, he'd gone crazy.

Maybe the true story was a combination of all those things. Or maybe the truth lay elsewhere entirely.

Lonnie didn't know. At the moment, more pressing matters were working over his already-battered brain.

When the General was stripped of his tack and rolling in a patch of soft dirt and pine needles, Lonnie sat down on the stone slope, in a patch of warm sunlight filtering through the pine boughs. His head ached and he was tired, not to mention disoriented as well as puzzled.

He looked at Casey. His expression must have been question enough.

The girl sat down beside him, doffed her hat, set it aside, and ran her hands back through her sweat-damp hair.

"When I rode back from the canyon," she said, "the sheriff was gone. I didn't know what to do, how to help you. Then I saw Mister Calhoun." She cast her gaze down to where the lanky ex-Confederate was gathering firewood. "He'd come out of a saloon with an armload of bottles for his saddlebags. I had no one else to turn to. I asked him if he'd help me find you. But then, when we were fixing to ride back to Skull Canyon, you rode in . . . tied to your saddle . . . with Halliday and the two Pinkertons."

"But the rope. The noose. How . . . ?"

Calhoun, heading back toward them with an armload of firewood, must have overheard their conversation. He chuckled, and said, "I recollect I told you when we first met I was a sharpshooter back during the War of Northern Aggression."

Lonnie remembered the jerk on the taut rope. That must have been one of Calhoun's bullets striking the rope but not severing it entirely. The man must have fired a second, more accurate shot, and that was what had sent Lonnie plunging to the ground.

Calhoun dropped the wood in a gap in the stone floor, near Lonnie and Casey. He looked a little sheepish as he said, "Sorry about that first shot. I used to prize myself on never wasting a minie ball." He scratched the back of his neck, glancing around, still sheepish. "I reckon my peepers ain't as good as they was when I was nineteen. But the second shot did the trick, eh, boy?"

Casey leaned toward Lonnie and pried up the bandage on his temple to look beneath it. She made a face and said, "Try as we might, me an' Mister Calhoun couldn't think of a better way."

The girl sighed as she rose and walked over to where her gear was piled near Lonnie's. She glanced back over her shoulder. "But it came down to our hopin' they'd hang you."

"Wait a minute," Lonnie said, staring at the girl in disbelief as he rubbed his sore neck. "You were *hopin'* they'd hang me?"

"Sure," Casey said, scooping her canteen up off her saddle. "After all, there's never been a boy more deserving."

She winked as she strode back to him.

CHAPTER 43

With a tin coffee cup, Calhoun scooped out a hole in which to build a fire. Casey was hard at work, cleaning out Lonnie's bullet-creased head with a short length of flannel dampened with tepid water from her canteen.

"Figured the only way we were gonna save your hard-luck hide, boy, was to wait until you had a little distance between you and Halliday and them two no-account deputies of his," Calhoun said as he worked.

"Ow!" Lonnie said as Casey rubbed the cut a little too hard.

Casey gave him a dubious look. "You were nearly hanged a couple of hours ago, and *this* bothers you?"

"You don't exactly have a delicate touch, girl!"

"Oh, shut up, or I'll let you clean your own dang wound!" Casey shot back.

Calhoun chuckled, shook his head. "You two have a curious relationship. Anyways, like I was sayin', we needed to get you some space from the lawmen. Figured a crowd would be good, too. Harder for a lawman to shoot into a crowd. And I knew that Nestor Polk always liked to hang his victims without cuffs or shackles on, so they could dance good for the crowd. So, I took my Sharps Big Fifty, holed up in the loft of the Federated Livery Stable, and waited for you to drop through the hole."

As Casey continued to clean Lonnie's wound, the boy gave Calhoun an incredulous look. "If that second shot would have missed, I'd have been doin' quite a dance for that crowd. And that rope would been movin' around way too fast for you to make another shot." Lonnie's heart quickened as he thought through all the grisly possibilities. "And . . . about now they'd be droppin' me in a pine box, maybe already shovelin' dirt on me."

"Yeah, well," the ex-Confederate chuckled as he shoved some dried pine needles and crushed pinecones into his fire hole, "it's best not to look too close at the more delicate smaller workin's of the past."

"Delicate smaller workin's," Lonnie said, rubbing his throat. He looked at Calhoun. "I'm glad you were there, Mister Calhoun. I reckon if it weren't for you . . . and Casey . . . I'd be for sure laid out in that box."

Now that he had time to reflect, the fear came up to wash over him good and hard. His heart was thudding, hiccupping. Fighting back the fear, he turned to Casey, who was pulling some more cloth out of her saddlebags.

"So . . . you did believe me," Lonnie said, haltingly.

"Oh, of course I believed you, Lonnie. I know you'd never have killed those men in cold blood. I saw right away through Halliday's lie. I didn't want him to think I was sidin' you too hard, though. I didn't want him to get suspicious and keep a close eye on me. If so, I might not have been able to get over to the feed barn and saddle your horse. I had both the General and Miss Abigail tied in an alley near the courthouse, just as Mister Calhoun and I had planned. Fortunately, Mister Hadley was helpin' the hangman with the gallows, so I got in and out of the barn without raising suspicion."

Hadley was the manager of the feed barn.

Casey smeared salve into Lonnie's wound. As she did, she looked at him.

"What're you thinkin' about?" the girl asked.

"You two are now as wanted as I am," Lonnie said as it

dawned on him just how much these two friends—really, his only two friends in the world—had sacrificed to keep him from hanging.

He shook his head as he slid his gaze from Casey to Calhoun and back to Casey again. "You'll never be able to go back to Arapaho Creek. Not in a million years."

Casey looked back at him. She'd obviously considered that possibility before the dustup in town. But now it was real. She was as much an outlaw as Lonnie. As much as Calhoun, even. That was beginning to sink into her now, just as all that had happened was hitting Lonnie like a runaway lumber dray.

"I reckon you're right," the girl said, a slight tremor in her voice.

"Ah, hell." Calhoun was crouched low over his fire, coaxing some flames to life by blowing on them. "Towns is overrated, anyways. Too many folks. Too much trouble to get into. You two can live out here with me. When our trail gets hot, we'll mosey down Old Mexico way. Good place to spend the winter, down there along the Sea of Cortez. There's a little village down there. *Puerto Peñasco,* they call it."

He made a motion in the air with his hands. "The *señoritas* down there—they come supple as ripe tomatoes, and filled out like . . ."

Calhoun let his voice trail off as he looked up at Lonnie and Casey staring at him skeptically.

"Well . . . I'm just sayin' it's nice down there, that's all," the ex-Confederate said, flushing, and continued to blow on his fire.

"No," Lonnie said, staring pensively off through the trees. "There's gotta be another way. Halliday can't win. He's a killer. He's the one who's got to hang."

"In case you didn't notice," Casey said, "we're a little outnumbered, Lonnie. There were a good dozen men in that posse of Halliday's. He's got the whole county convinced you killed the deputy marshal."

Lonnie shook his head, grimacing. "I know, I know. But there's got to be another way. I can't, won't, let that killer . . . that killer who brained me an' almost hanged me . . . I can't let him win. He was going to let me take the punishment coming' to *him*."

He gritted his teeth with determination. "And I won't let him win."

"Don't see how you can't." Calhoun laid a couple of large branches on the building flames. He looked at Casey and then at Lonnie. "Look at it this way. At least neither one of you is alone in your predicament. At least you got each other."

He pulled a hide-wrapped whiskey bottle out of his canvas war bag, and popped the cork. He raised the bottle in salute, and took a drink.

Lonnie glanced at Casey. She returned the glance and then looked away.

Lonnie looked away, then, too.

When they'd eaten a meager meal of wild berries and jerky washed down with coffee, or, in Calhoun's case, washed down with whiskey, the ex-Confederate hauled his gear into the ruins of the stone cabin, and went to bed. He said that an old man needed even a partial roof over his head, though Lonnie sensed that the real reason he retreated into the cabin was because he wanted to give Lonnie and Casey some privacy.

He probably sensed there were things they needed to discuss. He was right, but Lonnie didn't work up the courage to broach the subject until the fire had died and he and Casey lay in their bedrolls about six feet apart, both staring quietly at the stars.

"Casey?" Lonnie said, keeping his voice low. "You still awake over there?"

"I'm awake."

"I suppose you're thinkin' about fancy Da . . . er, I mean, Giles Gilpin."

Casey gave a sardonic snort. "It's Niles. But at the moment I reckon I got more important things to think about but him. Besides, there's probably not much to think about. He is, I am sure, well aware that I was the wild young lady who galloped off like Calamity Jane with Halliday's prisoner, leavin' a bullet-cut hang rope dangling in the air below the gallows."

"I reckon I pretty much cost you your chance of gettin' hitched to a moneyed fella, and not havin' to worry about supporting yourself anymore."

"I reckon you did, Lonnie," Casey said with a sigh, raising her arms straight above her, interlocking her fingers, and stretching. "Thank you very much, Lonnie Gentry."

"Sorry."

"You're not sorry."

"No, I reckon I'm not sorry about Giles. But I am sorry about gettin' you into so much trouble."

Lonnie saw her eyes sparkling softly in the umber glow of the coals as she turned her head toward him. "You didn't get me into this trouble, Lonnie. I got into it of my own free will. Because we're friends. You needed my help. And, since we are friends, I had to help you. You would have done the same for me."

"I reckon I would have. But I can't imagine you gettin' into half the trouble I've gotten into."

Casey chuckled softly, half to herself, as though she'd found what he'd said genuinely funny. "No, I can't imagine that, either. But, you never know. I am still young." She chuckled again.

"Casey?" Lonnie said after a stretched silence.

"What, Lonnie?"

"You mind if I bring my gear and lay over there beside you?"

She looked at him again, her eyes flashing as though tiny fires burned inside them. He could see the whiteness of her smile in the darkness. "No, Lonnie. I wouldn't mind that at all . . . as long as you can keep your hands to yourself."

"I will, I will."

When Lonnie had quietly hauled his gear over and was lying beside Casey, only inches away, so that he could feel the warmth of her supple body beside him, he said, "I reckon Calhoun's right."

"About what?"

"At least we got each other."

Casey turned her head to him. "Lonnie, I am not going down to Mexico."

Lonnie stretched his gaze to the stars twinkling high overhead, beyond the occasional breeze-jostled pine boughs. "I reckon you won't have to. I'm gonna get us out of this."

"What're you thinking?"

"I'm going to dig up that money tomorrow. I'll take it over the mountains again, just like last year, and get it into the hands of the deputy US marshal in Camp Collins. Then folks will have to believe I didn't kill that marshal, that Halliday did and that he's the one who was after the money."

Casey stared skyward for a time. Then she shrugged. "I guess it's our only option. It might work . . . if Halliday doesn't hunt us down first."

"Yeah, there's another problem."

"What's that?"

"Halliday might be figurin' that's what I'd do. He might decide to dig that money up now himself, and hightail it. We have to get to it before he can."

Lonnie jerked with a start as Calhoun's quiet, anxious voice sounded from the direction of the ruined stone cabin. "Will you chil'uns pipe down over there? We got company!"

Lonnie heard the man click a gun hammer back.

CHAPTER 44

"Company?" Lonnie reached for his Winchester and pumped a round into the chamber. He aimed the rifle into the darkness.

Casey lay beside him, keeping her head down, blankets drawn up to her chin.

Lonnie peered into the trees around the camp, caressing his Winchester's trigger with his finger, the blood rushing through his veins as he waited for the gun flashes and the bullets screeching toward him.

Calhoun ran down the slope, both his old Confederate Griswold & Gunnison revolvers in his hands. Cherokee came running out of the woods, barking, hackles raised.

"I don't see anything," Lonnie said, keeping his voice low.

"I don't, either," Casey whispered.

"I do!" Calhoun said, his voice echoing loudly in the quiet night.

Cherokee had followed its master and was barking furiously now.

Lonnie could no longer see the man's silhouette in the darkness. He jerked with a start when Calhoun fired one of his pistols. The report was a hard crack. The gun flashed redly, silhouetting the tall, lanky man against it.

Calhoun fired his other pistol. Again, Lonnie jerked, his heart hammering in his ears now as he waited for return fire.

Footsteps sounded as Calhoun continued running down the slope.

"I know you're out there!" he bellowed, triggering both his pistols again.

"Wait here!" Lonnie told Casey. "Stay low!"

Lonnie scrambled to his feet. He pulled his boots on and then ran with his rifle down the slope toward where Calhoun had fallen silent. The dog had stopped barking. The night as quiet as the bottom of a well now on the lee side of the man's pistol shots and Cherokee's barking.

Lonnie wasn't sure where Calhoun was. The moon had not yet risen, and not much starlight penetrated to the forest floor around him.

Calhoun's pistols barked loudly and flashed brightly to Lonnie's right and down the slope a ways. "I see you, you sumbitches!" the ex-Confederate shouted. "Come on out here and face me like men 'stead of possums 'fraid of their own shadows!"

He fired again . . . and again.

Lonnie couldn't help flinching at each loud report that vaulted around the forest, chasing its own echoes.

Lonnie pricked his ears as the echoes died. For the life of him, he couldn't hear anything more than the soft sighing of the breeze and the occasional, soft thud of a pine cone falling to the ground. No night birds hooted. No coyotes called.

There were no sounds of men moving in the forest around him.

The horses were milling back where they were picketed near the camp, but that had only started after Calhoun had started shooting. Cherokee was sort of mewling curiously deep in his chest, but he was no longer barking.

Lonnie said quietly, "Mister Calhoun, I'm to your left and behind you a little. Don't shoot me."

"I know where you are, boy," Calhoun said in his gravelly voice. "I got the ears of a bat and the eyes of a prairie falcon.

Been that way since the war."

"I don't hear anything," Lonnie said. "Are you sure they're out here?"

"I'm sure." Calhoun fired again. "Right there—you see him? Runnin' around like coyote scopin' out a fresh trash heap! Cherokee, get after him!"

The dog barked once but remained sitting to the ex-Confederate's right, staring into the darkness.

Lonnie dropped to a knee to avoid possible return fire. He looked in the direction that Calhoun had fired, the flashes of the ex-Confederate's pistol still flashing dully on his retinas.

"I didn't see nothin'," Lonnie said. "Didn't hear nothin'. I don't think Cherokee did, either."

"They're here, all right. Boatwrights. Sneaky sons of Satan!"

Lonnie frowned toward where he could make out the tall Southerner's vague shadow. "Who?"

Calhoun fired again. "Come on out here, Danny! Come out here, Collie! Who you got with ya? You got ole Cousin Earl Sapp here, too?" Calhoun chuckled and fired two more times.

Lonnie licked his lips and scowled skeptically. "Who're you talking about, Mister Calhoun?"

"Boatwrights," Calhoun said after a brief silence. "Virgil Allen Boatwright's mountain folk from Tennessee. Mangiest bunch of curs you'll find in any hollow in Appalachia. I shot Virgil when I found him with my dear sweet June, after the war. Shot the sumbitch in my own cabin, though shootin' was too good for him. He deserved slow Apache torture, Virgil did. I shot ole Virgil, and Virgil shot June as he fell. Shot her with a bullet meant for me. Killed her, the polecat. They both died. The Boatwrights been shadowin' my trail for the past twenty years. Followed me west to avenge their kin. They been shadowin' me ever since, bidin' their time. I even seen 'em a time or two when I was huntin' Injuns with the frontier army."

Calhoun raised his voice. "You hear that, Danny? You hear that Collie? Yeah, I know you're foggin' my trail! I've knowed it for a long time. Been waitin' for you to work up enough sand to face me like *men*!"

He fired again.

"That's probably been plum foolish of me, though, ain't it?" Calhoun said. "There ain't nary a Boatwright that's ever done anything a *man* would do. Not a real man. All the Boatwrights do is steal other men's women! While said men are off fightin' the war that the Boatwrights cowered from!"

Soft footfalls sounded behind Lonnie. Before he could turn around, Casey said quietly, "It's me."

Cherokee was whining now as he sank to his belly on the forest floor, ears pricked and looking around incredulously.

"Come on out here, Boatwrights!" Calhoun shouted into the darkness. He extended his left pistol. The hammer clicked benignly down onto the firing pin, empty.

Casey moved up to stand beside Lonnie. She held up a whiskey bottle. There was no cork in it. She turned it upside down to show that it was empty. She looked at Lonnie, pursing her lips.

Lonnie looked at Calhoun who had holstered one pistol and was now busily reloading the other one.

"Mister Calhoun."

Lonnie moved on down the slope. He stopped beside the tall ex-Confederate and looked at the revolver he was expertly reloading from the leather pouch on his shell belt. Lonnie could smell the sour stench of alcohol.

"I don't think there's anyone out there, Mister Calhoun," Lonnie said. "I haven't heard anything. Haven't seen anything, either. I don't think your dog has, either. I think you must've dreamed it."

He glanced over his shoulder at Casey moving on down the

slope to stand beside him.

Calhoun looked at Lonnie, frowning deeply. He looked at his dog.

He swung a look into the darkness again. He turned his head this way and that. Then he just stood there for a time, staring, listening.

"If that don't beat a hen aflyin'," Calhoun said at last, his shoulders relaxing. "I believe you're right, boy. I must have dreamed the whole thing."

"I think that's what must have happened," Lonnie said. "You'd best go on back to bed. Still a few hours before sunup."

"Yeah," Calhoun said, slowly easing the pistol into its holster. "Yeah . . . I reckon I'd best do that." He chuckled incredulously. "Imagine me . . . dreamin' the whole thing. I reckon I'm gettin' spookier'n a tree full of owls."

"It's all right, Mister Calhoun." Despite the brouhaha, Lonnie felt sorry for the man. Calhoun had left a trail of trouble behind him. And a trail of ghosts.

But, then, who hadn't?

Calhoun turned to start back up the slope toward the ruined cabin. Cherokee followed him.

He stopped and glanced back at Lonnie and Casey. "Them Boatwrights are right sneaky. That's why I dreamed it. They're out there somewhere. Maybe not close. Not tonight. But they been trailin' me a long time. They won't rest until they've settled up for me killin' ole Virgil. They'll be huntin' me till Gabriel blows his horn."

Again, he started walking away. "Virgil. Can't understand what my dear sweet Junie ever saw in that spineless scalawag . . ."

He gave a sardonic shake of his head as he climbed the slope in the darkness, his dog behind him.

"Whiskey and that man don't mix," Casey said when Calhoun

was out of earshot. "We should've remembered that from last year."

"No, they don't mix. Not with all the demons poor ole Calhoun's got lurkin' around between his ears." Lonnie glanced at her. "You go on back to camp. I'll stay out here a bit and keep watch. If Halliday heard them gunshots, he'll be comin'."

Casey sidled up to him, pressed her hand against his. "I wish the other men in this world were half the man you are, Lonnie Gentry."

She kissed him and walked away.

Lonnie stood there, staring into the darkness, his cheek on fire.

CHAPTER 45

Lonnie sat up the rest of the night, occasionally wandering around the perimeters of the camp, looking but mostly listening. He knew that the General would likely alert him to trouble, but he wanted to be on his toes when and if trouble came, though he had no idea how he'd fend off a dozen men.

Fortunately, he didn't have to.

The rest of the night was peaceful, with only a night bird hooting now and then and the breeze scratching around in the branches. He wondered where Halliday was. Had he lost his quarry's trail? Apparently, he hadn't been close enough to hear Calhoun's wild, drunken gunfire.

As soon as dawn brushed a pale blush across the eastern sky, the ridges standing black against it, Lonnie quietly gathered his gear and saddled his horse. Casey slept curled on her side. She did not stir as Lonnie walked back into the camp, stepped around her, and strode over to the ruined shack. He moved on through the low doorframe and dropped to a knee beside Calhoun.

He hesitated, wary of waking the man out of a dead sleep. Calhoun had proven himself to be one jumpy old soldier. One who slept with both his holstered pistols close.

Cherokee growled softly from a corner but flapped his tail when he scented Lonnie.

Lonnie silently slid Calhoun's holstered guns out of reach,

241

and placed his hand on the snoring ex-Confederate's left shoulder.

Calhoun was instantly awake, reaching for his pistols.

Whispering, the boy said, "Easy, Mister Calhoun—it's only me, Lonnie!"

"Wha . . . where . . . wha . . . ?" Calhoun sat abruptly up, blinking and looking around, maybe imagining Union soldiers or Sioux warriors overtaking his camp. "What is it? Where's my pistols?"

"Shhh!"

Lonnie glanced through an empty window frame toward where Casey lay asleep by the fire ring.

"Please, keep your voice down, Mister Calhoun. I don't wanna wake Casey."

"Why? What's goin' on, boy? Trouble?"

"No, no trouble," Lonnie said, shaking his head. "I'm headin' back to Skull Canyon. I gotta find that money, get it back to a bona fide lawman so I can clear my name. *Our* names, I should say," he added, glancing at Casey again.

He doubted that anything would be able to clear Calhoun's name, as there was a good possibility the old soldier had a long list of old warrants on his head. His most recent transgression, freeing Lonnie from the hang rope, was likely the least of his transgressions.

"Wait—what?" Calhoun scowled at Lonnie, blinking sleep from his eyes. "What are you talking about? Skull Canyon?"

"That's where the money is buried. Didn't Casey tell you?"

"No, sir. She never told me nothin' about Skull Canyon." Calhoun placed a big, strong hand on Lonnie's shoulder and leaned close. Lonnie could still smell the whiskey on his breath. "That canyon's a bad, bad place boy. You don't wanna have nothin' to do with it."

"You believe the old legend? You believe it's cursed?"

"Hell, yes, it's cursed. Listen, son, I come from the old South. The Appalachians. Back there, folks is taught to respect them old legends. Some places is haunted, and that's a fact. Restless souls, sometimes demons, lurk in places where bad things happened. I was raised near a hollow where a man killed and ate his whole family. Any man, woman, or child who visited that hollow turned into a bag of bones. I know that to be true, because one of my uncles wandered in there without knowin' it, huntin' coons. Guess what happened to him?"

Lonnie felt chicken flesh rising across the back of his neck. "He turned into a bag of bones?"

"That what my mother told me, and that woman wouldn't have lied to save her own son's soul!"

"The damage is already done," Lonnie said, darkly, feeling a deep chill. "I've already spent a night in the canyon."

Calhoun shook his head. "That ain't one bit good, boy. If so, you're likely wearing the curse on your shoulders. What you need to do now is not go back to that infernal place but find you a witch to get the curse lifted. Until then, draw a circle around yourself, wherever you're gonna be for any length of time, and try to stand in it as much as possible. And when you get home, hang a horseshoe on your door!"

"I spent a whole night in that canyon several nights ago, and I ain't dead yet, Mister Calhoun. And I ain't been drawin' no circles or hangin' horseshoes!"

"You ain't dead yet—no. But not because folks ain't been tryin'!"

Lonnie considered that. Calhoun had a point. "What about the money?"

"Forget the money!" Calhoun squeezed Lonnie's arm tighter. "Listen, I know an old Ute medicine woman. She lives over in—"

"Forget it!" Lonnie straightened. "I don't have time for none of that hokum. I have to get that money back and turn it over to the law. The *right* law. Standin' around here lettin' you scare my bones to putty ain't gettin' it done. The reason I woke you in the first place is I want you to take care of Casey for me. When she wakes, tell her to wait here with you. I'll try to be back before sundown. Whatever you do, don't let her come after me. It's too dangerous."

Calhoun stared in disbelief. He wagged his head slowly. "Well, if I can't talk you out of returnin' to that infernal place, you don't have far to ride."

"Huh?"

"Step outside and look to the northeast."

Lonnie did as the ex-Confederate had told him to. His blood quickened in his veins as he stared at the crags, including the giant stone skull, towering above the first near ridge. The first copper rays of the rising sun were touching it. Oddly, those rays touched none of the other formations around it.

Just the skull.

As if pointing it out to Lonnie staring at it now, mouth agape.

Calhoun stepped up beside him. "Ride on down this hill here. When you come to a big spruce tree, swing left. You'll run into an ancient horse trail. The Spanish or ancient Injuns likely carved it. Follow it out of this valley, and after a couple of hours, it will take you to a notch in the wall of Skull Canyon."

"How do you know?" Lonnie asked the man, skeptically. "You've never been to Skull Canyon."

"No, but I know what that demon sounds like when you get close. You'll hear him, too. If you're smart, you'll take heed and ride right on past!"

"You're talkin' about the way the wind sounds when it blows around the skull. Am I right?"

"You call it what you want, you mulish little polecat. The least you can do is turn your hat around." Calhoun grinned with cunning. "They say evil spirits have a tougher time recognizing you if you wear your hat backwards."

"Ah, balderdash," Lonnie grumbled, and started walking toward where the General waited, still tied to his picket line.

"Boy?" Calhoun whispered, glancing toward the sleeping Casey.

Lonnie glanced back at him.

"Don't you tarry now. Don't let another night catch you in that canyon, and once you're out, you boil you up some dandelion tea then count the leaves at the bottom of your cup!"

Lonnie gave a caustic grunt. "Just keep an eye on Casey, Mister Calhoun."

He walked away, mounted up, and quietly booted the General out of the camp. He tried to tell himself that what he'd heard was all hokum, but he couldn't ignore that gooseflesh had now risen over nearly every inch of his body.

It only got worse when he started to hear the Skull Canyon demon blowing its infernal horn.

CHAPTER 46

Lonnie heard the tooth-gnashingly eerie bellowing as he followed the ancient horse trail east of the camp in which he'd left Casey asleep and Calhoun staring after him, shaking his head.

The moaning had started about an hour later. He looked up to see that he'd entered a narrow valley over which the skull-like formation jutted with its accompanying crags ahead on his left. The wind was blowing from the north. It was being caressed, plucked at, and ripped by the giant skull, creating those bizarre moaning sounds that changed pitch from time to time so that occasionally it sounded like a throaty wail.

The sound would die for a time and then start again, softly at first but gradually growing in volume before dying and starting all over again.

Lonnie followed the trail through a copse of aspens and across a narrow creek, heading for the red, crenelated cliff jutting ahead of him, the sun caressing it gently, burnishing it, stretching dark-purple shadows out from lumps and knobs and boulders that had likely tumbled from the crest but had gotten held up on their way to the valley floor.

The sun was as clear as a lens. Everything appeared close. Lonnie could see every dimple and piece of shale along the side of that towering cliff.

Somewhere in that cliff, a notch opened, offering a way into Skull Canyon beyond.

Lonnie followed the trail over the shoulder of a gravelly spur.

On the other side of the spur, he could see the base of the sandstone cliff littered with stone rubble, twisted cedars, and pinyon pines. Another creek ran along the base of the ridge. Little wider than a freshet, the brown water glistened like copper in the intensifying sunlight as it rippled over rocks and gravel and sluiced around slab-sided boulders.

The General whinnied and shook his head so hard he almost threw his bridle.

Lonnie looked down at the horse. "What is it, General?"

As he continued riding along the trail now paralleling the ridge, Lonnie looked around cautiously. His belly had drawn itself into a tight knot. The horse had heard or smelled something that Lonnie hadn't detected.

He rode several more yards, following a slight curve in the face of the ridge, when he drew back on the buckskin's reins. A notch opened before him. It was like a half-open door sheathed in willows and tufts of green grass nourished by the freshet. Lonnie looked at the mud around the narrow creek, and the knot in his belly tightened.

Someone had been through here before him. The clear print of a horse's hoof marked the mud of the spring, to the left of a leafy willow, the indentation filled with water that was very slowly wearing it away.

Apprehension throbbed like a war drum in Lonnie's head.

He stared at the notch. He didn't want to ride through that ominously beckoning doorway and enter the canyon. But he had to. There was a chance that whoever had ridden through here before him was merely a line rider looking for cows. Maybe a prospector. Maybe a drifter. Lord knew there were all three breeds of men in these mountains, and more.

That hoofprint didn't necessarily have to belong to Frank Halliday.

Something, however, told Lonnie it did belong to Halliday.

He'd probably been scouring the canyon for the gold for a long time, after talking to the old posse rider, and had come upon this hidden entrance, which Lonnie hadn't known about until Calhoun had told him.

Lonnie reached forward with his right hand, and slid his rifle from its scabbard. Quietly, he racked a cartridge into the action, depressed the hammer, and set the Winchester across his saddlebow. He clucked to the General. As though sensing his rider's apprehension, the big buckskin moved slowly, haltingly forward.

The stallion's hooves made wet sucking sounds as it crossed the freshet. The willows brushed Lonnie's calves as he and the General pushed through the entrance. The skull blew its whining breath down from the ridge above Lonnie as though in warning. A warning that went unheeded as the boy and his horse followed a twisting path between steep walls of pink, eroded rock before coming out onto a ridge overlooking the main canyon, which swept wide before Lonnie, a good hundred feet below.

The skull moaned shrilly, and then the wailing died with the wind.

Lonnie halted the General and looked around, trying to get his bearings. He looked at the broad skull looming whitely high above on his left. Staring straight out before him and down, he saw a stretch of flat water beyond a fringe of pines. That must be the lake near the side ravine in which Crawford Kinch had buried the payroll loot.

Lonnie gigged the General forward. The buckskin took one step then stopped. The horse blew hoarsely, twitching his ears, staring off to the right and ahead.

"What is it, Gen—?"

Lonnie let his voice trail off.

The skull's ominous call was rising again, gradually.

Something moved among the rocks strewn along the base of the ridge wall, several yards above Lonnie on his right. A man was coming through a narrow corridor of rock that hugged the side of the steep ridge, heading toward Lonnie, whose heart was beating almost painfully now.

"Help," the man said. "Please . . . help me!"

At first, Lonnie thought the call was a trick of the rising wind. But, no. It was a man's voice. A familiar voice. The man's tall, black-clad figure disappeared behind bends in the narrow corridor, but now Lonnie could hear the man's footfalls, the ringing of his spurs as he continued moving down the crooked corridor toward Lonnie.

The moaning wind rose, kicking up dust around Lonnie and further obscuring the halting figure up the rise before him.

Lonnie aimed his Winchester toward the staggering figure, and clicked the hammer back.

The figure came out of the gap in the rocks. He stood there on a mound of slide rock, staring down at Lonnie. His shoulders sagged. His chest rose and fell heavily as he breathed. He wore a black frock coat. His hat was gone. A bandage shown whitely around the top of his head.

Halliday's eyes were still swollen from Lonnie's assault.

What looked like cherry jam stained the sheriff's coat, high up on his right side, just below his shoulder. But Lonnie knew it wasn't jam.

The sheriff clamped his left, gloved hand over the bloody wound. Blood oozed between the fingers of that hand. He held a pistol straight down along his right leg.

"Help me," Halliday said, breathless. He staggered forward. "Please, you gotta . . . help me!"

He stopped. He stared at Lonnie, frowning. Then he glowered.

"Ah, hell . . . it's *you*!"

He triggered his pistol into the rocks at his boots and then fell forward. Dropping the gun, Halliday rolled down the slope toward Lonnie, causing the General to fidget and sidestep, whickering nervously.

Dust rose around Halliday's violently rolling figure. The sheriff rolled up hard against a boulder with a sharp smacking sound, just ahead and right of Lonnie. Halliday grunted, wheezed.

"Ah, *Christ!*" he said, miserably. "You killed me, kid!"

The voice of the canyon's demon fairly bellowed as though in response to the sheriff's yell.

CHAPTER 47

Lonnie looked around for the man or men who'd shot Halliday.

Seeing no one, he stepped down from his saddle and walked over to where the sheriff lay on his back beside the rock that had so unceremoniously stopped his roll. The man was writhing in pain, wincing, stretching his lips back from tobacco-stained teeth.

"What do you mean I killed you?" Lonnie stared coldly down at the man. "Not that I wouldn't mind the honors, but I just got here."

"You as good as done it . . . when you . . . cheated the hang-man!"

Lonnie stared at the man, incredulous.

"I had to come out here . . . try to dig up the money . . . before you got to it." Halliday grimaced and shook his head. "I swear, kid—you're a pile o' of unfettered trouble. Now I'm lyin' here dyin' on account of you!"

"You got that wrong, you bottom-feedin' dung beetle. You're lyin' here dyin' because of *you*. What I want to know is: who shot you?"

Lonnie looked around again, cautiously.

"Why, the Pinkertons, that's who!" Halliday laughed without humor. "They must have figured it all out, after the other day. They must've followed me an' the posse out from town. When I cut the posse loose, I rode up to where I had you rebury the money, and the sons o' Satan shot me after I'd dug up the money. I managed to scramble away before they could finish the job."

"Where was the posse?"

"I sent 'em back last night, when we lost your trail. Kid, help me up. I gotta get back to town. I gotta get to the sawbones."

Lonnie took a step back. "Where are the Pinkertons?"

"Hell, I don't know. They gave up on me and rode on out of the canyon, I reckon. They'll probably climb up over Storm Peak Pass, head on over to the railroad line by Camp Collins. After that"—Halliday laughed in caustic frustration—"who knows? Likely, Mexico. That'd be the only place for a couple of crooked Pinkertons packin' a mother lode of army gold!"

Halliday extended his hand to Lonnie. "Come on, kid—help me up. I gotta get back to town, see that old pill roller!"

Lonnie looked off toward where the lake shone in the distance beyond the trees, glimmering in the sunlight. His heartbeat quickened. Mostly to himself, he said, "If they're heading over the pass, they'll need supplies and fresh horses. The closest place to find fresh horses around here is the Circle G—my own ranch!"

His mother was there alone with little Jeremiah . . .

Lonnie swung around and started back to the General.

"Kid, you gotta help me!" Halliday begged.

Lonnie turned to look at the man. He remembered how the rope around his neck had felt. He'd likely remember that feeling on his deathbed.

Fury welled up in the boy. He spat to one side, and said, "You die slow. Right here, all alone, listening to that demon breathing over you."

He glanced toward the pale, skull-like mass of rock looming in the north as the wind wheezed and moaned around him, lifting chalky dust.

He looked at Halliday once more. "Then you burn in hell!"

Lonnie started once more toward the General. He stopped dead in his tracks when he heard the unmistakable click of a gun hammer being cocked.

He turned around slowly. Halliday must have been packing a hideout pistol. He held the small, pearl-gripped derringer in his right hand. He grinned as he aimed the little popper at Lonnie.

Automatically, Lonnie swung his rifle up, aimed hastily, and fired.

Halliday triggered the derringer wide. The bullet plunked off a rock behind Lonnie. Halliday dropped the pistol and stared down in shock at the blood oozing from the hole in his chest.

He looked at Lonnie through the gun smoke billowing in the air between them. He frowned as though hurt that the boy would be so cold as to kill him.

Then his eyes rolled back into his head. He fell onto his back and lay still.

Lonnie looked at the rifle in his hands.

It was shaking.

Lonnie drew a deep breath, fighting the urge to be sick. He didn't have time for that. He had to get back to the ranch. He had to get his hands on the loot. Besides, who knew what the Pinkertons might do to his mother when they tried to steal the horses from the Circle G corral?

Lonnie glanced once more at Halliday. Then he swung around and ran over to the waiting buckskin, who thrashed his tail testily. Lonnie mounted up and galloped away from the dead sheriff.

Was it just a trick of the wind, or was the canyon demon laughing at him?

As he rode, heading for the canyon's southern entrance, where all the trouble had started, Lonnie turned his hat around backwards.

★ ★ ★ ★ ★

Lonnie was glad to ride out of the canyon.

But it took him another two hours to reach the outskirts of the Circle G. The pines and aspens at the edge of the yard glittered softly in the late-afternoon sunlight. Lonnie slowed the General down to a walk as he rode under the portal's cross-beam and into the yard.

He looked around cautiously, wondering if the two Pinkertons had already been here and left, or if they were still here. He got his answer when he spied the Pinkertons' two horses in the main corral off the barn's side shed. Lonnie's other four horses were there, as well.

The Pinkertons were still here. Maybe they intended to spend the night, enjoying the ministrations of Lonnie's mother, including her cooking, before getting a fresh start in the morning.

The cabin was quiet, vaguely ominous-looking. The front door was closed. The sunlight reflected off the dark windows.

Lonnie swung the General around and rode back out through the portal and into the trees west of the yard. He dropped the General's reins then slid his Winchester from its scabbard.

"You stay here, boy," Lonnie said softly, patting the horse's neck. "Hopefully, this whole nightmare will be over soon." He racked a shell into the Winchester's breech. "And I won't have a bullet in my hide for my trouble."

Lonnie removed his spurs and dropped them into a saddlebag pouch. He gave the horse another pat then strode up along a small creek to the north. He worked his way around the yard and behind the cabin then dropped to a knee to survey his surroundings.

The long, low cabin lay hunched before him, beyond the privy. The keeper shed, where meat was stored, lay to the far right of the privy. A small, roofed, open-sided woodshed sat between the privy and the cabin. More split firewood lay against the cabin's rear wall, peppered with pine needles. A rain barrel stood back there, as well. The pine needles as well as dead leaves left over from last fall blew in the wind gusting down over the western ridges.

Lonnie thought he could hear the skull's moaning in that wind, but it had to be his imagination.

He was a long way from Skull Canyon.

The cabin was ominously silent but he could smell smoke from the range issuing from the chimney pipe. Lonnie licked his lips, squeezed the rifle in his hands, and then started to push off his knee. A sound stopped him. He let his knee drop back to the ground.

A man's muffled laughter rose from the other side of the cabin.

Anxiety flared in Lonnie's veins.

The laughter grew louder and then Bill Brocius came around the front corner of the cabin, following the well-worn path around to the back. Lonnie jerked with a start, and retreated a few feet into the trees.

Brocius's laughter died as he moved toward Lonnie, following the path that led to the privy. The rogue Pinkerton drew on the cigarette smoldering between his lips then flipped the quirley into the brush, blowing smoke into the wind.

"Good way to cause a wildfire, fool," Lonnie muttered under his breath, hunkered behind an aspen bole, watching Brocius follow the path to the privy. The Pinkerton walked a little unsteadily, as though he was half drunk.

The privy door opened with a squawk. Brocius's boots thudded hollowly as he entered the privy and then closed the door and dropped the nail through the hasp, locking it.

Another wave of anxiety washed over Lonnie. He drew a deep calming breath and stared at the privy. "There you go, you snake," Lonnie said, nodding slowly, pulling the Winchester up taut against his chest. "Now, I got you."

He stepped out around the tree and began walking toward the privy.

CHAPTER 48

Lonnie walked up to within five yards of the privy and then dropped behind a tree stump, waiting. Inside the privy, Brocius grunted. The man's boots thudded and scraped.

Done with business.

Lonnie lurched up off his knee and strode quickly up along the side of the privy. He stopped, pressed his left shoulder against the privy wall.

The door opened with a squawk. Lonnie glanced around the corner to see Brocius standing in front of the door, crouched slightly, buttoning the fly of his wool trousers.

When the Pinkerton had finished the maneuver, he lifted his hat, ran his hand through his hair with a sigh, then set his hat back on his head, giving it a rakish angle, and started following the trail toward the cabin.

Lonnie fell into step behind the man, quickly caught up to him. He kept his voice low as he said, "Stop right there!"

Brocius stopped, shoulders tensed. Lonnie pressed his rifle barrel taut against the man's back. "If you call out, I'll shoot you. Now, nice and slow, ease those pistols out of their holsters and drop 'em on the ground."

Brocius glanced over his right shoulder. "Well, well, if it ain't the young fugitive."

"Drop your guns."

"What're you gonna do, kid?"

"You'll know soon enough . . . after you've dropped those guns."

"What're you gonna do if I don't?" Brocius asked, a defiant smile quirking his mouth corners. "Kill me?"

Lonnie kept his gaze level, hard. He'd shot Halliday, he told himself. He could shoot this man, too, if it came to that. "That's right."

Brocius studied Lonnie from over his shoulder. Lonnie glared at him. Gradually, the smile faded from the Pinkerton's lips. "All right." He lifted his two revolvers from their holsters. He held them up and then tossed them underhand. They landed in the yard several feet to his right.

"You got a hideout?" Lonnie asked.

"Nope." Brocius shook his head, grinning. "Two's enough for me."

Lonnie nudged him forward. "Get movin', then. Inside. Like I said, you call out, I'll shoot you."

"Okay, kid, okay. Take it easy. We wouldn't want that long gun to go off by accident—now, would we?"

"You wouldn't, that's right," Lonnie said.

Brocius started walking slowly forward. Too slowly. Lonnie nudged him again with the rifle. Brocius stopped, swung around in a blur of quick motion, slamming the back of his right hand against the rifle.

The move had caught Lonnie off guard. The rifle bounced off the cabin's stout wall and landed in the brush growing up along the stone foundation. Brocius continued to wheel toward Lonnie. Lonnie saw the savage glint in the man's eyes. And then he saw the man's left fist smash toward him.

It smacked Lonnie's right cheek, sending the boy flying backwards and sideways. Lonnie's head slammed against the cabin. Feeling like a rag doll given a thrashing by an enraged child, he dropped in the brush, his face on fire. The blow had kicked up the pain in his bullet-notched head, as well. It was a searing, blinding fury, momentarily paralyzing him.

"Thought you were gonna take the money from us—eh, boy?" Lonnie felt the man's hands on his back, pulling him up off the ground and lifting him several inches off his feet before slamming him back down on his feet and giving him a shove.

Lonnie lunged forward, hit the ground with a groan, and rolled. When he looked up, Brocius was on him again, the man's cheeks flushed with fury, his eyes small and round and filled with hate.

"I don't think so!" the Pinkerton said through clenched teeth, lifting Lonnie to his feet once more.

The man grabbed Lonnie by the back of his shirt collar, swung him around, and threw him toward the cabin's front corner. Helpless against this big, powerful man, his head on fire, his vision blurry, Lonnie bounced off the cabin. Brocius retrieved his pistols then grabbed Lonnie again and gave him another shove, sending Lonnie lunging along the front of the cabin to the front stoop.

At the steps, Lonnie swung around to confront Brocius, balling his hands into tight fists, but Brocius smashed the back of his left hand against Lonnie's right cheek.

Lonnie went down hard on the porch steps. His ears rang. He could already feel his right eye beginning to swell.

Brocius pulled Lonnie up by his shirt collar again and shoved him up onto the porch. The Pinkerton came up behind him, gave him another shove. Lonnie kept his feet moving so he wouldn't fall. He raised his hands as he flew to the door, but then the door opened.

Madsen looked incredulous as he said, "What the hell's—?"

He stepped back out of the doorway, and Lonnie went stumbling inside and falling across the eating table, scattering plates and glasses. A pan tumbled to the floor with a *bang!*

"Lonnie!" his mother cried, her back to the range.

Lonnie pressed his right cheek to the table, sliding his boots beneath him.

"What's going on?" May Gentry yelled.

"Got us a little problem here," Brocius said to Madsen, as he pulled Lonnie up off the table and hurled the boy into the parlor.

Lonnie hit the braided rug on the parlor floor and rolled up against the stone hearth in which no fire burned. From back inside the lodge, little Jeremiah began squealing loudly.

"My god!" May Gentry screamed, running toward Lonnie.

Lonnie looked up at her. She wore her hair in a neat chignon. It was shiny from a recent brushing. Her nicest house dress— pink with white lace—was drawn taut across her hips and bosom. Her cheeks, lightly rouged, were flushed with shock as she glanced behind her at the two suited Pinkertons standing just inside the parlor, staring darkly down at Lonnie.

Their Pinkerton badges were pinned to their wool vests. What a joke, Lonnie thought.

"Like I said," Brocius said grimly to Madsen, "we got us a little problem. Found him out back. Or . . . he found me, I should say. Stuck a rifle barrel against my spine."

"Lonnie?" May said, a vague tone of accusing mixing with the befuddlement in her face. "What are you up to? Where have you been these past several days?"

She looked genuinely bewildered by his absence. Obviously, neither Brocius nor Madsen had told her about the necktie party. She couldn't have come looking for him because she couldn't leave Jeremiah. She hadn't looked overly worried when Lonnie had first entered the cabin, however. It looked as though she'd been preparing a hearty meal for her guests, after she'd prettied herself up a bit.

No, she hadn't been too heartbroken about her missing boy to enjoy the company of a couple of two crooked Pinkerton agents, who were every bit as much outlaw as Shannon Dupree had been.

"Suppose you didn't know about that, May," Brocius said, mildly sheepish. "Your boy here was tried for murder. The judge was about to hang him when someone with a rifle and a keen shootin' eye saved his bacon."

"Murder!"

"He killed a lawman."

"Another one?"

"I didn't kill him, Ma. Halliday just *said* I done it . . ."

"Halliday? You mean *Sheriff* Halliday?"

". . . because he done it himself—shot Marshal Appleyard, I mean."

Lonnie's mother stared down at her son, bereft. "Oh, Lonnie—what kind of trouble have you gotten yourself into *this* time?"

CHAPTER 49

Lonnie was beginning to think that Skull Canyon's curse was riding him hard. He'd had a perfectly good year until he'd ridden past that forbidden ground up in those high and rocky reaches.

Then it was as though demons loosed from hell had started chasing him, and even after the four who'd nearly run him down a week ago were moldering on the floor of Skull Canyon, demons of their same ilk were still dogging Lonnie's heels.

Eventually, one of those demons was going to catch up to him and turn him toe down. Or maybe it would be two demons, like the two staring down at him now from over his weeping mother's shoulders—Bill Brocius and George Madsen.

Lonnie looked around. A pair of bulging saddlebags lay against the wall to his right, near the old bullhorn rocking chair in which his father had once sat, studying the Good Book on cold winter nights while sipping hot tea, his feet stuffed into elk hide slippers that May had sewn for him, from an elk that Calvin Gentry had shot himself up near Skull Canyon.

Lonnie pushed up onto his elbows and glared at the two Pinkertons. "Is that the loot?"

The two men glanced at the pouches.

"So what if it is?" Madsen said. "We're takin' it back to the army."

"If that's so, why'd you shoot Halliday and leave him for dead in Skull Canyon?"

The two men glanced at each other. They cast Lonnie a dark, menacing gaze.

"What's going on here?" May wanted to know. "Someone, please tell me!"

"Nothin', Mama. You don't wanna know." Lonnie looked at Brocius and Madsen. "You two got the loot. Your horses are probably rested by now. There's feed out in the barn—I'm sure you done already helped yourself to that. Why don't you just leave?"

May studied each man in turn, bewildered, as though they were all speaking a foreign language.

"And waste all that good food your mother's cookin'?" Brocius sniffed the air teeming with the smell of roasting elk, drawing a deep breath. "Wild game and onions and fresh bread? No man in his right mind could leave a meal like that!"

"Besides, we kinda like the company," Brocius added, glancing lasciviously down at Lonnie's mother.

"Besides," Madsen said, "we want our horses to be good and fresh when we leave in the mornin'. Got us a long ride ahead. We'll be takin' two of yours, as well."

"With two horses apiece," Madsen said, "we'll be able to ride harder and longer . . . until we get all the way to Mexico!"

Cold dread pooled in Lonnie's belly. He didn't like the look in these two rogue Pinkertons' eyes. And the fact that they'd just told Lonnie and his mother where they were heading didn't bid well at all.

Not at all.

"I don't understand," May said, straightening and turning her full attention to the Pinkertons. "What's this about loot? And . . . Mexico?"

Madsen walked over and picked up the bulging saddlebags. They looked heavy, both pouches deeply sagging. He slung them onto the table with a grunt. There was a dull clinking sound.

Madsen gave Lonnie a sly glance and then opened the flap on one of the pouches. He dipped his hand in and pulled out one of the canvas pouches stamped "US ARMY."

"Oh, my Lord," May said, staring darkly at the bulging sack.

Madsen untied the rope from around the lip of the pouch. He turned the bag over. The gold coins clanked and clattered onto the table, glistening in the waning rays of sunlight angling through the cabin's windows.

May gasped, covering her mouth with her hand.

"You ever seen the like, May?" Brocius asked her.

May stared at the gold, but she didn't look at all happy to see it. She looked scared, horrified. She sensed the trouble it had come wrapped in.

"Where did that come from?" she asked Lonnie, as though he would know even better than the Pinkertons.

"Skull Canyon," Brocius told her.

Jeremiah had been squealing since Lonnie had been thrown into the cabin. Now he was screaming even louder. May turned toward her bedroom as though she were hearing the infant's cries for the first time, and, rubbing her hands nervously up and down her thighs, she strode toward the bedroom door. "I . . . I have to see about the baby."

She went into the room, glanced worriedly back at Lonnie, and then closed the door, muffling the baby's cries.

Lonnie started to heave himself to his feet.

"Stay down there," Brocius ordered, aiming his cocked Colt at Lonnie.

"What're you gonna do with us?" Lonnie asked, sitting back down on the floor.

His eye was really swelling now but the pain in his head was fading. It had been replaced with the cold fear that these two rogue Pinkertons would kill not only Lonnie but his mother and baby brother, as well.

Maybe he shouldn't have come here, Lonnie thought. Maybe the Pinkertons would have just taken the horses and left in the morning with the loot, sparing his mother and baby brother.

By coming here and confronting the two men about the loot, Lonnie might have just made the biggest mistake of his and his mother's lives.

There was nothing to do about that now. He had to keep his wits about him and try to figure a way out of one more mess he'd gotten himself into.

If the curse would let him, that was . . .

When neither Pinkerton answered his question, Lonnie repeated it. "I asked you what you're gonna do with us?"

Brocius glanced at Madsen, and jerked his head at Lonnie. The men's faces were hard and blank. "Tie him," Brocius said. "Tie him good and tight. He has a way of getting out of tight spots, this one."

"Well, he ain't gonna get out of this one." Madsen grabbed a rope dangling from a peg in the front door. "We can't afford to let him get out of this one."

Brocius kept his eyes on Lonnie as he said, "What're you thinkin', George?"

"What do you think I'm thinkin', Bill? Make him promise to keep a secret for the rest of his life?"

"He's just a kid," Brocius said. He appeared genuinely reluctant to kill a boy. He was probably also thinking about killing the boy's mother and baby brother, as well. His lean, clean-shaven face was splotched white. He was thinking it all through, and he was feeling grim about it.

As Madsen tied Lonnie's hands behind a ceiling support post delineating where the kitchen ended and the parlor began, the bearded Pinkerton said, "If you know another way, let's hear it.

I'm open to suggestions."

"I won't tell," Lonnie said, shaking his head, not knowing if he was speaking truthfully or not. But he was desperate to keep his mother and little brother alive. "I promise, I won't. If it means you not harming Ma and little Jeremiah, I'll take the secret to my grave. Heck, no one would believe me, anyway. I'm wanted for killin' a deputy US marshal! I'll tell 'em I killed Halliday, too! *That* they'll believe!"

CHAPTER 50

Brocius crouched down in front of Lonnie. "You really expect us to believe that you'd hold to that story—long after we were gone from here and livin' high on the hog in Mexico?" He looked at Madsen. "Besides, old Pinkerton himself would figure it all out when we didn't show up at the home office."

"Nah, we can't risk it." Madsen turned to Lonnie. "No way you'd hold to that story, and there's a chance someone would believe the truth when you told it. You need to disappear. Folks need to think you killed Halliday and absconded with the loot. No one'll figure out our part in it for days, maybe weeks, and we need to buy as much time as we can. Sorry, kid."

As though he'd heard and understood what his older brother's fate was going to be, little Jeremiah began crying louder in May's bedroom. Brocius cursed and whipped an angry look toward the closed door on the far side of the cabin. "Dammit, May—will you quiet that child? I'm sick to death of hearin' that infernal squealin'!"

Lonnie heard his mother cooing to the baby. A few minutes later, when Madsen and Brocius had sat down at the table and poured themselves glasses of whiskey and started building cigarettes, the bedroom door opened. Lonnie's mother stepped out, holding the screaming, red-faced infant in her arms. May, too, was flushed with anxiety.

"Lonnie's the only one who can soothe him when he's like this."

May looked with beseeching eyes at the two rogue Pinkertons. Little Jeremiah continued bawling, raising his two, tiny, red fists in the air as though trying to squirm out of his mother's arms.

Both men stared at the woman, incredulous, wincing at every tearing scream issuing from the baby's mouth.

"Can't you please untie him, so he can rock little Jeremiah? He'll get him back to sleep in fifteen minutes. He always does!"

The two men looked at Lonnie then at each other.

"I'm all for it!" Brocius rose from his chair and walked a little unsteadily over to Lonnie. He pulled a big bowie knife from a sheath belted against his back. He held the wide-bladed, savage-looking blade up in front of Lonnie's face. "One false move, boy . . . once false move. Understand?"

He glanced at the blade then looked again at Lonnie, eyes filled with threat. "You'd best consider your ma and that screamin' little crib rat, too."

"I'm no fool," Lonnie said. "I won't try nothin'. Untie me, and I'll settle him down."

Brocius cut through the rope tying Lonnie's wrists together behind the ceiling support post. When the ropes were off, Lonnie climbed heavily to his feet and walked around the table. He took the baby out of his mother's hands then, rocking him gently in his arms and cooing to him, he slacked down into his father's old rocker, the same rocker in which his father had once rocked Lonnie to sleep when he was Jeremiah's age.

As soon as he started rocking, little Jeremiah's cries grew less shrill.

"Say, there," Madsen said as he shuffled a deck of cards, a quirley smoldering between his lips. "Sounds better already."

"Good to know the kid's good for somethin'."

"I'm going to go out and get some firewood," May said. "I have to keep the range stoked, so the food will cook. We'll be able to eat soon."

Brocius grabbed the woman's hand and pulled her toward him. He stared at her hard, then gave a stiff smile. "No tricks—okay, sweetheart?" He glanced with menace toward where Lonnie was rocking the baby.

"Tricks?" May said, staring at the man as though she didn't understand the word. "Bill, I swear . . . you have me fit to be tied!" Her lips quivered. Tears dribbled down her cheeks.

"All right, all right," Borius said, releasing her hand. "Don't cloud up and rain on us, now. Go out and fetch your wood. Hurry back, or I'll miss you, honey!"

He gave a wooden laugh as May turned around, rubbed tears from her cheeks with the backs of her hands, and left the cabin, leaving the door half open behind her. She returned a minute later with an armload of wood, which she dropped into the box beside the range. By now, Jeremiah had entirely stopped crying and was fidgeting contentedly inside his tightly wrapped blanket.

"Why, look there," Madsen said while he and Brocius played two-handed poker. "The kid really does have a hand with babies!"

He chuckled and shook his head.

"Keep him quiet, kid," Brocius said. "If there's anything I can't stand it's a squealin' crib rat." He dropped a card onto the table, looked at his partner, and said, "You're tryin' to fill a straight, aren't ya? By god, I know you are!"

Madsen chuckled as he refilled both their whiskey glasses.

May was making gravy at the range, stirring flour and water into the grease. As she did, she glanced over her shoulder at Lonnie. She appeared sick with worry. Her expression was a vaguely beseeching one, as well. The plaintive cast to his mother's gaze made Lonnie feel even worse than he had before.

She apparently wanted him to do something. To save them, somehow.

But, how?

When supper was ready, May began setting the pots and pans on the table. The men cleared away their cards and money. "Time to tie Junior back up," Brocius said.

"Oh, can't he please eat at the table with us?" May implored, wringing her hands. "I can't stand to see him tied down there against that post!"

Lonnie looked down at little Jeremiah. The boy was dead asleep, his little, pinched-up face turned toward Lonnie.

"Besides," May added, "I'll probably need him to quiet little Jeremiah when he wakes up for another feeding in an hour or so."

"Oh, I reckon," Brocius said, his voice thick with drink. "Can't hurt nothin'. He knows what's at stake, if'n he tries anything."

When all the food was steaming on the table, Lonnie handed little Jeremiah over to his mother. He took his father's old place at the head of the table, since Brocius was sitting in Lonnie's usual place. May returned from the bedroom, closed the door quietly until she heard the soft snick of the latch, then removed her apron and sat down beside Brocius, who had already started filling his plate.

Again, May glanced at Lonnie. When the boy met her gaze, she gave him a faintly crooked smile then looked away. Lonnie frowned.

She was trying to tell him something.

What?

Lonnie looked at her again, but now she wouldn't look at him as she passed the potatoes to him. She followed with the gravy bowl, still not looking at him. She was telling him something, all right, but for the life of him, Lonnie couldn't decipher what it was.

The Pinkertons wolfed their meals and then slid their plates away to continue their poker game. As May began to clear plates from the table, she glanced at Lonnie, giving that crooked smile, that same obscure look as before, and said, "Lonnie, honey, would you please fetch me a pail of water from the rain barrel, so I can wash these dishes?"

She held his gaze for about one second with her own. It was as though her eyes were burrowing into his. And then she smiled and turned toward the dry sink.

"Hey, wait a second," Brocius said, scowling at Lonnie. "Where's the rain barrel?"

"Out back," May said offhandedly as she scraped food scraps into a wooden bucket. "Lonnie knows where it is. While you're out there, honey, please grab a few more chunks of wood off the stack, too, will you?"

"I'll go," Brocius said, starting to heave himself out of his chair. "That kid ain't leavin' the cabin." He stumbled backward a little, drunkenly, before getting his boots set beneath him.

"Yeah, you go," Lonnie said, glaring at the man. "Just because you're rich don't mean you're above a few supper chores. I think I'll sit in Pa's rocker."

Madsen chuckled as he tossed out another poker hand. "The kid sure has sass. I for one ain't gonna be at all sorry to, uh . . ." He glanced at Lonnie pointedly then gave a fleeting devilish grin.

Brocius pulled his pistol and aimed at Lonnie. "You're gonna fetch the water and the wood. I'm just gonna tag along to make sure you don't get no ideas."

"What ideas?" Lonnie scoffed.

"*Any* ideas," Brocius said, clicking his Colt's hammer back. He wagged the gun toward the door. "Move."

"I so hate guns," May intoned, looking at Lonnie. There was something strange in her eyes again. "Lonnie, you know how much I hate guns. Please be careful!"

"I will, Momma, I will," Lonnie said, heading for the door.

CHAPTER 51

Brocius opened the door and backed outside onto the stoop, holding his cocked revolver on Lonnie.

Lonnie walked out onto the stoop, down the steps, and around the cabin's west front corner, heading for the rear. Brocius followed, his pistol aimed at Lonnie's back.

Halfway to the cabin's rear, Lonnie stopped suddenly. A thought occurred to him. Behind him, Brocius's foot thuds stopped. "What's the matter?"

"Nothin'," Lonnie said, his heart lurching, hands tingling.

His mother always kept one of her husband's old Confederate pistols in the drawer of a table near her bed. Lonnie had given her the pistol when he'd started staying away from the cabin overnight. He'd wanted her to have a way to protect herself if she ever needed to. He'd tried to teach her how to shoot the old Navy Colt, but she'd refused, regarding the old, brass-cased pistol as though it were a coiled diamondback.

Had she hidden the Colt out here somewhere? Is that what she'd been trying to tell Lonnie?

Probably not. He couldn't imagine her touching the gun much less finding the nerve to steal out of the cabin with it.

Still, Lonnie turned to the woodpile with his heart thudding in his ears. He stopped dead in his tracks again. His heart lurched violently into his throat. The brass of the pistol's case glistened in the late-afternoon light angling down from the western ridges. She'd partly covered the gun under a couple of

272

split logs. Lonnie could see the small screw at the base of the brass trigger guard.

He glanced behind him. Brocius stood off the cabin's rear corner, staring at Lonnie, head canted to one side.

"Will you stop your gallblasted fidgeting around, kid? I know what you're tryin' to do. You're wonderin' if you're fast enough to take me. You're wonderin' if you can get this pistol out of my hand." Brocius grinned darkly. "Go ahead. Try. Save me havin' to tie you up for the night just to shoot you in the mornin'."

"I'll get the water first," Lonnie said, grabbing the wooden bucket that hung from a nail in the side of the steel-banded rain barrel.

"Just to save time, I'll grab some wood."

Anxiety ripped through Lonnie like lightning. If Brocius grabbed the nearest top logs off the woodpile, he'd find the gun . . .

Lonnie's mind scrambled. He didn't know how he did it, but he found himself turning and giving the man an angry scowl and saying, "Yeah, make yourself useful. Here, I'll load you up."

Lonnie grabbed a couple of split logs off the top of the woodpile, to the right of the gun partly hidden on the pile's second tier.

"Hold on, hold on!" Brocius snapped, holstering his pistol. "Just remember, I'm faster'n greased lightning, so don't you try a damn thing—understand? Less'n you want your ma and little brother joinin' you in the same ravine."

When Brocius had holstered the pistol, he held out his arms. Lonnie grabbed several split logs off the pile and laid them across the man's chest. Next, Lonnie plucked up the log over the old Navy Colt. Lonnie grabbed the Colt, clicked the hammer back, and aimed the revolver at Brocius's chest.

The Pinkerton's eyes snapped wide and he took one step back, dropping the wood at his feet.

"Call out or go for your pistol, and I'll gut shoot you," Lonnie said, narrowing one eye and curling his upper lip, grinning with challenge. "Go ahead. Save me a lot of trouble."

Brocius stared at him, mouth half open. Shock glazed his eyes. He held his hands just above his hips, half open, palms down.

"You with me, now? Or do you want to make a play?" Lonnie took two steps back, so the Pinkerton couldn't easily lunge at him and wrestle the Colt out of his grip, like he'd done before. Lonnie didn't know if the old cap-and-ball would still fire. He'd fired it about a year ago, and it had worked fine. Still, he wasn't sure.

Lonnie grinned, fury surging in him on tidal waves of hot blood. This man had been going to kill him. He'd probably been going to kill Lonnie's mother and little brother, as well.

But now, Lonnie had him dead to rights. He was amazed at how light-headed and powerful that made him feel. This time, he would not squander his opportunity of removing this scum from his ranch cabin.

What he'd do with the two Pinkertons, he had no idea.

First things first . . .

"Easy, kid," Brocius said, nervously licking his lower lip, staring at the revolver in Lonnie's hand. "Just take it easy, now. You don't wanna do this. You might have me . . . for the time bein' . . . but you'll never take down Madsen, too. You're gonna end up gettin' your ma and little brother killed."

"Nah," Lonnie said, his mild expression belying the anxiety churning in his gut. "I'm gonna end up gettin' you killed if you don't slip those pistols from their holsters and toss 'em back behind you. Real slow! Use just your thumbs and first fingers."

Lonnie aimed his Colt at the man's head, narrowing one eye as he aimed down the barrel.

"Easy, now—easy, easy, easy!" Brocius slid the guns from

their holsters and tossed them out behind him.

Lonnie wagged his own Colt toward the front of the cabin. "Nice and slow. If you call out, try to warn your partner, I'll shoot you in the back. If you don't think I will, you're dead wrong."

"Tough guy, huh?" Brocius said as he started to walk toward the front of the cabin. "We'll see about that."

Having learned his lesson from before, Lonnie followed the man from seven feet behind, so Brocius couldn't turn and grab the gun before Lonnie could shoot him. They walked around the cabin's front corner. Brocius glanced over his left shoulder as he headed for the porch.

"Just keep movin'," Lonnie said softly, so Madsen wouldn't hear him from inside.

Brocius climbed the porch steps.

"Stop at the door," Lonnie said behind him.

"Whatever you want, kid. Whatever you want."

When he'd stopped before the door, Lonnie walked up behind him. He pressed the pistol against the small of the man's back and tightened his finger on the trigger. He was ready to shoot if Brocius began to make any quick move. Any quick move at all.

It would be easy. It was almost frightening how easy it would be to kill this man, Lonnie thought. His life and his mother and little brother's lives were at stake.

"All right—open it," Lonnie said.

CHAPTER 52

Brocius tripped the latch, shoved the door open.

Lonnie pushed Brocius inside. Madsen was sitting at the table, rolling a quirley. He frowned up at Brocius, looked at Lonnie. He lowered his gaze to the gun in the boy's hand.

"Stand up—slow-like," Lonnie said, keeping his pistol aimed at Brocius. "If you stand too quick or reach for your gun, I'll shoot your partner."

Madsen's face turned brick red. "What in the *hell*?"

The sudden outburst gave Lonnie a start. He took his eyes off of Brocius for half a second.

A half a second too long.

Brocius whipped toward him and nudged the Colt wide just as Lonnie fired. The bullet sliced through the air along Brocius's right cheek and clanked off an iron kettle hanging from a ceiling beam.

Brocius reached for the Colt, grabbed it, but Lonnie didn't let go. As he tried to pull it back away from Brocius, in the corner of his right eye he saw Madsen lurch to his feet.

As he did, Lonnie's mother screamed, "No!" and swung a cast-iron kettle around hard. It slammed against the back of the man's head with a loud, crunching thud. As Madsen fell forward, grabbing his head with both hands, Lonnie stumbled backward, tripped over a table leg, and fell to the floor.

He still had the pistol in his hand.

As Brocius came toward him, eyes wide and filled with fury,

Lonnie started to click the hammer back.

"Oh, no you don't!" the rogue Pinkerton snarled, and kicked the pistol out of Lonnie's hand.

The old Colt flew back over Lonnie's head. He saw it bounce off an arm of his father's rocking chair and fly to the floor on the chair's other side.

He heard his mother screaming and Madsen yelling, but there was nothing he could do for his mother now. Brocius kicked Lonnie in the side and then strode past him, reaching for the pistol.

Ignoring the ache in his ribs from the man's savage kick, Lonnie lunged for him. He grabbed him around the waist. Brocius cursed as he twisted around and flew backward. His head hit the side of the hearth with a dull smack.

"Oh!" Brocius said, wincing.

Lonnie saw the Colt lying on the floor.

"No, you don't you little devil!" Brocius kicked at Lonnie, who avoided the man's scissoring feet as he dove for the Colt. He hit the floor on his belly and chest. He grabbed the Colt, clicked the hammer back, and swung around just as Brocius gained his feet and lunged for him.

Lonnie gritted his teeth and fired.

Brocius stopped with a jerk.

Lonnie shot him again. He saw the two holes in the man's wool vest. Blood oozed from them. Brocius looked down at the blood. He staggered backward, flaring his nostrils at Lonnie.

His tone pitched with surprise, the rogue Pinkerton said, "Why . . . why . . . you killed me, you little . . ."

He let his voice trail off as he dropped to his knees, looked at Lonnie again then fell forward to hit the floor on his face. He shook, as he died, spurs rattling.

Lonnie heard violent scuffling sounds. Madsen cursed tightly.

There was the muffled pop of a pistol. Lonnie's mother screamed.

"Momma!" Lonnie shouted.

He gained his feet and ran to where Madsen lay atop May Gentry, facing her. Lonnie's mother lay taut against the floor, her head tipped back. She was wincing, her eyes squeezed shut.

Little Jeremiah's squeals issued from the bedroom.

"Momma!" Lonnie yelled again, staring down in horror at his mother, who lay shockingly still beneath Madsen.

"Get off her, you bastard!" Lonnie screamed, cocking the Colt again and aiming at the back of the man's neck.

But then Madsen turned and looked up at Lonnie. He had a faraway look in his eyes. As he continued rolling backward off of May, Lonnie saw the blood on Madsen's chest. Flames from the close gunshot licked at the man's shirt and vest. Acrid smoke filled the air.

Lonnie also saw the gun as the man drew his hands away from it. Now only May Gentry's hands were on the gun—Madsen's own Smith & Wesson. Her right index finger was curled through the trigger guard.

Lonnie's mother opened her eyes and stared up at Lonnie. Her eyes were glazed with shock. She looked down at Madsen and then up at Lonnie again. Her dress was bloody, but it didn't appear to be her own blood.

Madsen sighed. His eyes rolled back in his head, and he lay still.

"Momma!" Lonnie cried as he dropped to the floor and threw his arms around May Gentry's shoulders, holding her tight. She tossed the gun away and returned the boy's hug, sobbing quietly against his shoulder.

Lonnie held her like that for a long time.

Finally, May drew her head away from his, and tried a little smile though her eyes were still bright with the awe of what they'd both been through.

"Lonnie," she said in a thin, faraway voice, "would you mind . . . looking in on . . . your brother?"

Lonnie laughed at that. It was as though a dam had burst inside him. Relief washed through him like a warm soothing wave.

"Sure, Momma," he said, rising. "I'd be happy to."

He went into the bedroom, plucked the screaming infant out of his bassinet and carried him outside, away from the smell of wafting gun smoke and spilled blood. He walked out into the yard, jostling his little brother in his arms.

The thuds of an approaching rider grew louder. The sun was down but there was still enough light left in the valley for Lonnie to see the blonde rider gallop under the ranch portal and into the yard.

Casey stopped Miss Abigail just beyond Lonnie. She stared at him, wide-eyed.

"I heard the shooting," Casey said, her voice trembling. "I thought . . ."

She swung down from the saddle and walked over to where Lonnie stood holding his baby brother.

"Everything's fine," Lonnie said. He couldn't quite believe those words himself, so he said them again. "Everything's . . . fine." He frowned at her. "I told Calhoun not to let you come after me."

"What was he going to do—hog-tie me? Thanks to the skills you taught me, I tracked you here."

"Did you find Halliday?"

Casey drew her mouth corners down, and nodded.

"Where's Calhoun?"

"I don't know. He wanted nothing to do with Skull Canyon. I'd venture to say that after I left him, he headed in the opposite direction—rather quickly." Casey heaved a sigh of relief.

"Oh, Lonnie."

She threw her arms around him and Jeremiah, who had quieted considerably. The baby poked his tiny index fingers up at Casey and gurgled contentedly. She squeezed one of the little fingers and gave Lonnie and the baby another hug.

"You know, you're gonna make a good father someday, Lonnie Gentry." She kissed him straight on the mouth, then brushed her nose against his.

Lonnie was not so stunned by all that had happened that he couldn't appreciate the rich suppleness of the girl's lips on his. Every taut muscle in his body turned to warm mud.

"If the curse of Skull Canyon don't get me first," he said.

"You forget that old legend," Casey said. "If there's really a curse, it's a curse on bad men. Good men ride out alive. And you're one of the best men I've ever known, Lonnie Gentry."

Lonnie arched a skeptical brow at her. "What about . . . fancy Dan?"

"You forget about him," Casey said, pressing her cheek to his. "I know I have."

ABOUT THE AUTHOR

Western novelist **Peter Brandvold** has penned over ninety fast-action westerns under his own name and his penname, **Frank Leslie.** He is the author of the ever-popular .45-Caliber books featuring Cuno Massey as well as the Lou Prophet and Yakima Henry novels. The Ben Stillman books are a long-running series with previous volumes available as e-books. Recently, Brandvold published two horror westerns—*Canyon of a Thousand Eyes* and *Dust of the Damned.* Head honcho at "Mean Pete Publishing," publisher of lightning-fast western e-books, he has lived all over the American west but currently lives in western Minnesota with his dog. Visit his Web site at www.peterbrandvold.com. Follow his blog at www.peterbrandvold.blogspot.com.